T5-DHE-719

# SURPRISE!

After a long time, Slocum heard the soft clopping of hooves. Slowly a figure, leading a horse, came into Slocum's view. Through slitted eyes, Slocum strove to focus on the assassin. Another twenty paces and he recognized the reputation-hunting kid he had wounded the night before. He had a Winchester slung in the crook of his left arm, a big bandage making a bulge on his right shoulder.

That accounted for the lack of accuracy, Slocum surmised. He forced himself to relax and look dead. The kid came closer, ground-reined his mount, and walked in close. He stopped over Slocum's body and gazed down at the blood that spread on the ground. He licked nervous lips, which began to tremble, then uttered a muffled curse.

"I got him!" he gloated. "I killed John Slocum!" The kid raised his eyes to heaven, as though defying God to contradict him.

"Wrong," Slocum told the exulting kid as he came back to life and drilled the youthful murderer through the heart.

Slocum came to his feet and kicked the Winchester out of reach. He toed the slack corpse over with one boot and stared into unseeing, pale blue eyes. In their glazing surfaces he saw only a reflection of himself.

"Damn. Why do some of them never learn?"

## OTHER BOOKS BY JAKE LOGAN

RIDE, SLOCUM, RIDE

SLOCUM AND THE CLAIM JUMPERS

SLOCUM AND THE CHEROKEE MAN-
HUNT

SIXGUNS AT SILVERADO

SLOCUM AND THE EL PASO BLOOD
FEUD

SLOCUM AND THE BLOOD RAGE

SLOCUM AND THE CRACKER CREEK
KILLERS

GUNFIGHTER'S GREED

SIXGUN LAW

SLOCUM AND THE ARIZONA KIDNAP-
PERS

SLOCUM AND THE HANGING TREE

SLOCUM AND THE ABILENE SWINDLE

BLOOD AT THE CROSSING

SLOCUM AND THE BUFFALO HUNTERS

SLOCUM AND THE PREACHER'S
DAUGHTER

SLOCUM AND THE GUNFIGHTER'S
RETURN

THE RAWHIDE BREED

GOLD FEVER

DEATH TRAP

SLOCUM AND THE CROOKED JUDGE

SLOCUM AND THE TONG WARRIORS

SLOCUM AND THE OUTLAW'S TRAIL

SLOW DEATH

SLOCUM AND THE PLAINS MASSACRE

SLOCUM AND THE IDAHO BREAKOUT

STALKER'S MOON

MEXICAN SILVER

SLOCUM'S DEBT

SLOCUM AND THE CATTLE WAR

COLORADO KILLERS

RIDE TO VENGEANCE

REVENGE OF THE GUNFIGHTER

TEXAS TRAIL DRIVE

THE WYOMING CATTLE WAR

VENGEANCE ROAD

SLOCUM AND THE TOWN TAMER

SLOCUM BUSTS OUT (Giant Novel)

A NOOSE FOR SLOCUM

NEVADA GUNMEN

THE HORSE THIEF WAR

# JAKE LOGAN

## SLOCUM AND THE PLAINS RAMPAGE

**B**

BERKLEY BOOKS, NEW YORK

SLOCUM AND THE PLAINS RAMPAGE

A Berkley Book / published by arrangement with
the author

PRINTING HISTORY
Berkley edition / January 1991

All rights reserved.
Copyright © 1991 by The Berkley Publishing Group.
This book may not be reproduced in whole or in part,
by mimeograph or any other means, without permission.
For information address: The Berkley Publishing Group,
200 Madison Avenue, New York, New York 10016.

ISBN: 0-425-12493-2

A BERKLEY BOOK ® TM 757,375
Berkley Books are published by The Berkley Publishing Group,
200 Madison Avenue, New York, New York 10016.
The name "BERKLEY" and the "B" logo
are trademarks belonging to Berkley Publishing Corporation.

PRINTED IN THE UNITED STATES OF AMERICA

10  9  8  7  6  5  4  3  2  1

# 1

A barn burned furiously. Silhouetted against the magenta and purple of the far western horizon its wooden roof, rafters, and doors roared and crackled. Trailing eddies of orange sparks, a column of black rose in the Kansas sky above it. The hungry flames illuminated the farmyard, which aided the hard-faced men in their grisly task.

From the house, a turf-block and clapboard soddy, came a flurry of shots that sent several of those men scurrying for cover. One yelped and stumbled into a corral rail.

"Bastard winged me!" he shouted to his companions.

Livestock lowed and whinnied and rolled white, frightened eyes. Wood splintered where two frantic horses broke through the corral fence. Three of the attackers rushed the house with flaming torches. When they reached a suitable spot, they heaved the blazing brands onto the roof. Ignoring the occasional hum and crack of bullets, the leader stood spread-legged over the corpse of the farmer in the center of the yard. He wore a faded gray Confederate tunic and campaign hat. Curly yellow locks spilled to his shoulders below the stained brim.

"You died for a glorious cause, friend," he told the dead man, his voice low, a hypnotic caress. With exaggerated calm he surveyed the destruction and laughed softly in satisfaction.

• • •

A cool night breeze wafted through the window of a third-floor room in the Brown Palace Hotel in Denver. It carried the acrid odor of coal and woodsmoke, horse manure and pine boughs. The olfactory signals failed to disturb the man and woman on the bed. John Slocum and Hope Vanneman clutched each other tightly as they made a slow, delightful love.

"John, ooooh, John," Hope gasped with a shudder. "D-don't ever let it end."

"Hummmm. You're so fine," Slocum murmured as he slid his fevered organ out to the leafy fronds that guarded her pulsing passage. "Keep with me, Hope, keep with me."

Hope sucked in a mighty draft of air and her legs rose from the sheets to entwine around his waist. "Harder, darling, harder. Make . . . me . . . come!" she ended in a thin wail.

Slocum drove into her then, hips undulating powerfully with each thrust. His lips found one nipple and covered it, tongue teasing the rigid nub of flesh to greater excitation. The bed creaked and groaned. Tingling waves of euphoria washed over the amorous couple. Hope moved one hand down his back and between his legs. Her fingers cupped his tautly drawn sack. She began to knead his cods, which set off new tremors of delight. Slocum increased the force of his plunges, which brought a squeal from Hope.

"Yes! Aaaaah, yes-yes——YES!" she hissed through clinched teeth.

With a mighty stroke, Slocum hilted himself and Hope erupted in a frenzy, head thrashing from side to side, eyes wide, glazed, and unfocused. She made a fist and pounded his back. She rose up and her lips closed over the straining muscle at the base of his neck. He'd have a suck mark the next morning, Slocum thought detachedly. For now, though, that didn't matter a damn sight. Hope's pelvis lurched and steadied in matching rhythm. Her stout nails dug into his back. Slocum redoubled his efforts.

"Oh—yes! Oh—oh—oh—yesssss. Oh-oh-oh-OOOOOO-OHHHH!"

Hope's stomach cramped and she achieved a convulsive, magnificent climax. Slocum never slackened his pace, his humping body the walking arm, his rigid phallus the piston of a mighty steam engine. Starbursts of awesome sensation raddled his muscular frame. He snorted, grunted, and gasped his way toward his own completion, sent ripples of renewed delight through Hope as their ardor grew and intensified until the delirious moment of mutual release.

"My God," Hope moaned. "Wh-what did I do for love before I met you?"

"You're pleased?" Slocum asked, slowly withdrawing his still-erect member from her heated compartment.

"Pleased is not the word. Enthralled comes closer. You've stolen my heart, John Slocum."

"And you have bewitched me." Moving gently, Slocum lay down beside her. "Hope, I had no intention of spending spring in Denver. I wanted to get shut of Colorado for a long while. Now . . . I've even taken a job."

"You did?" Hope blurted, surprised and pleased.

"Yes. I followed your advice and saw Wade Burton at the mine. I'm going to be in charge of security for him."

Hope clapped her hands. "That's wonderful. You'll have to find a place. Staying in this hotel is too expensive. We'll be able to go for long rides, have picnics out in the woods. I—I'd ask you to move in with me, but . . ."

"The neighbors, your boss," Slocum named off, nodding knowingly. "People talk. And they don't like seeing people doing what they hardly dare dream about. That don't mean we can't have a lot of fun. I might be able to make this last through the winter."

"What sort of hours will you have? Will you be required to stand guard?"

"I'll have banker's hours. Being in charge of security means planning and supervision, not parading around the fence line. We'll have plenty of time for ourselves. Which reminds me," Slocum concluded as he bent and began to nuzzle a slight fold in the creamy skin of Helen's belly. "Do you think . . . we might . . . find time . . . for a little . . . more of this?"

Hope shivered to the feathery touch of his lips and thrilled to the hot puffs of his breath. "Yes, I—I do indeed th-think we'll ha—Oooooh, Slocum," she moaned as he brought her to full arousal.

Accompanied by the alarmed gabbling of three geese, four men charged across the backyard of a farmhouse and crashed in through the kitchen door. Crockery scattered and a woman screamed.

"Get that one," a voice commanded.

A muffled shot followed. A higher, younger voice took up the shrieking. "Momma! Oooh, Momma!"

Two of the brigands dragged a man in his early forties out the front door of the sod and fieldstone building. Behind them came the other pair with a boy in his early teens.

"Down. On your knees," one raider growled.

From their kneeling position, father and son stared at the man who approached them a moment later. He had a stocky build, with a round head, cup-handle ears, and long, dishwater blond hair. His wide-set, hypnotic eyes glowed as he spoke in a soft, faintly effeminate voice.

"Well, what fine specimens we have here. You two have been chosen to play a key role in the cleansing of Kansas. We're going to purge the land, and you will help rid the state of human vermin. They are filth, who don't deserve to live. The two of you should take joy," he went on, drawing his revolver from the black, flap holster, "in being martyrs to the cause of abolition."

"Mister, that's a crock of shit," the farmer gamely spat. "We didn't take sides in that war, got no interest in its outcome. Not any more than you're a rebel officer," he concluded.

"Ah, well, some of us never see the significance of our roles in the future," the leader lamented as he made a step behind the kneeling men and quickly shot them both in the back of the head.

His breath roughened, as though sexually aroused, and the front of his trousers bulged at the groin as he watched their final spasms. A faint smile spread his thin lips and he licked them in a sensuous manner. When the frail youth twitched his last and his sphincters relaxed, the leader made a soft sound like a moan of ecstasy. From inside, feminine screams attracted his attention.

"Hold her legs, dammit, I can't get it in," a rough snarl overrode the wails of terror.

"Hurry up, Alf, I wanna wet my wick, too."

"There's the li'l girl," Alf suggested.

"Yeah. Right. C'mere, sweetie."

"No. Oh, please, don't," came a frightened appeal.

"Git them clothes off," a snarl demanded.

"Stop! Stop! Oh, please stop it. You're hurting Momma," another child begged.

"Bud, yank that dress offen her."

Cloth tore as the leader stopped in the doorway to take in the scene. His smile widened at the sounds of pain and misery coming from the woman. Alf looked up and nodded.

"Want we should save a little for you, Cap'n?"

Captain Godfrey Howard shook his head. "You boys enjoy yourselves. I've other work to do."

Howard turned back to the yard as the smaller girl howled in agony at the brutal violation. Captain Howard walked away and around one corner of the farmhouse. Thin, reedy yells of protest came from two wriggling, naked boys that one of his troopers held by the scruff of the neck as he exited the washhouse.

"They was takin' their Saturday night bath," he informed the captain.

"Put them down there is good enough," Howard ordered.

"What'd you do to our Paw?" the older lad demanded.

"Why'd you come here?" his younger brother asked, lower lip trembling on the edge of tears.

Godfrey Howard looked closely at the bare children. They couldn't be more than eight and ten. "Why, to make you-all a rallying cry. You're going to be famous."

"You're a liar," the defiant one said hotly, water dripping from his sun-browned skin.

"It's not nice to talk to your betters like that, boy," Captain Howard chided as he drew his Colt model '60 Army conversion and shot the boy between the eyes.

"Jimmy!" the younger brother shrieked.

A bullet from Howard's .44 silenced him. An intense, orgasmic sensation flooded Godfrey Howard as the children jerked and writhed in their death throes. He would have to see Stella the moment they got back to Topeka. He'd not been this aroused for a long time. His groin ached and tingled. The splashes of blood, bright red and dark, were an aphrodisiac of unequaled strength. He quivered and the breath rasped in his throat. Captain Howard forced himself to turn away from the scene he found so erotic and banish the image from his mind. Later, there would be time for that later.

"Set the other outbuildings on fire," he commanded the men

standing nearby. "Then the house. Send someone to tell those randy stallions in there to finish up and be done with it."°

New flames began to crackle in the grain elevator, a toolshed, and in the kitchen of the house. Pistol shots from inside the dwelling informed Howard that the women had been taken care of. For a moment he regretted not availing himself, but the image of his bare posterior flashing in the lamplight to the bawdy comments of his command rose to dissuade him. Wouldn't do at all for discipline.

No. They had too many things yet to accomplish that would demand absolute obedience, utter respect, and the impersonal relationship that could not be among men who had shared a woman. Command was a cold and lonely pinnacle, upon which he alone must stand.

"Sergeant Banks," Captain Howard called out. "Mount the men. We've finished here."

"Yes, sir. Trumpeter, sound recall."

Brassy notes spilled from the dented instrument and the troops hurried to their horses. Banks, a burly barrel of a man in his late thirties, filled leather lungs. "Troop, prepare to mount. . . . Mount!"

Crackling flames made happy music for Captain Godfrey Howard and First Sergeant Isaac Banks as the troops cantered lightly away from the ruined farm. After they had ridden off, the dying farm wife fought valiantly to drag herself from the burning house. Wounded twice, blood stained both sides of her torn dress and the tears ran freely. Not for herself, shot and violated, but for the ruined bodies of her daughters, now stiffening in death. She had to live, she told herself. She had to tell someone. It—it was important. The murderers who had ravaged their home were not what they seemed.

"Red legs," she panted aloud. Then she repeated the seemingly senseless phrase with stronger emphasis. *"They had red legs."*

He would leave it all to Howard. The tall, thin, angular man pacing the drawing room of his suite in the Kansas Hotel in Topeka lowered himself into a Queen Anne chair and leafed through the papers in front of him on a matching rosewood table. Where next? He would have to decide and get word to Howard.

That man. Godfrey Howard had an absolute talent for refined butchery. Only the best good fortune had put him in the way of Captain Howard. He knew the type existed, men who had never grown tired of, or sick of, the bloodletting of civilians during the great war. Some said they had no souls. He believed differently.

Their souls had been soaked in the blood of their victims for so long that they could kill and feel nothing. All in all, Howard and the men he led would move the plan forward much faster than anyone had anticipated. So long as the senator and his cronies kept their noses out of "field operations," all would be well. Squimishness had no place in his plans. Anticipating a rosy future, he felt his stomach give warning of approaching hunger.

He hadn't eaten in over thirty hours. Time enough for that now, he reasoned. With the grace of a mountain lion he rose and crossed to a bellpull. Two firm strokes set a distant tocsin to tinkling. He wet his lips with a pink slice of tongue and crossed to the sideboard. There he poured a small brandy. A little appetite stimulant was in order for all his long abstinence from food.

"I would like a veal steak, fried potatoes, and three eggs, please. Biscuits and orange marmalade. Coffee to go with it, and a quart pitcher of beer." His slight, well-modulated Southern accent went well with his gracious manners.

Tomorrow, he thought after the waiter departed, would show the world more of the horrors visited by the mysterious night riders. The knowledge comforted him.

# 2

Like squirrels preparing for winter, Slocum and Hope stored up four days and nights of delightful romps in bed and country-side after that marvelously rewarding night. Hope Vanneman's attitude altered markedly after Slocum informed her he had been accepted for the job of security chief at the mine. The Vanneman name had gone a long way toward insuring his success and Slocum appreciated that. What set him a bit off-balance was her immediate assumption that he should acquire domesticity along with employment. For all of that, he didn't let her nest building interfere with their pleasure. He lay beside Hope now, one hand lightly cupping a bare breast. She muttered into her pillow and turned to present him her lovely, sharp-angled face. Slocum kissed her nose.

Hope giggled and reached out to tweak his semierect phallus. That sensitive and well-worked organ responded instantly by elongating and, to Hope's immense delight, stiffening. With a whoop of joy she rose like a phoenix in triumph and straddled the supine man she loved so dearly. With infinite care, Hope lowered herself onto this protuberant shaft, wetly ready to take it in its magnificent entirety. She had impaled herself on half of the silken length when Slocum spoke softly, big hands holding her waist, stopping further progress.

"Whoa. We'll have to make this fast. I start work today," he reminded her.

"Oh, pooh on that. Wade Barton will excuse you being an hour or two late, if he knows it's what I wanted." Hope wriggled in an attempt to take in more of his manhood.

"Hope, bad habits are hard enough to break. Good ones are nearly impossible. Believe me, it could become all too easy to spend an extra hour or two every morning in such pursuits as this."

"And why not? I love every minute of it, and so do you. We have to have some time for ourselves."

"We have all night. Sundays too," Slocum offered.

"That's not nearly enough," she protested. Lifting her legs off the bed, she uttered a soft grunt as gravity gave her the desired results and she slipped his reddened prong fully into her tightly clutching canal. "Aaah, John—John, how wonderful you are. Love me, darling. Love me long and hard and throw worry to the wind."

Slocum surrendered to the inevitable and did his best. It proved enough, for Hope soon wailed and keened her delight, shuddered and squeezed and coaxed him to yet another explosion of vitality, then left the damp bed singing, to prepare a tremendous breakfast. On his way out the door, after eating, Hope handed him a cylindrical tin pail.

"Your lunch. It has two roasted pork sandwiches with horse-radish, a big pickle, and a piece of apricot cobbler."

"Where did you get the fruit?"

"Dried, beloved. Thank nature for a large crop and lots of sun last year. Now hurry on, you're already an hour late." She gave him a long, inviting kiss that nearly brought an end to his budding career as a security supervisor for failure to report for work.

Slocum's route to the Columbine mine took him through a stretch of factories, small shops, and saloons that composed a suburban business district. A thin, pale-faced, barefoot youngster in unbuckled knickers, a too-large hand-me-down shirt, and a seaman's cap hawked newspapers on one street corner. His too-bright shoe-button eyes and nervous movements betrayed his constant hunger and, Slocum suspected, the desperate plight of his family.

"Kansas in flames! Read all about it," the little lad bellowed in a high, cawing voice. "Night riders rampage farms. Paper, mister?"

Usually disinclined to keep up with events through the purple prose of bombastic newspaper reporters and their hyperbolic editors, Slocum nevertheless delved into one pocket for a coin. His gaze remained fixed on the bold, black headline:

INSURRECTION IN KANSAS! BLOODY-HANDED REBELS!

The subhead provided more information: "*Farms Burned by Unreconstructed Rebels. Whole Families Murdered in the Night.*"

Slocum handed the boy a dime and took the paper. "Keep the change."

"Thanks, mister," the astonished lad chirped.

Quickly Slocum scanned the article. "Raising frightening memories of Bloody Bill Anderson and the butcher Quantrill, rebel irregulars brought fire and death to Kansas farms over the past week," it read. The reporter had relied heavily on such inflammatory phrases as, "Women ravaged, their menfolk executed in cold blood," and "Few witnesses have survived." But, he assured his readers, "All of those who lived through these terrible rampages have agreed in their descriptions of the dastardly perpetrators. The leader, a cold and heartless man, wore the hated gray of the recent rebellion, as did many of his henchmen."

Slocum blinked and reread the passage. Something about it didn't ring true. It seemed all too pat and assured. Witnesses, particularly when they were also victims, rarely agreed on any two details, let alone such accurate recounting of appearances. Shrugging, he folded away the pages of the *Denver Post* and continued on to work.

With the routine established before him, Slocum spent little time giving instructions to the guards. After introducing himself he stood before the gathered day shift with hands behind his back.

"Remember, we're not looking for anyone to attack the place. Your job is to make sure of the identity of everyone entering the mine property. Also to keep an eye on the powder magazine, toolshed, and stamp mill. We don't want anyone helping themselves to small items that can be carried in lunch buckets."

"Do we search the miners coming on shift?" one not-too-bright guard asked.

"No. We search those going off duty. No one is going to steal something and carry it around all day."

"What about union organizers?" asked a man with metal sergeant's chevrons on his round, blue cap.

"Orders from above that they're not welcome here. Politely escort them from the premises."

"What if they don't want to go?" A small titter of laughter followed.

Slocum frowned, as though concentrating on a world-shaking problem. "Then escort them off not so politely."

Rich, full laughs complimented his repartee. "Seriously, I have nothing for or against unions. The orders come from the top, so we follow them. Our main concern is to prevent pilferage. A clever miner can steal a hundred dollars' worth of gold per day under his fingernails."

"The boss ain't kiddin'," the sergeant offered gratuitously. "One mine I was workin' in, we got to losin' gold at a steady rate, the same amount every day, like clockwork. We searched and checked everything we could think of. Finally the owners made the men change into work clothes in a small shed, leave their shift stuff behind. We still lost gold. So we went to searchin' them while they was stripped down to change to street clothes. I found one bog-county Mick with three ounces, the exact amount always missin', stuffed in his foreskin." An uproar of boisterous laughter followed.

"What were you doin' when you found it, Tiny?" an anonymous voice came from the ranks of guards.

The sergeant flushed a deep crimson. "Step out here an' ask me that again," he challenged. "I'll show you what I was doin'."

More laughter. Slocum dismissed the men and headed for his office. He intended to review the personnel records of his security force. First, though, a cup of coffee and another look at that disturbing news article.

He found it no different from before. Something didn't seem right. Shaking his head, Slocum put the paper aside and settled down to earn his day's pay. For him the steam whistle ended work at four o'clock, leaving the rest of the afternoon open to his own pursuits. Slocum walked in company with Sergeant Tiny Felsen to the nearest saloon. Already Slocum found the dark, intense, middle-aged Felsen to have a priceless sense of humor and an expert's knowledge of what could or could not go wrong at a gold mine. In order to avail himself of this wealth of information, he offered to buy.

After the barkeep sat a large tin bucket of beer on the table between them, Slocum poured and handed a schooner to Felsen. "To you, Tiny," he toasted. "I can only have one. I'm going back in a while to meet the night shift."

"Awh, they're a lot like the rest of the boys. Only they're owls. Me, I figure night is for sleeping. Cheers, boss. I've got a feeling you're going to be the best security chief we've ever had here."

"Thank you, Tiny. Now, tell me—"

Before Slocum could get any further, another hollow-cheeked, barefoot lad shoved a copy of the evening paper in front of him. "Paper, mister? There's bloody uprisin's in Kansas. Just a nickle, sir."

For an unprecedented second time, Slocum bought a newspaper. He spread it on the beer-stained table and began to read. Under a bold subhead—"*Renegade Leader Identified*"—he found the name Ewan McDade. Reading further, he discovered McDade's name prominent throughout. His formerly relaxed, congenial expression became thunderous with suppressed anger. Now convinced that something was decidedly wrong with this account, he fumed at his own enforced inactivity. He positively knew that someone was lying.

He accepted that as fact because he knew Ewan McDade. They had served together during the war. He cleaned off the top half of his beer and rose, mind working on the contradictions presented in the articles. Gone was any thought of reviewing the night shift. Hastily he made his excuses to Felsen and departed.

When he arrived at Hope Vanneman's small house, she instantly sensed that something was distracting him. His responses, when he gave one, had little to do with what she had said. Vexation mounting, she at last snapped at him and jerked his thoughts to the present.

"Wh-what was that?" Slocum asked her, blank-faced.

"I said, you're getting ready to leave me, aren't you?"

"Why—ah—no, not at all," Slocum stammered, guilt igniting a slow burn in his stomach from the knowledge that leaving was *exactly* what he was thinking of.

For a brief second, Hope's eyes narrowed and her anger flared. Then, in an effort to sustain the atmosphere of romance she had worked so hard to achieve, she offered small talk about the dinner she had prepared and alluded to the pleasures of the night.

"I, ah, found something special at Giselle's today," she informed him.

"Such as?" Slocum had to keep his mind focused to ask.

"Do you like it?" she prompted as she shrugged her shoulders out of the dressing gown she wore to reveal a gossamer creation that tauntingly revealed more than it concealed.

Slocum sucked air fast enough for the breath to qualify as a gasp. A big, lusty smile split his lips to reveal the white palisades of his teeth. With a hesitance born of awe, he reached out one hand to gently smooth the filmy garment to the pleasing contours of her full-blown figure.

"Even a blind man would like this," he said honestly. "How easy is it to get out of?"

"Is that *all* you think of?" Hope snapped in mock criticism.

"It's what I'm thinking of now," Slocum told her.

"We eat first," she stated firmly. "I suppose I should have saved this for later."

"Why?"

They both laughed in appreciation, and Slocum's outlook improved markedly. Not for long, though, as images of a young Ewan McDade, and of the murderous Kansas Jayhawkers they had fought together, returned to tug at his sense of responsibility. Hope, after receiving only muttered responses to her increasingly salacious thrusts, gave it up and resigned herself to only a halfhearted performance by her lover. Slocum did not even acknowledge her change in mood.

Tall windows, each masked by thick, rich burgundy drapes, lined the two long walls of the opulent private dining room of the Jayhawk Hotel in Topeka, Kansas. At the far end of the room more twelve-foot windows looked out on the grounds of the state capitol, two blocks west of the hostelry. Potted ferns adorned large brass braziers atop mahogany columns in the design of the portico of the Acropolis. Several long trestle tables had been joined together to form a buffet line, and muted illumination from myriad candles and the huge oil chandeliers cast a soft, golden glow on the men gathered in their finery.

Each guest wore the red-white-blue rosette of the Union in his lapel. They wore evening dress, opera capes abounded, and black patent leather shoes sparkled. Savory aromas rose from the juicy rare baron of beef, mounds of fresh oysters on beds of ice, salmon in aspic, roasted partridges refitted with their plumage, and deep chafing dishes of meatballs. Silver trays of frogs' legs, fresh-baked bread triangles, smoked buffalo tongue, and forcemeat tarts completed the lavish repast. To one side a barman kept busy at the portable bar, pouring bourbon, champagne, rye, and brandy. A steady burring undertone of conversation undulated around the room. The host, Cyril Anstruther, rapped musically on a champagne glass with his gold cigar clipper to attract attention.

"Gentlemen, welcome to my modest festivities," he pronounced oritorically. "I am greatly pleased to see all of you here."

"What's the occasion, Cy?" Senator Victor Dahlgren asked. He stood along one wall with newspaper editor Walter Albert Black.

Anstruther chuckled softly. "Now, now, Victor, not until we've all gorged ourselves on this fine array. When everyone has made at least three rounds of the buffet and bar, I'm sure one of us will volunteer as bartender and another for carver and let these good folk go about their business. Then we'll get to the heart of this gathering." Secrecy had become second nature to Anstruther over the years since 1863.

"We can't let our host go around with an empty glass," Justice John Duffey of the Kansas Supreme Court brayed. "Come on, Cy, I'll race you to the bar."

An hour crept by before Cyril Anstruther could dismiss the restaurant staff and securely lock the door behind them. He turned to his coconspirators with a hand-washing gesture and nodded to Captain Godfrey Howard, who stood at the brass rail, drink in hand.

"It's time we had a report from our good Captain Howard. Godfrey, if you please."

Captain Howard drank off the remaining inch of clear seltzer water in his glass and set it aside. "Gentlemen, the groundwork has been laid, as I'm sure you know. Our plan is ready to go into action. The adjutant general has authorized my company to conduct punitive measures against the rebel scum in southeastern Kansas." A few knowing chuckles interrupted him. "Once the governor concurs, we are free to use 'any means at our disposal to bring an end to the depredations.' And I'm quoting the AG when I say that." Godfrey went on to outline in detail the immediate measures he would be putting in force to squelch the insurrectionist activities of the Southern sympathizers. Again this brought a few sniggers. He concluded with a stunning announcement.

"I'm going to use the writ of marital law to carry out summary executions, by hanging, of all seditionists captured alive."

Anstruther had some difficulty clearing his throat, then spoke effusively. "Thank you, Godfrey. Thanks for an excellent report. I'm sure everyone here is anxious to hear of big things from you." He nodded toward Senator Dahlgren. "You've put the machinery in place to process confiscated landholdings to the, ah, right claimants?"

"All set, Cy."

"I still don't understand why we're going through all this involved legal process," complained the governor's personal secretary. "Why don't we just grab the land, throw the damned rebels off it, and do as we please?"

"Because," Anstruther explained patiently, "if we do that, the actual homesteaders will still retain legal title. They can sue for reinstatement of their title. We do that and we're out. Not only that, but we'd be wide open to criminal charges."

Walter Black, a relative newcomer to the cabal, spoke up with a question always asked by everyone Cyril Anstruther had contacted. "What's so important about this particular land? Surely you're not merely exercising a hatred for all former rebels?"

"Certainly not," Anstruther barged in. "The reason is purely one of economics. There is a lot of land in the tallgrass region of this state just waiting for the plow. With immigrants pouring in, particularly the religious dissidents like the Mennonites, German folk from Russia, prices will be soaring. The only problem in the way of developing that land in question is that it is claimed and occupied by former Southern sympathizers and out-and-out ex-Confederates. They don't see the advantage in exploiting the land the way we do." He paused and accepted a fresh drink from Godfrey Howard, who as the person of least importance—and a teetotaler—wound up tending bar.

"Those who came here from the South don't operate like we do. To them, land is not a commodity, to be bought and sold, or traded for profit. Mostly, they farm small portions of the vast prairie, usually forty to a hundred and twenty acres per family, to provide for their own table and winter feed for livestock. The rest of their homesteads or purchased land is left in open-range pasture. Their main source of income comes from beef cattle and dairy herds." Anstruther took a long draft on his bourbon and sampled a sliver of smoked buffalo tongue.

Licking his lips in appreciation, he continued his narrative. "Someone is going to farm that country. With this new, hard winter wheat, Turkey Red, the Mennonites are bringing in, dry farming in Kansas is going to be revolutionized. Yields as high as twenty to twenty-five bushels an acre could be achieved. Those who own the most acres will become enormously rich. Large concerns back east demand more and more cereal grains. Corn alone can not fill the need. What we intend to do is obtain title to all of that land, sell off the poorer portions, and plow under the whole tallgrass prairie to be turned into vast wheat fields. Needless to say, the Southerners are resisting this. They want to preserve the blasted country the way it is."

"And that's why Captain Howard here has been arranging, ah, incidents that will create an atmosphere wherein confiscation of insurrectionists' property can be accomplished as a punitive measure," Walter Black declared triumphantly, putting the whole plot into perspective.

"Exactly, Walter, you have it in capsule, so to speak," Anstruther lauded him. "It all depends now on how the Southern hotheads will react when Godfrey and his troops enforce the governor's new edicts. If Captain Howard does his job right, the Southerns won't be owning that land for long."

# 3

*Bullets whined and cracked through the air. One struck the barrel of a wrecked cannon and moaned off at an obtuse angle. Smoke obscured the battlefield at Manassas Junction. Slocum knelt beside the bleeding man. "Go on, keep up with the men, dang it," Sergeant Ewan McDade forced through gritted teeth. "I'll be all right. It's only a nick. The hospitalmen will take care of me. Go on, John." Slocum rolled restlessly, his movement arrested when he bumped into Hope's side.*

*Young Frank James, his kid brother, Jesse, at his side, crouched in the burr-oak thicket, looking down on the blue-belly patrol camped in the southern Missouri glade. A few feet away, standing with Lieutenant Ewan McDade, Captain John Slocum, CSA, observed the intensity of their expressions. There was more here than a desire to defeat the enemy. Something deep and wild drove these boys. Jesse, barely fifteen, glanced up at the captain, the youngster's face split by a mirthless grin. "I'm gonna kill me a Yankee," he said, his voice echoing in Slocum's mind.*

Slocum snorted and turned in the bed. His mind swirled, muddied, cleared again. *A prancing bay twinkle-footed down the lane. Seated in the fringe-topped surrey, at the reins, a portly man in a somber suit. He reined in beside the split-rail fence of the field John Slocum tilled. "You're working my land," the man said in a hollow voice. "Ah, I mean, the*

17

*new government's land."* Judge Garth, the carpetbagging, corrupt Reconstruction judge, come to steal Slocum's birthright. Slocum groaned and his hands balled into fists.

*"For God and Our Right!"* The rallying cry rebounded over and over in Slocum's head. With a shout, he sat upright. Sweat oiled his forehead and chest. His waking reflections went to how it all began.

Slocum had journeyed east from his Georgia home in 1861 to join the Army of Northern Virginia. There he had met Ewan McDade. McDade had been a natural soldier and earned promotions with the same speed and ease as Slocum. Then Slocum had received his commission and outranked McDade. Not for long, for McDade distinguished himself at Gettysburg and earned promotion to lieutenant. When Slocum was promoted to captain, and received orders to report to General Sterling Price's command in the Army of the Trans-Mississippi, he asked that Lieutenant McDade accompany him. Outside of his brother, who had died tragically at the foot of Little Roundtop, Slocum knew no man so well as Ewan McDade. He knew him well enough to be certain McDade would not be leading a band of murdering rabble. That sort of thing ended with Quantrill and Bloody Bill Anderson. Ewan McDade was in trouble and Slocum knew he had to make good on his promise to himself. His outburst had awakened Hope Vanneman, who blinked and strained to focus gummy eyes in the dimness of the bedroom. Slocum shook his head in a vain attempt to clear it.

"Honey? What is it, John?" Hope asked in a soft tone, concern coloring her words. Shyly, she touched his arm.

"I . . . it's . . . " Slocum sighed heavily. "It's no use trying to put off what I have to do."

"You *are* leaving me," Hope pouted.

"Yes. But not for the reason you might think. Ewan McDade needs whatever help I can give him."

"Who's Ewan McDade?" Hope asked pettishly.

Slocum hesitantly explained, his delivery broken because he was putting his convictions into words for the first time. He ended on an interrogative note, hopeful that Hope Vanneman had understood. The crow's-foot frown between her brows disabused him of any notion of success.

"I don't understand why you feel you owe these men something. After all these years . . . and they did join your army voluntarily, didn't they?"

"I made them go places all reason and sanity told them they shouldn't. I led them to death, maiming, terrible mental anguish. *I* did that, not some anonymous general in a far-off headquarters. And they followed me. Did what I ordered with a will. Sometimes they—they even sang, riding into battle. That sort of loyalty deserves some reward."

"John, you have a good job, what I hope is a nice place to live, and you have me. How could you possibly . . . ? Oh, John, how can I make you understand?"

"No. No, it's you who has to understand. I'm doing what I *have* to do. I'll be leaving first thing in the morning. Before I go I'll write a letter for you to give to Wade Barton at the mine. I . . . " Slocum sighed and embraced her, buried his head between her full, globular breasts.

His sigh had been one of regret. For all the marvelous bedroom athletics he had been enjoying for two weeks, he knew that no appeal she could make would stop him.

"They's 'nother one ovah theah," the lanky redhead shouted to his companions. "Y'all get him, heah?"

Three other youths reined their horses around and headed for the obstinate heifer that refused to leave its imagined security of a thorny bush. The eternal wind of Kansas bent the tall grass to the northeast. Few in number, the trees in the area inclined in the same direction. A hot spring sun beat down, encouraging the youngest of the quartet, Davey Varney, to loop his reins around the saddle horn and tug the tails of his shirt from behind his belt. He undid the buttons and wriggled out of the long sleeves.

His skin prickled at the touch of sunlight and free air. Pasty white from the long winter, he looked forward to the gradual browning process that would signal the welcome months of summer. He stuffed the shirt under the cantle of his saddle and waved to his brother, Nathan, who rode to his right and slightly ahead.

"Nate, hey, Nate! Lemme chowse this one out, huh?"

Nathan Varney studied his twelve-year-old brother for a moment. Davey was so skinny his ribs stood out like a skeleton. Yet he ate enough for two grown field hands. Nathan envied his

brother for that, thinking of the single roll of fat that marred his
own otherwise flat, smooth belly. Couldn't step on him all the
time, he reasoned.

"Sho' 'nuff," Nathan called in his slow, Georgia drawl.

Working to the calf's left flank, Davey edged closer, swinging his rope with a slack loop at the end. The brushy wash
in Clay County, Kansas, had always been an irritant to their
father. Even full-grown cattle got trapped in it, though most
could crash their way out again. Worse were the calves. Far
too often they got hung up, to die of thirst or starvation. The
onerous task of rescue devolved onto Nathan and his brother
and their two cousins, Fred and Ansel Gregory. Davey slowed
his pace, in order not to startle the calf.

Davey eased closer, then paused to swiftly snap his Lariat
forward and back, with a result similar to that of a whip. The
running loop sizzled along the hempen cord, to end in a knot at
the end, which struck the furry-faced Hereford on the rump.

With a bellow of alarm, the four-month-old critter leaped
forward and upward, freeing itself from the underbrush. It
bawled its protest and cast a baleful look over one shoulder
in the direction of Davey as it trotted toward the gather the
boys had rounded up that morning.

"Okay, kid," Nathan praised his brother, genuinely pleased
at Davey's success.

"Let's go get some more," eager Davey urged.

Ansel Gregory stayed behind with the collection of strays,
while the other youths set off to search deeper in the wash. At
only a year older than Davey, Ansel had already hurtled the
chasm of puberty. He had filled out in chest, arms, and legs.
He no longer shared with his cousin that androgynous figure
that might be a girl with the wrong fixtures stuck on. In a way,
Ansel felt sorry for Davey, who had not yet experienced the
heady rush of approaching manhood. Most of the time, though,
Ansel felt proud of his new status. It took a man to keep the
runners, like these strays, in a gather by himself. Ansel knew
himself to be capable of it. In the distance, down where his
brother and cousins had disappeared, Ansel heard the drumroll
of pounding hooves.

"What the hell are they running for?" Ansel asked aloud of
his horse. "Fred knows better than that."

A moment later, the three boys came into view, riding as

if the devil nipped at their heels. When the wind blew away the dust, Ansel saw that they were being chased. Men in blue coats and forage caps rode hell-for-leather after them. With less than three hundred yards to cover, the troopers managed to catch up before the trio joined Ansel.

Menaced by the barrels of revolvers, the boys reined in and raised their hands. "What is this?" Fred Gregory demanded. "Why'd you chase after us?"

"Well, lookee here, Sergeant," one rat-faced trooper declared. "We caught us some kid rustlers."

"We ain't rustlers!" Nathan Varney shouted hotly.

The rat-faced trooper backhanded him with a gloved fist. "Shut your mouth, you thievin' Southern trash."

Nearly knocked from his saddle, Nathan reeled a moment and clapped a hand to his bleeding mouth. "You got no call . . . ," he began, then ducked to avoid another blow.

"Round 'em up," Sergeant Isaac Banks growled. "You men drive those cows. We'll take these brats to the cap'n."

"Hey, those are our cattle," Davey Varney protested.

A florid-faced, pudgy trooper smashed a fist into Davey's bare chest. For a moment he went numb. Then it felt as though all his ribs had broken. Davey winced and fought to hold back the tears that came.

"Leave him alone!" Nathan raged.

"You want some more?"

Nathan looked at the rodent visage and noted the drawn revolver. He had no doubt he would be pistol-whipped at the least if he defied them further. Yet, Davey was his brother. He worked up a gobbet in his mouth and spat at the trooper.

"Blue Belly scum," he snarled.

"Rebel shit," the weasel-face growled.

Then bright lights exploded behind Nathan's eyes. His senses disfunctioned, sending confused messages through his body. Dully he felt more pain and could hear, as though at a great distance, Davey's voice.

"Stop it! Y'hear, stop it! You'll kill him."

"Now that ain't likely, youngster," Sergeant Banks said jovially. "At least not until after the cap'n sees the bunch of you. Move out, men."

Twenty minutes later, the prisoners and escort arrived at a stunted grove of cottonwood trees atop a small knoll. Banks halted the detachment and saluted when an officer came forward.

"What do we have here, First Sergeant?" Captain Godfrey Howard asked.

"Caught four rustlers. Kids, but they were stealing cattle anyway."

"We aren't rustlers. Those cattle have my father's brand on them," Nathan Varney blurted.

Captain Howard showed them a patient, if amused, expression. "It doesn't matter whose brand is on those cattle," he told them. "If Sergeant Banks says that you four are rustlers, then you are rustlers."

"That won't never stand up in court," Fred Gregory, the oldest, stated confidently.

Howard underwent a transformation. A certain amusement and an obviously erotic preoccupation suffused his features. "Out here, *I* am the judge, *I* am the jury . . . and *I* am the executioner. I hereby find you guilty of cattle rustling. Get down off those horses."

"No," Davey Varney barked defiantly. "You can't make us."

An odd glow brightened Captain Howard's eyes. "I'd hoped you would say that," he remarked. "First Sergeant, have three men knock those other rebel cow thieves off their mounts. I'll take care of this one."

He advanced and reached out, closing his big hands around Davey Varney's chest and lifting him from the saddle. The boy kicked and squirmed and Howard hugged him close. After a protracted moment he set the boy's feet on the ground. Slowly he slid his hands down to Davey's waist. Almost reluctantly he released the lad.

"You men, rig four ropes and fix them over that lower limb." Captain Howard pointed to the largest cottonwood on the knoll, an ancient, grayed, gnarled specimen with thigh-thick lower branches.

Nathan Varney struggled in the grip of the man who held him. *"No!"* he shrieked as he realized Howard's intent. "You can't do that. You can't hang us!"

Captain Howard jerked his fixed gaze away from Davey and laughed uproariously. "What do you mean? That's exactly what I'm doing."

"We have a right to a trial. You can't take it on yourself,"

Nathan babbled on, dredging up the scraps of law and the Constitution he recalled from his infrequent schooling sessions.

Howard licked his lips and returned to his perusal of the shirtless boy. "Oh, but I already have. When those saddles are off," he continued, addressing his troops, "take the horses over there and put these insurrectionist rabble back on them. Sergeant Banks, will you take charge of fitting the ropes in place?"

"Indeed, sir. With great pleasure," Banks responded.

Burning with resentment and shame at the close scrutiny given him by Captain Howard, Davey forgot his fear and his tears. His cousin Ansel discovered his and wept bitterly. When two troopers took his arms and bound them behind him, he began to sob wretchedly.

"Noooooo! Oh, nooooo," Ansel moaned. "P-please don' do that to meeee!"

"Listen to me," Nathan demanded in desperation. "Those are our cattle and we're not rustlers. What you're doing is against the law."

Howard spared him a surprised, disbelieving look. "No, son," he said softly, then added with voice ringing, "I am above the law. I am the legacy of John Brown. I am sent by God to avenge Father Brown on all the filthy Southern trash. I'll laugh while you die and I'll piss on your grave."

"Jeez, the old man's slipped a cog again," Davey heard one of the troopers who was manhandling him tell another from the corner of his mouth.

They stopped him under the big cottonwood. The sergeant he'd heard called Banks fitted a rope around his neck. Then they lifted him and set him bareback on his horse.

"Don't move, Nellie, please don't move," Davey implored the gentle, obliging mare.

Davey began to cry. He felt no shame in it, for he saw Ansel blubbering and begging their captors not to kill him. Fred Gregory wept also, as did Nathan. Fred's shoulders writhed and his lips worked awhile before sound came.

"Ain't you gonna do somethin'? Ain't you gonna say a prayer for us, or anything?"

"Stand ready, men," Captain Howard commanded.

Half a dozen troopers, rifles at port arms, stood behind the horses. With each of Howard's commands they moved in unison.

"Ready . . . aim . . . *fire!*"

Four horses stiffened and flinched in reaction to the gun-shots so close and unexpected behind them. Then they leaped forward into an agitated run. Fred Gregory had time to scream in horror before his neck broke with a dry-stick crunch. His little brother had already voided his bladder and he went to his reward with a single pleading word.

"Momma!"

"Murdering bast—," Nathan Varney managed before his neck snapped.

"Help me, Jesus!" Davey blurted as he felt Nellie writhe and bolt forward.

Davey fell and the rope elongated. Eyes tightly squinted shut, he heard the creaking sound of stretching rope and felt a terrible burning around his throat. From far off, echoing as though from the bottom of a well, he heard the voice he hated most.

"Leave 'em strung up for their folks to find," Captain Howard commanded. "Sergeant, mount the troops."

"Sir! Pre—pare to mount! . . . Mount!"

"Column of twos to the left, for—ward march!" Godfrey Howard ordered.

Forming up, the troops rode past the dangling bodies. Captain Howard spared a long, contemplative look at the youngest. His bare belly still heaved as he tried to suck in air. Too bad he could not have been spared, Howard mused to himself. He was—*interesting*.

Through slitted eyes, Davey watched the troops until all had their backs to him. Then he struggled with the loosely fastened rope around his slender wrists. Too light for his own weight to break neck—though he wasn't aware of the cause—Davey had not died instantly as his brother and cousins had. Now he fought time and gravity to free his hands and pull himself up the rope before he strangled. One item, one small and to him important detail, kept repeating in his fevered brain.

Through bloodied lips, he kept repeating in a harsh whisper, *"They had red legs."*

# 4

Dawn came clear and chill in the mile-high city of Denver, Colorado. With the prospect of better than seven hundred miles to cover, Slocum wisely chose to take the Kansas Pacific Express at least as far as Salina, Kansas. The final leg of his journey, he reasoned, would be better spent on horseback, which would give him the opportunity to gather more information on the situation. It would also keep him away from the prying eyes of curious lawmen, who habitually observed who came and went by train. The huge Baldwin $4-6-0$ huffed and snorted, the engineer's cab wreathed in a white cloud, when Slocum arrived at the depot.

He had paid his bill at Hobson's Livery and now sought the stockcar that would transport his supple bay gelding, Ol' Rip. Slocum generally considered horses the way most men would any handy tool and rarely owned one with any name other than "horse." Ol' Rip deserved his rare exception. The big gelding had a devilish personality that suited his name, with a strength and endurance Slocum admired. He walked the animal to where a conductor stood by a loading ramp and showed his ticket.

"All the way to Salina, eh?" the man in a blue suit and round bill cap observed, reading the destination. "We don't get a lot of business going this way, so he'll not be too crowded, I'd wager. Take him on up, or do you want me to get a baggage handler to do it?"

"I'll take care of it, thanks," Slocum said sparely.

"Fine by me. There's sawhorse stands at the front for tack."

Five minutes later, a pair of oversized saddlebags slung over one shoulder, Slocum again presented his ticket and boarded a first-class car. He found his seat to be large and comfortable. Small wonder the railroads were rapidly taking over stage-coach business. Large signs, in bold red ink, at each end of the coach informed passengers: THIS IS NOT A SMOKING CAR. SMOKING PERMITTED ON THE VESTIBULE AND SMOKING CAR ONLY.

Well, no one wanted folks smoking in their parlors at home, either, Slocum thought, amused. Since early childhood, he recalled the end-of-meal ritual, especially after Sunday dinner. The menfolk went out onto the porch, or into the yard, for a cigar or quirley and to pass the jug of white whiskey. It was one of those "it's always been this way" things. After easing his burden onto an overhead metal rack, Slocum took his seat. The cleverly designed plush chairs of George Pullman's would convert at night into comfortable bunks. Well and good, Slocum considered, since he'd be on board for two nights, barring breakdowns or obstructions such as cattle or buffalo snoozing on the tracks. He looked out the window and twisted his lips into a wry grin.

He had managed to jolly Hope into a final, delirious bout of lovemaking before morning came. He hadn't convinced her to come down and see him off. Women tended to limit their men, Slocum thought philosophically. If thwarted in that goal, they became sulky. He had had every intention of returning to Hope Vanneman, yet she saw his leaving as an absolute. No appeal would change that, which left their relationship in ashes. Still, he might come back someday. In the twenty minutes that followed, the coach filled to half its capacity. The steam whistle hooted and the driver wheels spun when the engineer threw a valve and released live steam into the cylinders. Pistons hissing and weeping, the Baldwin No. 6 overcame inertia and began to stretch out the couplings.

With a creak, bang, and violent jerk, the train went into motion. Three hundred thirty miles to go, alone as usual, Slocum summed up with a rueful shrug. He would eat and drink and sleep in luxury, and then back to his real world. One of dust and danger.

For good or bad, Salina, Kansas, had never attracted the cattle business. Abilene had given way to Ellsworth, and then much further south, to Dodge City, for the mighty trail herds that came up from Texas. The only rowdy element in the city, where the Methodist Church was already talking of establishing a university, came from the small army garrison outside town on the Smoky Hill River, which had charge of supervising the Smoky Hill Indian Reservation. The small detachment was far from its station at Fort Riley, and thus out of direct observation of ranking superiors. So, Salina basked in late-afternoon placidity when the KP Express rolled into the depot and discharged half a dozen passengers, including Slocum and his horse.

Too late to set off for Chase County that day, Slocum decided. He searched out a livery, put up Ol' Rip, and set out for the Hay Hotel. Along the way, he noted that the Kansas newspapers made an even bigger ballyhoo over the depredations attributed to "rebel insurrectionists." That stood to reason, Slocum reckoned; after all, it was their state. He purchased two different issues and took them along to his room.

What he read did nothing to improve his mood. If he had been more susceptible to hyperbole, Slocum might have believed the editors of the two papers—one was the *Emporia Light* —who were bent on crucifying Ewan McDade and the other Southerns. Their prose waxed almost hysterical. In the *Light*, the editor had gone so far as to call for summary executions of "all rebels in our great state."

Disgusted at such blind prejudice, and alarmed for his friend, Slocum ate a light supper and spent the evening preparing for his overland journey. Memories of Hope Vanneman still fresh, he even shunned the company of a willing, compliant young female who approached him in the hotel's small saloon.

"You look lonely," she had announced when she sidled up to him.

"I am. I left a wonderful woman back in Denver to come . . . here."

"Oh?" from pouting lips, with arched brow.

"Oh," Slocum bit off shortly.

"Sounds like you could use a little tender loving. My name's Kitty."

"Meow," Slocum responded cattily. "I've been on a train for three days and two nights, Kitty, and all I need is a good, long sleep."

"Alone?"

Slocum answered with a crooked smile.

"Don't you like Kitty?" she pouted.

Slocum's long, up-down gaze could have undressed her right there. He produced a sensuous smile that completed the effect and brought a blush to Kitty's cheeks. Slowly he shook his head from side to side.

"You're a fine enough woman, Kitty, but I'm just not in the mood."

Kitty appraised him for a moment, then rose on tiptoe and planted a wet kiss on one cheek. "At least I know you're man enough, if you had the inkling."

She ambled off, seeking another patron. Slocum appreciated the churning motion of her posterior, visualizing two squabbling wildcats in a satin bag. He finished off his drink and went to his room and to bed at once.

In the lower altitude of Salina, Slocum awoke, dressed, and left the hotel into a pleasantly cool predawn. He had Ol' Rip saddled and provisions stored in a single carpetbag pannier, slung on the animal's left rump, before first light. He cleared the town's limits and let the prairie swallow him as the first faint line of pearly white delineated the eastern horizon. It looked altogether like a perfect day.

Long before Kansas achieved statehood in 1861, someone had coined the phrase "If you don't like the weather in Kansas, wait half an hour and it'll change." Slocum became aware of the truth of this adage before the sun reached the meridian.

Huge thunderclouds, black on the bottom, growing and soaring in roiled columns of deep gray, their upper reaches opalescent at over forty-five thousand feet, formed to the southwest. They continued to spread and blot out light while inexorably moving closer through the noon hour. Slocum kept a chary eye on them, noting the faraway flickers that indicated intense electrical activity. By two in the afternoon, fully two-thirds of the sky's dome had been blotted out. The air seemed charged with invisible particles and the wind died. Slocum's skin itched and his nostrils tingled. The first blinding flash and cataclysmic burst of thunder nearly took him out of the saddle.

All around the crackling air smelled of ozone. Slocum winced at the fading tumult and kicked Ol' Rip to a quick trot. Three more times dry lightning blasted the prairie, striking randomly around him. The sky turned black and huge drops began to patter in the dust, raising puffs at first, then spreading out to dampen the soil. The racing globules grew thicker, harder. A midair sibilance and tin-roof rattle on the hard ground announced the rapid approach of a swath of hail. Slocum knew better than to shelter under a tree during a thunderstorm. Yet, depending on the size of the hail and the altitude from which it fell, it could severely injure or render unconscious man and beast. A quick glance to the rear and he set Ol' Rip to a gallop.

White ice balls the size of walnuts pelted downward. Ahead, jagged bolts of blue-white illuminated a low ridge. Slocum headed that direction. The first of the hailstones smacked Ol' Rip's rump and Slocum's back when they topped the rise. Another brilliant zigzag of electric energy laddered through the clouds. In its actinic light, Slocum saw a rectangular yellow shape. It had to be a house.

Slocum reined Ol' Rip to the right and bolted for the promised safety of the dimly seen dwelling. His curiosity increased as the distance diminished. For all the storm's darkness and fury, he could not make out the slightest glow of a lamp at any window. He approached to the point where he could see the rough-hewn character of the native limestone that formed the outer walls. Still no light. A shutter came free and whipped violently in the gusts.

With a howl, the wind increased in force and set up a screech-bang flapping of the loose boards. The house must be abandoned, Slocum realized with a sinking feeling. Beyond it now he could make out the charred, irregular wall studdings, so many blackened teeth in the skull of Mother Earth, that marked out what was once a barn. If the place was abandoned, Slocum considered in a detached, unreal set of mind, then no one could object to Ol' Rip lasting out the storm in the kitchen. Another fifty yards and they would be there.

Soaked through, teeth chattering from the severe temperature drop, Slocum swung out of the saddle and, keeping one hand on the reins, walked up the crumbling steps to the sagging porch. The door failed to yield to his touch, so he stepped back and gave it a powerful kick. It flew open, the creak of its hinges loud enough to be heard over the storm. Slocum took a look around inside and led Ol' Rip into the front parlor. Left behind, a potbellied stove remained attached to the chimney.

Slocum stripped off his leather vest and flannel shirt and used a pair of long johns from his saddlebags to wipe dry his face, arms, and torso. Then he set to breaking up some scraps of furniture, a built-in bookcase, and then prying off some of the mopboard. The latter he split with a hand axe and arranged as kindling in the stove. This he lit with a lucifer match and added more fuel. He and Ol' Rip would soon be dry.

Before wiping down the wet, shivering horse, Slocum stripped out of the rest of his clothes and set everything to dry by the stove. Naked, his flesh goose-bumped at once. He lost the tingle of cold by removing the saddle and slicking the rain from Ol' Rip's hide. The bay gelding whuffled gratefully and edged closer to the stove.

"All the comforts of home, Rip," Slocum announced. "We'll get you dry and set up in another room. Then I'll have fatback and beans ready in an hour."

Mourning doves greeted a leaden morning sky with appropriate lament. By the time Slocum had his gear stowed on Ol' Rip the rapidly thinning clouds had pink fringes. He studied the sodden terrain with startlingly clear green eyes and developed a trio of parallel lines on his forehead. A light breeze stirred his longish raven's-wing hair. His full lips pursed and he gave a slight shrug in full opinion of the slow progress he knew he would make.

By evening, Slocum knew he had overestimated his ability. He had made barely twenty-five miles slogging through the gummy mud of Kansas. He and his horse showed signs of extreme fatigue. Not inclined to spend a wet night on the clay-based ground, he continued to urge Ol' Rip forward. With the orange, magenta, and purple bars of sunset a memory, and even the quail bedded down, Slocum spotted a tiny pinprick of yellow in the distance south of him. Encouraged, he drubbed heels into Ol' Rip's sides and headed there.

His hoped-for shelter turned out to be a ramshackle combination of at least three shacks shoved together to form one large building. The sign outside identified it as Haven's, a low dive of dubious reputation. Slocum didn't give a damn. In his present condition the road ranch beckoned like a siren. To one side, a pole corral and low barn offered shelter for animals. Slocum dismounted and led his horse there.

"One night?" the hostler asked, as though anyone would voluntarily stay there longer, Slocum thought.

"Yep."

"Two bits. Four if I grain it."

"Here's half a dollar. Snap the feed bag on him while I do a rubdown. D'you have any liniment?"

"Dr. Sloan's, dollar six bits a bottle."

Double the usual price. "I'll take one."

Slocum spent half an hour grooming Ol' Rip, making generous applications of liniment to each leg joint. Then, his rumbling belly leading the way, he entered the road ranch. The odor of rancid grease that had assailed his nostrils outside disappeared in the rich aroma of a stew, baking biscuits, and tobacco smoke. Slocum ordered a beer and a bowl of stew. They arrived with a thick slice of fresh-baked bread.

While he ate, Slocum took in his surroundings. A scant dozen men occupied the central barroom. Five played a desultory game of poker at a stained green baize table in one corner. One rose from his seat after a short while and walked to a scratched and weathered piano. He flexed his fingers and began to bring forth music. A sad ballad, rather than the bright, tinkly tunes of a saloon, filled the smoky air. Two men stood at the bar between Slocum and a youngster who steadily knocked down shots of whiskey and criticized everything and everyone present. Slocum gnawed on the unidentifiable meat and chewed hard on the gritty bread.

At least, he consoled himself, it was hot and filling. His meal completed, Slocum asked for a cup of coffee and a shot of whiskey. The coffee was bitter, the whiskey of surprisingly good quality. He raised his eyes to study the youth in the backbar mirror when the slender young man raised his voice.

"There's not a one of you here who can fuck or fight. It

takes balls to do both." He laughed coldly at his own gibe.
"This place is the final refuge for losers."

"You don't like it, kid, there's a wide trail out there," one
of the poker players paused to say.

That earned him a sneer. Then the teenager noticed Slocum's
scrutiny in the mirror. "You find something interesting to look
at, mister?"

"Not really," Slocum answered mildly. "I've seen dozens
just alike."

"Got a bur under your saddle?" the kid bristled. "What's
the matter with you, mister? Awh, hell, you're like all the
rest . . . no balls."

"Didn't your momma ever teach you manners?" Slocum
snapped, abraded by the youngster's hot tongue.

After exchanging a concerned glance, the two men between
them abandoned the split-plank bar for a table well out of the
line of fire. "Manners is what you use on folks you respect. I
ain't seen anyone around here fits the bill."

Slocum's ire rose hotly. "You could be making a bad mistake."

For the first time, the kid looked directly at Slocum. A mad-
man's smile flickered briefly. The youth took a step away from
the bar. "Well, as I live and breathe. You're a gunfighter, ain't
ya? I think I know you, seen your likeness somewhere. You're
a fast gun named John Slocum, right?"

"Who I am doesn't matter. If you're that set on bein' on the
prod, take it somewhere else."

Wondering expression adding to his boyishness, the kid
shook his head. "No—no, I don't think I can do that. I
recognized you the minute you rode in. So, there's no backin'
down now. Y'see, I intend on makin' my reputation by being
the man who got Slocum."

"You're on a fool's errand," Slocum cautioned. He didn't
want a confrontation, not when bound on a sensitive mission
like the one he had undertaken.

"That's for me to decide. I figger I'm better than you, faster."

Slocum sighed. "A lot of men have thought that. I'm still
around."

The kid brightened, said almost lightly, "Then you are
Slocum. I've a mind to settle this right now."

"I've no wish for a shooting," Slocum protested in a soft, low voice, his green eyes narrowing, changing to a flat, troubled sea tint.

"Slocum, *make your play!*"

Slocum's right hand snapped across his belt line and closed on the butt grips of his weapon. His .45 Colt Peacemaker cleared leather a half second ahead of the boy's. The prodding youth hadn't even leveled his piece when Slocum's hammer dropped. The discharge rang loud and painful in the low-ceilinged dive. His aim had not been hampered by his drinking, Slocum observed as the kid staggered backward a step and dropped his six-gun.

A red stain began to spread on his shirt in the right shoulder area. He blinked and dropped to his knees. His good left hand rose to cover the numbing wound and tears filled his eyes. He took his fingers away from the entry hole and looked at them.

"It wasn't . . . supposed to . . . be like this," he panted out. Then he fainted.

"Shit!" Slocum grunted as he reholstered his revolver. "I didn't even know his name."

# 5

"Now, don't you worry about that wild hair you tamed last
night," the proprietor of the road ranch informed Slocum in
the faint light of false dawn. "More'n enough witnesses who
saw you was pushed into it. 'Sides, since liquor is outlaw in
Kansas now, this place ain't supposed to exist, so nobody'll go
reportin' the shootin' anyhow. You was smoother than silk, an'
quicker than a rattler, Mr. Slocum. It was a pleasure to watch
you work."

"It wasn't for that kid," Slocum reminded him sourly.

The owner of the road ranch had spiffed up somewhat over
his previous appearance, vicarious pride in the besting of the
hot head inspiring him to make a better effort. He pondered
Slocum's words a moment and shook his head in agreement.

"Nope. I suppose what you say is rightly true."

"And it wasn't any pleasure for me. You think on that."
Slocum swung into the saddle and headed Ol' Rip down the
short lane to the main road south.

A meadowlark gave an alarmingly bright, heart-painingly
sweet call as Slocum eased his mount into a gentle lope. He
had a lot of distance to cover, some to make up for, the way
he saw it. He settled into the smooth, comfortable rhythm of a
mile-eating gait and considered again the problems facing his
friend and former brother officer.

Ewan McDade had the temperament for sudden, harsh anger,

34

but his even nature quickly moderated that and reason generally prevailed. In fact, Slocum could recall only one time McDade had lost it entirely. Their intelligence-gathering patrol had come upon a pro-Southern farm near Branson, Missouri. The house had been burned, barn also. Two bodies, of a man and a half-grown youth, lay in the yard. Victims of Jayhawkers, obviously, had been the verdict. Then Ewan McDade had discovered the woman and three children.

The mother of that brood had been violated before she died, as had her six-year-old daughter. One of the boys showed evidence of having been sodomized before being shot in the back of the head, and the other had been cruelly trapped inside the flaming house and burned to death. Ewan McDade made a personal vow to track down the vermin responsible and deal with them in a manner not at all prescribed by General Sterling Price's orders.

In the end, he had. It took more than a month, then a chance remark from a captured Yankee irregular identified the five men who had done murder and worse. Three of them were also captives. One McDade branded and emasculated, the other two he hanged. A week later, during a foray into Kansas, McDade and three of his enlisted men visited the homes of the other two Jayhawkers. Their families he spared. The houses he burned. And the men died shrieking in terror and agony, bullet-shattered legs preventing them from escaping the flames that devoured their dwellings.

Could something, equally barbaric, have set Ewan McDade off again? Slocum didn't have time to contemplate that possibility. A hot pain and tearing sensation erupted in the flesh of his left armpit. A moment later he heared the crack of a rifle. Using the force of the impact to direct him, Slocum went slack and propelled himself off his horse as if he had taken a fatal shot. Not ten miles from the road ranch, he thought. Damn.

Eyes slitted, Slocum lay on the ground, waiting out the hidden assassin. While the long seconds crept by, Slocum considered his ruse a gamble. Whoever had shot him might not be curious enough to come down and make certain. And all the while, he lay bleeding. Although not incapacitating, the wound began to sting and throb. His blood loss would be profuse. He might stay there, growing weaker, until he exsanguinated and died, never knowing his murderer.

After what seemed a disproportionate time, Slocum heard the soft clopping of hooves. Slowly a figure, leading a horse, came into Slocum's view. Through slitted eyes, Slocum strove to focus on the assassin. Another twenty paces and he recognized the reputation-hunting kid he had wounded the night before. He had a Winchester slung in the crook of his left arm, a big bandage making a bulge on his right shoulder.

That accounted for the lack of accuracy, Slocum surmised. He forced himself to relax and look dead. The kid came closer, ground-reined his mount, and walked in close. He stopped over Slocum's body and gazed down at the blood that spread on the ground. He licked nervous lips, which began to tremble, then uttered a muffled curse.

"I got him!" he gloated. "I killed John Slocum!" The kid raised his eyes to heaven, as though defying God to contradict him.

"Wrong," Slocum told the exulting kid as he came back to life and drilled the youthful murderer through the heart.

Slocum came to his feet and kicked the Winchester out of reach. He toed the slack corpse over with one boot and stared into unseeing, pale blue eyes. In their glazing surfaces he saw only a reflection of himself.

"Damn. Why do some of them never learn?"

With his wound bandaged as best he could manage one-handed, Slocum continued southward. A hot spring sun that summoned forth the green shoots of new life soon soaked the armpits of his shirt. The bullet gouge smarted and Slocum harbored no doubts about the need of proper treatment. Without it, infection would soon set in. A man alone, in even so settled a land as Kansas, could easily come to grief. Occasionally he would hum a little snatch of a half-forgotten song.

He was thusly engaged in midafternoon when he came upon a small farm, tucked in a fold of the rolling plain. Slocum rode up to the tie-rail outside a weathered, once-white picket fence that described the scraggly yard of a clapboard house. The house showed obvious signs of "tack-ons" as the family grew. Two barefoot boys, cotton-top mopheads of about eight and ten, peered at him from the gnarled branches of an ancient cottonwood. Another lad, in his early teens, stopped forking hay down from the open loft of the barn to study the stranger. From inside the house he heard a woman's startled expression.

"Land sakes, we've got company. Jessie, you get some shoes on, ya hear?"

"Yes, ma'am," a more musical, younger female voice answered.

Slocum remained in the saddle, patiently waiting. After a moment the door opened and a woman in her early to mid-thirties stepped onto the small porch. She wore an apron over a blue-gray housedress, and a smudge of white on one cheek indicated she had been engaged in baking when he arrived. Hair pulled back in a severe bun, she cocked her head and stared boldly.

"You're new to these parts," she stated as acknowledged fact. "Neomi Sweet. Step down and state your business."

"Slocum's the name," he gave for answer. He freed his right leg and swung away from the saddle, winced at the pain in his left side. "I've been, ah, injured. Someone shot at me."

Ice clouded Neomi's deep blue eyes. "A posse?" she asked coldly.

"No. It's a long story. Suffice that a hotheaded kid with a hanker to make a name for himself ambushed me. First time he tried it, I let him go with a bullet in the shoulder. The next, he back-shot me."

"What happened to him?" Neomi inquired, her lips in a thin, hard line. A frown of disapproval creased her forehead above arched, nearly invisibly light brows.

"He, ah, went off to meet his Maker."

Her sudden change of mood and appearance shocked Slocum. "Good. My man, he ran into one of those. Made me a widow. Not that I hold with violence and killing, but the Good Lord must allow honest folks a little payback time."

"About the, ah, scrape I got. Is there a doctor nearby?" Slocum pressed.

"Nope. There's just me. I make do for my family and critters, any neighbors who can't help themselves. Though there's few enough of them, God knows. C'mon in, Mr. Slocum, I'll do what I can. Jason, Jeremy," she called, raising her voice to a bellow. "Get down outta that tree and make yourselves useful. I'll need another bucket of water, some of that cotton gauze, the sticking plaster, liniment . . . " Her voice faded as she went inside.

Slocum followed and found a seat, as directed, in the kitchen. The two small boys scampered in a moment later. One grabbed up a wooden bucket, while the other turned bottom end up over a deep drawer in a free-standing cupboard with pressed metal panels in the doors.

"Get outta that shirt," Neomi demanded.

For the first time, Slocum noticed she was a handsome woman. A bit rawboned and weathered, but not showing age at all. No gray streaked her coppery yellow hair, nor had wrinkles invaded the corners of her eyes or mouth. She moved with a lithe smoothness that revealed promising curves in all the best places. He shrugged out of his shirt after undoing the buttons and laid it aside.

"You got another? My man's stuff is still here if you have need."

"In my saddlebags," Slocum told her shortly.

"Jessie! C'm here, girl." A remarkable beauty appeared from another room, a duplicate of what Neomi must have been in her youth. "This is my oldest, Jessica Sweet. Jessie, go out to the man's horse and find a clean shirt. This one's got a bullet hole through it and more blood than's decent."

"Yes, Momma," a voice to match her family name responded.

Neomi produced a large bottle of Dr. Latham's liniment and daubed a large quantity onto a square of cotton gauze her youngest son had produced from the cupboard. It stung like hell. Slocum took his mind off the cramp-generating effect by reflecting on the daughter. Jessica could hardly be called a child. She had the full bloom of a woman and eyes that seemed to undress him when they were introduced. The liquid torment over with, Slocum found himself startled anew to discover the same intense scrutiny on the part of his benefactor.

A stray whisper of a smile and a knowing boldness about the eyes revealed an interest on Neomi's part beyond giving succor to a stranger. While she cleansed and dressed the scrape, she made an expert assay of his rippling muscles, the scars and discolorations of past encounters, and the elastic youthfulness of his flesh. Clearly what she saw evoked memories of past splendor, betrayed by a wistful smile and heartfelt sigh.

"It's been three years." Neomi might have read his mind. "Jerred, that's the oldest boy, begged his poppa not to go to town that day. Almost like he had a premonition. He was eleven that year, and Robert forty-one. It didn't matter, him being seven years older than me. It does now," she added in a tiny voice. "There, all patched up. That should hold you good enough." She tied the last binding.

"Thank you," Slocum said sincerely. "I really owe you for this."

"Stuff and nonsense," Neomi answered. "I've been doin' for my family and other folks long enough to qualify as a doctor in some parts."

"I'd be obliged if there might be some small chores I could do to repay you for this, a meal, and a night's rest."

Neomi flirted with big eyes. "Why, Mr. Slocum, you've no need. But . . . now that you mention it, there's a broken hinge on the big barn door. Too heavy for Jerred an' the little boys to handle alone. Then there's the privy. Seat's taken to splintering and a new one could be nailed in place. O' course there's always a need for split firewood."

"Point me to them," Slocum interrupted before she could recollect more.

Jerred turned out to be fourteen. Long, lanky, but remarkably strong, the lad worked with a will. The barn door took an hour. When Slocum started on the outhouse seat, Neomi joined him and kept up a steady chatter. It had more purpose than might appear on the surface, Slocum soon realized. Her glib patter wove a clear tapestry. One that loudly declared how badly she needed to lie with a man once again. Slocum suppressed an anticipatory grin and bided his time.

A full moon turned the Kansas prairie a ghostly white. At its zenith a man could read a newspaper by its light. Slocum had eaten a satisfactory supper of fried chicken, with plenty of potatoes, gravy, and all the trimmings. Afterward he sat on the porch and smoked a thin, pungent cigar and listened to Jerred enthusiastically describe all the other projects he would like to get done, if only he had some help. Considering the attractive widow and her obvious willingness, it made a tempting proposition. Yet, the plight of Ewan McDade and his neighbors

called stridently to Slocum. He bid the family good night along
toward nine-thirty and went to his blankets in the barn loft.

With the moon on the westering side of the sky, Slocum
awakened shortly after midnight. The short, strident creak of
the hinges on the small access door to the barn had cut through
his slumber like a thunderclap. Years of being on the edge sent
his hand to the smooth walnut grips of the .45 Colt. Slowly his
sleep-clouded eyes cleared and focused.

A feminine figure stood outlined by the pale alabaster light.
Silently the visitor entered the barn and walked to the ladder
that led to his sleeping place in the haymow. Slocum felt the
vibrations of each footfall on the cross rungs. A cloud of yellow hair, loose now and afloat on the rising warm current of
barn-scented air, rose above the flooring. Slocum relaxed and
returned his six-gun to its leather. When he looked back, his
surprise redoubled.

His visitor revealed herself to be not the ripe and wanting
Neomi, but her lovely, and equally needful, daughter. Jessica
was barefoot and her feet hissed through the loose hay. She
wore a dress now instead of the mannish jeans of the afternoon.
With one finger to her lips to signal silence, she swayed her
way into Slocum's arms.

Her kiss was soft, vibrant, and incredibly sweet. Her breath
and mouth smelled faintly of peppermint. Like that of a child.
For a moment, his rapidly rising ardor cooled. No, children
were never possessed of the large, firm, full breasts that pressed
desperately against his bare chest, their rigid nipples prominent through the thin cloth of the dress. His loins grew warm,
extending his manhood and quickening it to solid erectness.

Jessica's jaw sagged and her tongue probed at his mouth.
Sweeter still. Slocum's breath grew ragged and irregular. One
hand slid down her taut back to the wonderful curve of her
buttocks. He squeezed and she moaned. She thrust her pelvis
against his extended phallus and ground into it. Their embrace
ended and Jessica pushed away.

Bending, she caught at the hem of her garment and began
to hoist it. Silver moonlight revealed the delightful curves and
hollows of her womanly body. Slocum gasped at the dark rings
from which her nipples protruded, and then again as his eyes
traveled to her narrow waist, perfect navel, and the wispy thatch
that graced, but did not hide, her swollen pubic mound. The

cleft pinkly glistened, wet and ready. A rapidly retreating part of Slocum's consciousness started to protest that she was but a child.

"Jessie, we can't . . ."

A finger to her lips silenced him again. "Don't worry," she whispered hoarsely. "Everyone is sound asleep. I'm seventeen and I *know* what I'm doing, know what I want."

"But you're . . ." Slocum again raised objection, though with hardly convincing effort.

"Innocent? Hardly," Jessica informed him. "I'm far from that. Five years ago, with malice aforethought as they say, I gleefully surrendered my maidenhead to a farmhand we had working here. He was twenty-five and saving to homestead his own place. Charlie was so handsome," she sighed. "And awfully shy. I almost had to crawl into his bed to get him to understand what I wanted." Then her passion-bright features altered, became sad, lower lip out in a pink pout.

"When Poppa died, we had to let him go. Since then I've been doing without and it's driving me crazy," Jessica concluded. Her hands cupped the lovely globes of her breasts. She undulated her hips in invitation. A sleek and desirable sea nymph, she danced in the dust motes captured in moonbeams.

Slocum's last fragment of hesitation shredded with the first tender touch of her lips against his chest. She nuzzled him like a hungry colt, slithered across his firm skin, and closed tightly to suck at his nipple. With one hand, Slocum examined the front of his long johns and found he inhabited a red flannel Sibley tent. Deftly Jessica's fingers found the drawstring and untied the bow. She slid him out of his only garment and knelt at his feet.

Featherlight, her warm, soft, moist fingers and seeking lips located his swaying manhood. They charmed, teased, coaxed him to even greater hardness and length. His knees trembled as Jessica opened wide and took his fullness deep within her mouth. A long, soft sigh banished all cares. Slocum sought only delight.

With consummate skill Jessica brought him to the peak, then released his throbbing member so that he slid down the incline of excitement and achingly called out for more. Greedily she obliged him, each time consuming more of his rich endowment, sucking harder, head and shoulders bobbing as she exerted fantastic energy into delivering every bit as much pleasure as she received.

"Th-that's—that's un—*unbelievable!*" Slocum groaned as his ecstasy mounted.

"Umhum-hum-hum," Jessica chortled. "I thought you'd like it. Now it's my turn. Now, now, you big, randy stallion, take me."

Shivering with erotic abandon, Slocum lowered her slender, lively figure to the blankets and insinuated his hips between her upraised, wide-spread legs. The silken skin of her thighs brushed his muscular body as he lowered himself and plunged full length into her portal of forgetfulness. The passage behind the gate gave slowly, reluctantly, turning his penetration into an odyssey of heroic proportions.

Jessica beat tiny fists on his naked back. "Hard! Hard! Do it harder, dear love. Drive me . . . D-d-drriiiive meeeeeee wiiiiiilld!"

Slocum did his absolute best to comply. Jessica keened, and wailed, and groaned, and howled her utter rapture at his possession of her body. She bucked and slammed her pelvis against his until they both ached; she pounded his back, bit and scratched and squeezed with bareback horse–strengthened legs. All of which put Slocum into a frenzy he'd not known since that magical time, so many long years in the past, when he had claimed his first erotic victory.

Oblivion came as relief. Panting and groaning in weariness, Slocum lay beside her. His heart rate had hardly subsided to normal when he felt her inquisitive fingers searching his groin. A few deft strokes and he found new life. Once more he mustered the strength to rise expectantly and drive deep within her tender, yielding flesh. Swaying and thrusting, the occasional nag of his wound banished, Slocum brought new joy to his hungry partner. In reward he received a clinging kiss and soft, sweet words.

"I'll never forget you, Slocum. Never. What I knew before is fit only for a child. You are the man every real woman dreams of."

And then she was gone. Slocum found repose without effort. His deep slumber, devoid of even the barest primal caution, masked the furtive sounds of movement in the barn. He knew nothing until he awakened to find the naked widow astraddle his loins, her distended and welcomingly open cleft poised above his supine manhood. Her first cool, soft touch brought it eagerly to life. While his reason screamed for escape, his lusty nature called for yet another round.

They loved in a tangle of arms and legs, pumping bodies, soft calls and coos. They loved long and well. Fatigued parts revitalized in order to match the urgency and heated demand of Neomi's body. Exerting every drop of his resources, Slocum made certain she lacked nothing in achieving blessed completion. Not once, but twice, and a third delirious time she made her carnal demands. Slocum never flagged. By sunup he had been thoroughly drained, but was determined to continue if called upon. When at last she signaled her surfeit, her soft, teasing words bemused and perplexed the ex-Confederate.

"Was she as good as that?" Neomi asked.

Slocum slept until nearly ten o'clock. Both smirking happily, Neomi and Jessica fed him a huge breakfast, frequently suppressed outbursts of giggles, and waved him a fond farewell.

# 6

At first sight, McPherson, Kansas, didn't look like much to Slocum. The skyline featured more outhouses then multistoried buildings. The native fieldstone courthouse was still under construction on the upper story and dome. A larger-than-life bronze statue of Union General James Birdseye McPherson on the scraggly lawn gave him a distinct chill.

General James B. McPherson had been at Gettysburg. He'd also been the commander in the field for General Wm. T. Sherman at the battle of Atlanta. "Butcher" Sherman's fair-haired boy in the abattoir of the Georgia campaign, until his death on July 22, 1864. There had been some celebrating in the Army of the Trans-Mississippi when word of that reached them. A lot of the younger rank and file had gotten soundly drunk. The older, combat-weary veterans, Slocum and Ewan McDade among them, had expressed their joy quietly, often in prayer that the loss of McPherson would end, or greatly slow, Sherman's march that was ripping out the heart of the Confederacy. Yet people here, in the center of Kansas, had chosen to honor McPherson by naming their town after him and erecting a huge statue to that monster.

Slocum could readily see how that would raise the ire of former Southerns, exiled to new homes in Kansas by the exigencies of war and the reign of terror called Reconstruction. Would it be enough to bring on the bloody reprisals he had

44

been reading of? Slocum meant to find out.

An accommodating clerk at Slocum's hotel gave him a note of introduction to a private "gentlemen's club." Even before the gubernatorial edict outlawing booze, McPherson had been dry since its inception. That didn't prevent a sub rosa society of "members only" saloons, thinly disguised as fraternal or patriotic organizations. There, in the reading room of the Loyal Order of Hibernians, Slocum paged through several recent newspapers for more accounts of the atrocities allegedly committed by Ewan McDade and his "gang of unrepentant rebels."

Slocum soon discovered a new note had entered the editorial remarks. Everyone with even vague connections to the Old South was being blamed for the depredations. One editor in particular, Walter Albert Black of the *Emporia Light*, was easily the most vituperative.

"The evidence of a vast conspiracy is obvious," Black stated in a half-page editorial three days earlier. "Led by agents of the black cabal, the Knights of the White Camellia, these dregs of the vanquished Southern aristocracy are banding together to defy the will of the people and establish a new slave state here in Kansas. This Pit of Gehenna must not be allowed to emerge into the light. The Kluxers, as they call themselves, are the servants of the Dark Powers. It is manifest that we decent folk of this great state crush their evil before it multiplies."

"Would you like this refreshed, suh?" a white-jacketed colored waiter asked Slocum deferentially.

"Ah-umm, yes," Slocum answered. "There's no such thing as *one* mint julep, is there?"

"Nawssah, there sho' ain't."

Slocum wondered whether the waiter would be making reports on his activities. The cotton-haired old man had slipped into the speech pattern and rhythm of the plantation-born when Slocum had first spoken. The ex-Georgian speculated whether the man truly considered himself better off now that he worked for wages and had to provide a home, purchase food and clothing and every essential of life for his family.

Although Slocum's father had not owned slaves, members of the Slocum clan had, and some of their immediate neighbors had as well. Slocum cared neither one way nor the other about slavery. Contrary to the new versions of history being written by the victors, the war had not been fought over the issue of owning slaves. Like most wars, the acquisition of power, in this case absolute power, had been the underlying factor. That and the eradication of states' rights, that most jealously guarded keystone of the Constitution. One could not throw out the economic domination of the South, either. Slocum had seen the Constitution trampled in the mud, along with the corpses of the flower of Southern manhood. He had watched an all-powerful, centralized federal government reel drunkenly in the heady intoxicant of its newly acquired importance. And he had seen the lawful, rightful owners of plantations, farms, and businesses stripped of all they possessed through the convenience of Reconstruction.

The South had been reconstructed all right. It had been built afresh in the image of New York City. Slocum had seen his way of life destroyed and had been, like his peers, helpless to prevent it. He'd be damned if he'd let the possibility of being informed on to rabid Unionists in this covert McPherson saloon bother him. The waiter returned with his drink, a tall silver tumbler filled with crushed ice, trickled through with sugar syrup, lemon juice, and bourbon. A jaunty sprig of fresh mint garnished it. Slocum paid the bill and sipped deeply. His eyes strayed back to the biased harangue of Walter Black.

"Reports of rebel assaults on farmsteads and small communities as far west as Hutchison continue to come in. Make no mistake. We are in deadly peril from this Confederate menace. The time for night riders and the lynch rope has not arrived, as yet. It can hardly be far away if these atrocities are allowed to continue."

*Everyone* would be in deadly peril, Slocum thought, if this radical's ideas came into popularity. Another long pull on the mint julep washed away the bitter taste. Slocum began to plan for the remainder of his journey.

"I realize," Cyril Anstruther declared following a tinkling of crystal water goblet to command silence, "that having a meeting at noon is the same to some of you as being called out before breakfast." His pause was filled with polite chuckles. "All the same, it is of paramount importance that we are all together at this time."

"How's that?" a white-bearded member of the cabal asked

from far down the long table in the elegent private dining room.

"Yes, and how soon will we be able to buy up land in the counties south of Emporia?" Senator Dahlgren asked pointedly.

"Justice Duffey, Senator, I'll answer both with the same remark. The time is close. Within a month, two at most, we can have all the land we want virtually for the asking."

"Not soon enough, Cy," Senator Dahlgren snapped. "I have a significant number of constituents—major contributors to my campaign purse, I might add—who are eager to profit from the Southerners' misfortune. Even the governor," Dahlgren hinted without finesse, "is anxiously awaiting the removal of the rebel menace. I'm not talking about his political rhetoric, I'm talking pocketbook here."

"Events can move only so fast," Anstruther reminded him and the others. "Captain Howard's company can spread itself only so thin. About the best we can ask is that he be in two places at the same time. One for setting up, ah, unfortunate rebel atrocities, and the other for chasing down real rebels to blame for them."

"Then I suggest Howard's company be reinforced by at least two platoons of mounted militia," the Kansas senator stated forcefully.

"Now, Victor, please understand," Anstruther protested. "The men in Howard's company are all handpicked. Godfrey Howard and Isaac Banks screened them to make certain their sympathies lay in the, ah, right direction. All of them are Jayhawkers to the core. Bringing in new men, of questionable loyalty, could be a disaster."

Senator Dahlgren hurrumphed over that, adjusted his position in his chair, and banged a silver fork on the table. "I'm certain I can provide just the sort of men needed. If Howard still feels uncomfortable with them, why they can be put to the task of rounding up the rebel scum. Then Howard's men can be left to the job of creating incidents. Uh, by the way, I hope you are making certain Howard's pillaging is being done only against suitable targets."

"Yes, Victor," Anstruther assured him. "The farmers picked for extermination are all registered members of your opposition party. As to your offer of men able to lend their talents to barn burning and child killing . . ." Several members of the conspiracy winced at such blunt talk. "If you can find them, get them."

Before Slocum left McPherson he received chilling news in the form of a praise-filled article in the *Emporia Light*, substantiated by similar, albeit more restrained, reportage in the local *Times-Republican*.

### MARTIAL LAW DECLARED!

A banner headline screamed the news. Under the special executive powers reserved by the governor of Kansas, that worthy had enacted a state of martial law in Lyon and the twelve counties south of Emporia. "Frequent, ruthless attacks against the citizens of Kansas" were cited as the reason for the governor's action. A separate headline, MILITIA CALLED TO EMBATTLED COUNTIES, topped an article revealing that the governor had dispatched an additional ninety-six mounted troopers to serve under the command of Captain Godfrey Howard, headquartered in Emporia, for the purpose of stamping out rebellion among the dissident former Confederates residing in the specified thirteen counties.

It sickened Slocum. Memories of the last days of the war filled his consciousness. Federally activated Kansas State Militia units had been sent into the field in Missouri and Arkansas to accept the surrender of Confederate irregular units. Bloody Bill Anderson had gone in, only to be cut down with his men in a hail of .45-70 slugs from a concealed Gatling gun. The duplicity and dishonor of the Kansans caused the bile to rise from Slocum's stomach even now.

Long before the treachery of the ambushed surrender parlays, most of the Kansas state militia had been men he and many others, both military and civilian, had come to hate. Jayhawkers, they proudly called themselves. Kansas Redlegs. Slocum knew them to be bloody murderers of women and children, house and barn burners, looters and burners of churches and stores, and generally the scum of the earth. They made Anderson and Quantrill look like pussies.

They arrogantly proclaimed themselves to be the legacy of John Brown. Some had even fought at Harper's Ferry. Any thought of fairness for a former Confederate would be a laugh-

ing matter among such animals. Worse, Slocum reasoned, by
the governor's decree they had the "pretense of law" to protect
them. Loud voices from the common room of the Loyal Order
of Hibernians caused Slocum to put aside the newspaper and
stroll into the saloon.

"Gentlemen, to the Jayhawk Militia!" a beet-faced, pudgy
man in an expensive business suit toasted.

"To the Jayhawkers," other voices joined him.

"The only good rebel's a dead rebel," a hatchet-faced man
with too little bristle of mustache declared solemnly.

"Let's hope this here Captain, ah, Howard knows what to
do."

"Yeah," another tippler joined in. "The rope and the firing
squad. That's what's good for Johnny Rebs."

"I'd like to get my sights on a couple of 'em," the beefy
man with the purple face said wistfully.

*You'd shit yellow mustard, too,* Slocum wanted to snarl at
him. Instead, he wisely kept his own counsel. As never before,
the urgency of reaching Ewan McDade goaded Slocum. He
updated his departure. He'd leave that afternoon.


South of McPherson, an unceasing vista of unpopulated rolling prairie presented itself to Slocum's view. Hardly a tree
provided a splash of green more intense than the waving buffalo grass. For aeons the great shaggy beasts had roamed this
land, eating everything they came upon. Rooters, like pigs, the
American bison could and did consume any sort of vegetable
matter. Except along the main watercourses, they had left a
swath of land from the Neosho River in eastern Kansas to the
foothills of the Rockies in Colorado, and from Texas to the
Canadian border, denuded of trees. Even the hearty sage and
chokecherry bushes struggled for continued existence.

It left bleak country to ride across. Nothing, except the
native Osage, Kiowa, and Cheyenne Indians, could hide in
this undulating vastness. Given normal sight, a man could
most days see the maximum fifteen miles to each horizon.
To Slocum's reckoning, he crawled over this stark terrain with
the speed of an ant. About as big in the scheme of things, too,
he acknowledged.

He had made better than twenty-five miles out of McPherson
when he came upon a damaged stagecoach. The illusive appa-

rition he had been watching for some while resolved into a collection of stranded passengers and the injured driver. It was possible this had something to do with the dead man he had come upon earlier. Slocum walked Ol' Rip in close and remained in the saddle.

"You folks appear to have hit upon misfortune," he observed laconically.

"You might say that," came a waspy whine of a voice from an obese man with pudgy fingers, moon face, and thick, protuberant lips of a nasty red-blue coloration.

He wore the typical checkered vest and broad-striped suit of a traveling salesman. At once, given Slocum's state of mind, the lardy drummer reminded him of the carpetbaggers. The man wetly smacked his overfed lips and pinned Slocum with a pointing forefinger.

"Well, young man, are you going to do something to help us or just sit there and gloat?"

"I'm contemplating conducting a short course in manners, suh," Slocum replied, temper enhancing his slight Georgia accent.

Flushed scarlet, the drummer's moon face changed to a disk of outrage. "Why, you young whelp, I've a mind to thrash you properly for your arrogance."

"You'd pay hell doing it," Slocum growled.

"Now, gentlemen, please," an attractive, auburn-haired young woman spoke conciliatorily. "Mr. Dobbins, sir, if you would only reconsider and one of you tender an apology . . . ?"

Slocum wore an expression of regret. "I'll not apologize to this pompous lard bucket."

"I shall certainly not beg the pardon of a . . . a saddle tramp," Dobbins pouted pettily.

Slocum's expression silenced the mouthy salesman, which allowed the raven-haired man to inquire into the cause of distress. The injured driver spoke up first.

"Damn badgers musta dug 'em a cave to expand the family in," he jawed around a chew of Union Leader cut plug. "Wheel dropped through the roof and broke. Pitched me clear'n hell offa the seat. Busted my leg when I hit."

"What about your assistant, the shotgun guard?" Slocum probed.

"He was the only one of the two of us fit. He sort of half-ass set my leg and took off for McPherson for help."

"I see you have the coach horses staked out to graze," Slocum remarked, chosing not to mention the dead man some thirteen miles south of McPherson. "Why didn't some of you accompany the guard on horseback?"

"There's Injuns still around these parts some. Cheyenne, 'specially," the driver told him. "That and road agents. Not so safe for ladies, in particular, and what with no saddles . . ." He let it hang.

"Our biggest problem, Mr., ah . . ."

"Slocum."

"Vivian Ballard," the attractive redhead responded, then went on. "Staying behind wasn't so wise, we discovered, Mr. Slocum. There was no food and little water. We've been here since yesterday shortly after noon."

"Why didn't you go to the creek? You had to have crossed it a short while before the accident."

"Yes, of course. But you see, like the driver said, there are Indians."

"Miss Ballard, I wouldn't worry myself a great deal over Indians unless I saw some. Besides, they don't kill people out of hand simply because they come upon them. It's hardly a mile to that creek. You can see it clearly from here."

"Walking would be no problem except for the shoes I'm wearing." Vivian Ballard displayed a fine turn of ankle when she drew up her skirt hem and showed one of a pair of patent leather high-button shoes.

Slocum nodded understanding and turned on the pushy drummer. "Why didn't you go?"

"Me? Why, it's the stage company's obligation to provide for their passengers," he blurted in an offended tone. "Far be it for me to undertake their responsibilities."

"Don't you have some whiskey samples or something?" Slocum asked.

"Certainly not! I travel in ladies' unmentionables."

Slocum eyed him askance. "I wouldn't, ah, spread word of that around, if I were you," he told Dobbins with a straight face.

The porcine features flushed and Dobbins fairly gobbled in anger. "Now see here, young man. I'll not brook insults from trashy inferiors of your ilk."

Slocum's eyes narrowed. "You'll 'brook' a whole hell of a lot if you're in the mood to be helped out of this."

"We certainly are, Mr. Slocum," Vivian Ballard intervened. "For the rest of the passengers and poor Mr. Jaeger, we'll be grateful for whatever you can do."

"I'm obliged. Now then, Miss Ballard," Slocum began.

"Please, call me Vivian."

"Vivian, the first order is to replenish the water supply. Why don't you gather the canteens available and get up here behind me on the saddle."

"I will, gladly," Vivian told him.

When she had completed the task, and had wiggled into a comfortable position astride Ol' Rip, Slocum reined his mount around and started for the creek.

"What about us?" Dobbins blurted. "What are we supposed to do?"

"You might gather some wood," Slocum advised. "Maybe I'll scare up some game." Then he heeled Ol' Rip into a brisk trot.

# 7

For aeons water had run through this course, eating into the rich, black soil of the prairie, laying bare ledges of lime- and sandstone, here and there a granite boulder and other, harder rocks. Near the point where it widened and became shallow to allow the ford, Slocum reined in and presented an arm so that Vivian could dismount.

She did so with easy grace. Slocum joined her a moment later, retrieving his own canteen. Side by side, they walked to the water. Vivian seemed more animated here, away from the others and the mute evidence of their hazardous condition. She managed a warm, if fleeting, smile.

"I feel so much . . . safer with you here, Slocum. In fact"—she paused to look up and down the creek—"I feel sort of foolish for not having come after water before. It's—the Indian scare, I have to admit. I was brought up on the edge of Cheyenne country. We never had any real trouble, though one neighbor lost some cattle and another had his haystack burned."

"Are you still living there?" Slocum inquired.

"Oh, heavens no. I've been in Salina for some time. Actually, I'm on my way to Wichita, to get a connecting stage to Emporia."

Slocum frowned briefly. The town's name had come up often in the reports of supposed guerrilla raids. "What takes you there? I don't want to pry, but I understand there's some sort of uprising around Emporia."

"Oh, that. Yes, it's why a vacancy came about. I'm going to accept a job as a teacher. The former schoolmistress resigned because of the disturbances."

"Do you feel safe in doing that?"

"Oh, of course. I find it hard to believe that anyone would make war on women and children. Our newspapers do tend to distort the facts."

They bent and began to fill the water bottles, which relieved Slocum of the necessity of making an answer. When they had completed the task, and set the canteens aside, Vivian cupped her hands and lifted water to her face. She splashed herself liberally and made cooing sounds of relief. Then, to Slocum's surprise she began to undo the buttons of her high shoes.

"It feels too good to resist," Vivian said by way of explanation. "I'm going wading."

Amused, Slocum didn't try to avoid the tease. "There's bound to be snapping turtles."

"Oh, pooh, they'll get away when I stir up the sand with my feet." With which she hiked her skirt and waded into the stream.

For obvious reasons, Slocum realized, that suggestion worked better on small boys swimming naked. "You take to the water quite naturally," he remarked.

"I was a tomboy until I entered the normal school."

Wading into deeper water, Vivian raised her skirt higher. A flash of creamy white thigh commanded Slocum's attention. The effort he had to make to control his stirring emotions was not lost of Vivian. She found herself amused and aroused in turn by his reactions. If they had been further from the coach, or entirely alone, she might strip to the buff and see what happened, she considered.

Tightly reined, Slocum forced himself to turn away when she returned to the bank. His keen hearing brought him a hint of a stifled giggle. Cloth rustled and Slocum noticed a series of short, harsh gasps.

"Oh, damn, I should have remembered a buttonhook," Vivian muttered.

She certainly showed little of the primness attributed to those in her profession, Slocum thought. "We—ah—had better be heading back," he suggested.

"Fine with me. Oh, but I'm hungry."

They returned to the damaged coach with the water. Also three rabbits and four prairie chickens Slocum shot on the way. From a distance, Slocum could see the agitated gestures of the fat drummer.

"You shouldn't have done that," Dobbins snapped the moment Slocum reined up. The heavy jowls of his hog's face wobbled indignantly. "That shooting will attract Indians. Worse," he added darkly, "it might bring those rebel brigands down on us."

"I think we stand a better chance of being killed by a chunk of the sky falling on us," Slocum riposted dryly.

Slocum kindled a fire and Vivian set to feeding it while the ex-Confederate cleaned the game he had bagged. All the while, Dobbins muttered darkly to himself. Slocum found his patience rubbed raw. The best he could do, he decided, was to ignore Dobbins. When he had the meat prepared, he broke out a telescoping trestle set and drove the spikes into the ground at opposite sides of the fire. Putting the spit in place, he leaned the green wooden sticks that held their meal against it. Then he went to see what more could be done for the driver.

"Ain't nothin' much," Kurt Jaeger protested when Slocum unbound the crude splints that supported his leg.

"This doesn't appear to have been set properly. If you don't get treatment soon, you'll lose the leg," Slocum told him after examining the limb.

"You talk like a doctor," Jaeger observed, punctuating his remark with a squirt of tobacco juice.

"I saw plenty of broken legs during the war, and since," Slocum advised him.

"Well, it's certain sure I ain't goin' anywhere for a while. You folks will have to send a doctor back for me."

"What about your partner?" Slocum asked evasively.

Jaeger lowered his eyes and nervously munched his cud of Union Standard. "Ain't a day's ride from McPherson. Way I figger it, Jed didn't make it for one reason or the other."

Quietly, to prevent the others from hearing, Slocum told him about the body along the road. Jaeger nodded thoughtfully. Then he wet his lips and looked searchingly into Slocum's eyes.

"You're gonna have to help them, you know."

"I have other commitments," Slocum protested.

"Shucks, what's that amount to when you've got a pretty gal in distress?"

Slocum shrugged. "You've a point there, Jaeger. I'll think on it."

"You do that. And bring me one of them prairie chickens, hear?"

After the food had been consumed, the passengers began to express their urgent desires to Slocum. They all wanted to leave, right then, for the closest town. Back to McPherson, Slocum told them. They agreed, provided he led them.

"We'll be quite helpless without you," Vivian added her appeal. "We'd only have . . ." Her disdainful glance took in Harvey Dobbins.

"All right," Slocum curtly agreed.

Reluctantly he found himself protector of this unlikely group. Vivian, he felt certain, could make the trip without undue strain. The other two women presented a possible weak point. One, a large, portly dowager with rigidly fixed ideas, came close to having the vapors whenever the word *Indian* came up. Her daughter was still in her teens and every bit as flighty. Slocum was willing to bet they would hold out for sidesaddles when they learned how they would be traveling. Well and good, he thought uncharitably. If they didn't like arrangements, they could walk.

Dobbins he considered a greater liability. Then there was the other man, if that term could be applied. Small in stature, with a thin, willowy figure and overblown gestures, he had identified himself as an "Ac-*tor*," with exaggerated emphasis on the last syllable. Slocum considered him likely to wet his trousers if he saw an Indian, any Indian, over the age of ten.

"We ride out of here, folks," Slocum announced after completing his evaluations. "Vivian, if you'll help me get the remaining coach horses ready?"

"Sure enough, Slocum," Vivian agreed.

"Young man," the dowager cawed at Slocum. "The coach will not move. How are we expected to use those horses?"

"Ride them, ma'am," Slocum answered bruskly.

"Why—why—that's patently outrageous. I can't possibly do that without—"

Slocum didn't congratulate himself on his perspicacity, he merely completed her sentence. "Sidesaddle. There aren't any, nor any other kind of saddle, ma'am. So, if you want to come with us to McPherson, you'll ride astraddle."

"Impossible!" she snapped. "No lady ever—"

Interrupting, Slocum spoke through a mischievous smile. "You'd be surprised what a lady can do if she's being chased by a few Cheyenne warriors."

"*Mother!*" her daughter wailed. "Don't let him do this. It will *ruin* me."

"It's ride, walk, or stay here," Slocum stated bluntly.

Then Vivian entered the breach in an attempt to smooth the ruffled sensibilities. "Don't worry, honey, it takes more than one ride to tear your secret veil. I rode for nearly a year before it broke my maidenhead. And I was only seven and it was a big horse."

The matron spluttered a moment before she could form words out of her violated sense of propriety. "Y-you—you have a foul mouth for one in your profession, Miss Ballard. No person of breeding discusses such—such intimate topics openly, let alone in front of men. I've a mind to write your superiors."

"Go right ahead. As it happens now I'm not employed. For that matter, as I recall, I don't remember ever having any, ah, superiors. Now, come on and let me help you get mounted, or you can, as Slocum says, walk."

"Atta girl," Slocum whispered as Vivian walked past.

Crimson-faced, Harvey Dobbins bustled up, his portly body inflated for a windy protest. "By God, it's me you'll ruin, Slocum. I'll—I'll be—be crushed."

"Before that can happen," Slocum stated softly, so that none of the others could hear, "you've got to have something to crush."

Then he turned away to mount Ol' Rip. "Jaeger," he called to the injured driver. "You've got a whole cooked rabbit, a full canteen, and enough ammunition to last you until tomorrow. Someone should be here early in the morning."

"Thank you, Slocum. Be sure to tell the doc about hurryin'. I don't hanker to go around with a peg leg."

Slocum nodded and led out, accompanied by the loud, uncomforted protests of Harvey Dobbins.

• • •

Early-spring crickets chirped outside the dimly lighted office of the *Emporia Light*. Editor Walter Albert Black, index and middle fingers of his right hand stained purple-black by ink, bent over the sheet of foolscap. The neat, precise lines of his copperplate-lettered text showed several drops and splotches where personal emotions had surfaced. He paused, sighed, and looked out at the dark street.

There would have to be some strikeouts, some words changed. His personal rancor against those with Southern sympathies came through entirely too clearly. Where should he begin? Here? No. That was entirely too perfect. Lifting the page, he began to read aloud.

" 'Once a seditionist, always a seditionist. Secession from the Union was an act of sedition, if not open treason.' Beautiful, just beautiful. 'Since this applies to those who harbored sympathies for the defunct Confederacy, under the equity of law provision, as well as those who actively supported it, it is *pro forma* that they should be stripped of their rights and assume a status like that of the American Indian. Indians do not, and cannot, own land, nor can they vote. Should those who equally spurn the blessings of our strong federal system enjoy more simply because their skins are white? Therefore, it is with clear conscience—' Ah, no, that's a bit too much." Black drew a line through the words and wrote in above them.

" 'Therefore it is with moral certitude that we call upon the legislature of this fair and bountiful state to initiate and support a bill that will—' No. Ummmm." Walter Black scratched and scribbled again.

" '—initiate and support a bill that when made law will deny property rights in Kansas to those of proven past disloyalty to the Union.' Ah, yes. That's it."

Jingling loudly, the bell over the door announced a visitor. Black pushed back his green eyeshade and looked up at his office manager. The man wore a contrite expression.

"What is it, Norville?" Black asked.

"I got home, Mr. Black, and discovered a letter got stuck to some of my mail. It's for you, and from the feel of it, it must be important." Norville offered the thick, creamy, rag-bond envelope tentatively, as though expecting a sharp reprimand.

Instead, Walter Black chuckled tolerantly. "The way some

of our compositors swing the glue pot, it's small wonder, Norville. Here, let me see it."

The office manager complied and Black sat a few moments weighing the heavy object. His expert knowledge of paper and ink gave him considerable appreciation of the quality. He nodded in dismissal and reached for a long, silver, Italian filigree letter opener. With a single deft slash he opened the sealed missive. Pursing his lips, he began to read aloud.

"Mr. Walter A. Black. Greetings. Your presence is requested at a dinner party . . ." His voice trailed off as he assimilated the importance of the invitation. When he finished reading he set it aside for later filing. Whistling softly, eyes alight, Black returned to editing his column.

"We'll probably never know, will we?" Vivian Ballard asked of Slocum.

Slocum looked up from where he was adding to a pot of boiling water the cut-up carcasses of four rabbits he had shot a short distance from their night camp. He also had some wild onions and young cattail shoots to flavor the stew. He knew at once what she referred to.

"No. Not unless someone comes clean about it."

They had come upon the corpse of the shotgun guard just under two hours out from the damaged stage. Slocum had stopped to examine the body and declared that Indians had not done it. The dead man still had his hair and he had not been mutilated, nor wounded by an arrow. Right away everyone started talking about those terrible Southern renegades. Careful to keep his inquiries casual, Slocum used the opportunity to pry further into what had been going on. What he heard he didn't like.

Over several weeks before the news spread outside Kansas, the farm homes of pro-Union families and of Union army veterans had been attacked by unidentified brigands. The men and boys had been killed outright, the women violated and killed. Everyone "just knew" that murdering Southerns had been responsible. One child had survived long enough to describe the leader as wearing a gray army tunic with officers' shoulder boards and gold buttons. As to how or why Slocum's friend and former subordinate officer had gotten involved, he learned nothing.

"You're sure it wasn't Indians?" Vivian's question snatched back Slocum's wandering thoughts.

"Positive enough," he told her. "The lack of broken arrows or arrow wounds isn't absolute proof, but there was no sign of unshod hoofprints leading off anywhere. Indians aren't much for traveling on the white man's roads."

Standing over him, Vivian bent and reached out impulsively to give Slocum a big hug. "Oh, I'm so glad you came along. The others, they would have done something foolish when they discovered that poor man's body."

Slocum reacted to another fire—in the one in his loins rather than the willow and buffalo chip fire that cooked their meal. His whole body thrummed like a plucked string on a harp. He moved slightly in her embrace to ease the tension of his swelling manhood.

"If you keep holding me like this, I'm afraid I'll make some improper suggestion."

Vivian gave a tiny giggle up close to his ear and whispered. "Nooo. Anything you suggested would be decidedly proper. But not here and now. Later."

Awakened passions leading, Slocum suggested, "After we eat. When everyone gets drowsy. We can slip away and find a place. . . ."

Slocum loved the sound of her voice. Having seen a good deal of her legs, he had the feeling he'd love a whole lot more of her, given the chance. That chance came around nine-thirty, when a laggard moon rose huge and slow over the rolling land, preceded by a ghostly band of orange-white. The opalescent disk gained height as they strolled away from the campsite, where the exhausted passengers had taken to what comfort they could arrange for a deserved sleep.

"It's beautiful," Vivian spoke softly. "All of this, and the moon makes it sort of magical."

"Do you believe in magic?" Slocum asked.

Vivian paused and looked up into his face. The rugged but handsome features had been softened by alabaster light and stygian shadow. At an inch over six foot, Slocum towered over her by a good eight inches. In a rich shaft of moonlight, her auburn tresses looked almost as dark as his collar-length coal black locks. Impulsively, she reached out and took one of his big, square hands.

"You're all the magic I need, Slocum." A little gasp escaped her and she glanced away. "My God, that sounds so brazen."

"No more so than I feel," Slocum assured her.

"Do you? I—I, ah, mean . . ." She stopped then when Slocum took her in his arms.

Their lips met, hers soft and pliable against his, firm but yielding. Her bite relaxed and Slocum instantly probed with his tongue. Vivian's defenses gave way to his assault and he joyfully explored the sweet mysteries of her mouth. Vivian pressed her pelvis against his lean, hard body and returned the passion of his kiss with her own growing ardor.

When the embrace ended they walked on until they came to the moss-covered rocks of a creek bank. There Slocum located a comfortable place, a spoon-shaped depression in a large slab of limestone. He reached for her and undid the top button of her dress. Vivian, to her surprise, experienced a flash of embarrassment. She stepped away from him a pace and began to disrobe.

She turned back to face him, to discover Slocum had shed his clothing and wore only the bottom half of a pair of long johns and a huge erection. Her full lips spread in a sensual smile and she opened her arms in invitation. Slocum eased into her embrace. Deftly he began to pull drawstrings and loosen her undergarments. Vivian cooed in his ear and wriggled her enlarged pubic arch against the solid bulk of his maleness.

One hand she slid under the waistband of his underdrawers and sought out the upthrust organ that so tantalized her heated flesh. Long fingers closed around the shaft and slowly stroked him. They kissed . . . exchanged sighs . . . kissed again.

"I—ah, didn't expect this when I came upon that stage," Slocum murmured.

"Neither did I. At least not for the first minute," Vivian admitted.

Slocum found her moist and vibrant cleft. He dipped two fingers within and Vivian shivered. Her manipulation of his upcurved phallus increased in strength. He answered with practiced pulses that opened her portal, a magnificent flower awakening.

"Oooh, oh—God, Slocum, take me," Vivian moaned.

In no time they lay naked in each other's arms. The moss provided a resilient cushion as Slocum turned Vivian and spread her legs. His lean frame settled between creamy thighs and he lowered his large manhood and made a tentative thrust that buried the sensitive purple tip.

Vivian shivered in delight and hunched her hips. Slocum answered with a more powerful drive that seated him deeply within the tight channel. Rapid contractions of her powerful muscles brought a message of rapture to Slocum as his third penetration hilted his throbbing shaft. Vivian suppressed a squeal and constricted her passage even more. Slocum groaned as he began to withdraw.

"Y-you're going to pull it off," he whispered urgently, only half in jest.

"Oh—oh, I hope so. Then I'll have it all the time."

"You mock me, woman."

"Then punish me."

"I will," Slocum gusted.

What he did was propel them into a cascade of sheer ecstasy and bring on a cataclysm of exquisite completion. This would be, Slocum considered blissfully, a night to be remembered.

# 8

Barefoot children shrilled as they swarmed down Crawford Street in Emporia, Kansas, still captivated by their enforced nonattendance at school. A scruffy yellow dog yapped past after them. One of the team of dapple-grays stamped a foot nervously and caused the buckboard to inch forward.

"Easy, Silvester," a young man with a pronounced Southern accent spoke to the animal.

His three companions deposited heavy bags of beans, rice, and flour into the wagon bed. Once unburdened, the eldest put hands on hips and glared after the yelling boys.

"Dang kids. They oughta have better manners."

"They're Yankees, Melvin," a burly young man in suspenders and butternut trousers responded, saying all that was needed.

"Yo right on that," the driver remarked as he gave a pat to the silken flank of the gelding named Silvester. "I don't know why we come in ta this place."

"Because the prices are cheaper, Beau. Your family nor ours can afford the prices they charge down Yates Center or Neodesha," Melvin answered him.

Beauregard Calhoon regarded him a moment, then shook his head. "Let's get shut of this and go have us a beer."

"Sounds fine to me," Melvin agreed. "Lester? George?" he consulted his brothers.

Lester grinned broadly. "Didn't hear me complainin', did you?"

"Where we gonna get us a beer?" George asked. "These damyankees done voted the place dry."

"Pappy voted dry, too. Us Baptists is teetotalin' folk, 'member?" Melvin teased his peers.

"Sho'. That's why your grandaddy Spears ran a still up Cherry Hollah, huh?" Beau joined the banter.

"White lightnin's medicine, y'all know that," Melvin defended.

The quartet of strapping Southerns laughed together. Two barrels, one of molasses and the other of pickles, needed loading. Beau and George set up a ramp and the more muscular Melvin and Lester rolled the first one in place.

"Goll-dogit, the molasses weighs a ton," Lester complained.

"Think what it'll taste like on your grits," Beau offered.

"Fine thing," Lester riposted. "There be any trees in this godforsaken place and we could have honey."

"Never you mind, Lester," Beau taunted. "Jest you bring them pickles."

"With your sour puss, who needs a pickle?" Lester goaded back.

"Beer, my good boys. Beer. Hold that thought," Beau said grandiloquently.

Heavy boots clomped on the roofed-over planking outside the general mercantile. Engaged in their task of hoisting the barrel, the four young men ignored the sound. Their attention came around quickly enough when a harsh voice brayed at them.

"Won't be no beer for you rebel trash."

"Who says?" Beau challenged, turning around and dusting his hands together.

Four uniformed members of the Kansas State Militia stood on the porchlike platform outside the general store. Three more joined them as the quartet of Southerns stared in uneasy suspicion. The leader, a man with a narrow hatchet face and the stripes of a sergeant, clapped gauntleted hands together and spoke to his comrades.

"Well, look here, fellers. We caught us some of them rebel night riders."

"Sure looks that way, Sarge," a pop-eyed, froggy-faced private responded.

"You boys picked the wrong time to come into town," the sergeant snorted softly.

Beauregard noticed all seven wore red flannel leggings over their uniform trousers. A chill flirted with his spine and he found an empty ache in his stomach. The sergeant's full lips curled in a sneer and he stepped forward.

"Seems to me we should teach these Gray Ghosts a lesson."

"Whoopie!" another trooper cheered. "I get the one with the funny buck teeth."

"We'll just take our time and get a turn on each of them," the sergeant suggested.

"We aren't lookin' for trouble, Sergeant," Beau found his voice to say. "We're no kind of night riders or anything else. All we want's to be left in peace."

"Like you did that family over Eureka way?" the sergeant taunted. "You butcherin' secessionist scum. Get 'em, boys!"

The fight didn't start, it exploded. Fists and feet flew in every direction as five more Redleg troopers joined the fray. Outnumbered almost two to one, Beau and the other Southerns put up a good fight, though a hopeless one. From the first shout and soft thud of fist into flesh, a crowd began to gather. Several of the men watching shouted encouragement.

"Break their heads."

"Kick their balls off."

"Kill those Southern filth."

"That's it—that's it! Get him down. Stomp his face."

Hard knuckles and young, powerful bodies kept the militiamen from responding to their fans. Beau sank his fist nearly to the elbow into the fat gut of a trooper and then banged his knee upward against the bent-over face. The soldier grunted and did a pratfall. Two more leaped onto Beau's back.

He tried to swing around, only to be borne to the ground. Then one of his assailants rose and started to kick him in the ribs and stomach. Air whooshed out of Beau's lungs and he felt afire. Dust blinded him and he could not move to escape the powerful blows, held from behind by another Redleg who tightly gripped his shoulders. Dimly he saw George go down, to be kicked and stomped by three men. In desperation, Beau threw his free arm up and back.

His fingers closed on a greasy hank of hair. With all his strength he yanked and the trooper holding him bellowed in pain, his grip loosening. Beau sprang free and aimed a kick at the other Redleg's crotch. Contact jarred him to his hip.

Rewarded by a high, thin shriek that faded to a gurgling sob, Beau slammed his doubled fists against the base of the injured soldier's skull. Beau yelped in triumph and turned to find himself facing a cocked and leveled revolver. To his right he saw the sergeant kick Lester in the mouth. Blood and shards of broken teeth spewed out in a circular pattern. The sergeant drew his own service revolver. Slowly the fight ended.

Only yapping, snarling dogs and blood-crazed small boys made any sound for long seconds. Then a soft, mutual "Oooh" rippled over the crowd. One of the spectators found his voice.

"Shoot 'em. Shoot the bastards down."

"Naw," suggested another. "Let's string 'em up. Get a rope."

"HOLD IT!" the sergeant bellowed. "There'll be none of that. These insurrectionists are our prisoners. They'll be treated according to the law. All of you go about your business. We'll take care of them."

"What are you gonna do?" a skinny man in derby and rimless spectacles asked.

"We'll take them to Topeka for trial. *Then* we'll hang 'em."

A bloodlusting roar came from the crowd. Face beaming, Walter Black set off for his office to write words of glowing praise for the Jayhawker troops. "Heroes of Kansas," he spoke aloud, savoring the phrase, "who are valiantly ridding the state of poisonous vipers." Yes, he'd use that.

Early morning had brought grief for Slocum, too. It came in the form of more complaints from Harvey Dobbins. Bitching up a storm, the fat drummer found fault with everything, Slocum in particular.

"I can't understand why we don't have coffee," Dobbins wailed upon seeing strips of meat roasting over a bed of coals and no coffeepot.

"Because we don't have any," Slocum told him patiently.

Actually, he had coffee beans and a small granite pot in his pannier but was disinclined to provide any for this ingrate. The others could endure the lack, and it gave some small satisfaction to see the pampered buffoon discomforted. Pulling a wry face, Slocum chided himself for being petty. He retracted the self-criticism a moment later.

"And whose fault is that? Yours, of course, for not properly providing for us," Dobbins sneered.

"Look, Dobbins—," Slocum began hotly, to be cut off by Vivian.

"You can't blame Mr. Slocum for that, Mr. Dobbins. After all, he didn't know he would come upon us as he did."

Dobbins subsided for a while, content to mutter to himself and cast scowling glances in Slocum's direction. When breakfast had been attended to and the horses readied, Slocum directed everyone to mount up. He assisted the ladies and turned to Ol' Rip.

"Well?" Dobbins inquired imperiously.

"Well, what?" Slocum fired back.

"Aren't you going to assist us?" His sweeping gesture took in the actor.

"You've got plenty of space between your trouser legs. Swing a leg up and mount yourself, help each other, or walk. I really don't give a rip."

Dobbins blanched, read the expression on Slocum's face and bit at his lower lip, then turned to grab a hank of mane. On his third try he made it. Slocum raised his hand.

"Let's move out," he commanded.

Dobbins continued to speculate to himself and to cast a jaundiced eye on Slocum. Each time the ex-Confederate spoke, Dobbins's eyes narrowed slightly. An hour of steady, if slow, progress went by before he began to mutter with increasing volume.

"That's it. I know it has to be. Yes. Why were we so blind? Now he has us in his power, whatever can we do?" He girded himself and tried to put strength into his watery voice. "I've got your number, Slocum. I know what you're up to."

Slocum sighed and halted his horse. "What's that, Mr. Dobbins?"

"That accent. It's Southern, isn't it? From Mississippi, or . . . or . . ."

"Georgia," Slocum informed him. "What has that got to do with anything?"

"You're a Judas goat, sent to lead us to the slaughter!" Dobbins fairly shouted. "You're working with those rebel firebrands. Oh, I know it all now. You can't fool me."

Dobbins's constant carping had worn too thin for Slocum.

This latest absurd accusation settled it. Despite his best efforts to remain calm and unaffected, Slocum grew livid as the tubby ladies' undergarment salesman went on with his diatribe.

"You're all alike, treacherous, ill-begotten dregs. Why, it's nothing for me to prove that no white man born south of the Mason-Dixon line is anything but lowlife trash—degenerates and perverts. The spawn of England's jails, brought over here to rid the motherland of undesirables. Furthermore—"

"That's enough," Slocum said softly as he reached across the small space separating them and yanked Dobbins off his horse.

Finding himself suspended in midair, the loudmouth bleated in fear and wriggled ineffectually. Taxing the power of his arm, Slocum pulled the babbling drummer up until they were face to face. Dobbins choked off further protest when he saw the tiger-fire of fury in Slocum's green eyes.

"You've said all you're going to, Dobbins," Slocum growled. "One more word, you spineless piece of dung, and I'll break your face and stir the pieces with a spoon."

Gulping back his sudden rush of fear, Dobbins made to protest while his pudgy hand delved in the rolls of his fat. "H-how dare you? You c-c-crude animal," he wailed.

Dobbins reached the tucked-under edge of his vest and delved fingers into a pocket. He came out with a .41 Remington rimfire derringer. Before he could cock it, Slocum slapped the popgun out of his hand and dropped the fat salesman to the ground. Feet free of the stirrups, Slocum followed a moment later.

He landed with his knees in Dobbins's well-larded gut. The rotund salesman lost his air and tried to vomit, bile burning in his throat. Slocum came up quickly and jerked Dobbins to his feet. Three times he coldly and methodically backhanded the drummer. Dobbins' lower lip split and blood trickled to his chin, to drip on the front of his white shirt.

"You have the manners of a billy goat, Dobbins. No, that's an insult to the goat. You have the manners of a Mongol savage, the breeding of an alley cat, and less brains than an ant. That sewer mouth of yours is going to dig your grave someday."

"Y-y-you can't talk to me that way," Dobbins whimpered.

"You're even stupider than I thought. If I can't, what the

hell do you think I'm doing? Now, while we're at correcting your misguided way of living, you should give a little thought to this. Don't pull a gun on a man unless you are fully ready to use it. Hell, Dobbins, you didn't even cock that whore's toy. Second, you had better choose something with a cartridge powerful enough to stop whomever you shoot. Third, you had better be certain that when you pull that gun, the person you intend to use it on has at least no more skill than you. The cemeteries in every town west of the Mississippi River are full of men who didn't abide by that rule."

By then, Slocum had run down some and Dobbins had gathered what little courage he possessed. "Are you quite through?"

Slocum laughed. It sounded terribly nasty to Harvey Dobbins. "Through? I've hardly started." Slocum paused and looked around, noted the sun's position, climbing high into the morning sky. "But we haven't time. I'll just tell you a little something about the South, so that perhaps you'll gain a little knowledge.

"No doubt what little brain you have got thoroughly soaked with the lying, hypocritical propaganda of such panderers of hate as Harriet Beecher Stowe, John Brown, and their ilk. The truth is far from their hysterical outcries. Not one man in five owned slaves in the South. My father never did, and neither did I, nor did most of our neighbors. But, when the call went out, those of us of an age put aside the plow and went to serve our country. I was an officer in the Army of the Confederate States of America. We weren't fighting to keep a rich few in possession of their slaves. That wasn't even an issue. We fought to protect our states and our own precious land from the avaricious, bloodless tyranny of Washington City, that we saw growing more all-encompassing every year.

"Just like King George and his Parliament dictated every aspect of the colonists' lives and commerce, the rich and powerful industrialists, bankers, mine and mill owners of the North sought to get absolute domination over the South through the corrupt politicians they bought and voted into office. We fought for our rights under the Constitution, for justice, for what was ours, and asked not a thing for anyone else. We fought . . . and we lost. But we have put all that behind us. We're not brigands, outlaws, or degenerates. We're men, proud and free. And I for one intend to stay that way."

*Jesus, had he said all that?* Shock hit Slocum hard. Then he saw Harvey Dobbins twist his face into a snide and mocking mask.

"You do well at speechifying, Slocum," Dobbins purred. "Maybe you should have been one of those politicians you defamed so roundly. However, I remain utterly unimpressed."

Regardless of his effort to maintain an emotionless expression, Slocum's right eyebrow rose in an interrogatory manner. "If I failed in that purpose, let me introduce you to this. It was written and delivered by a man who had known much pain and suffering, few moments of elation, and had faced the ultimate humiliation of defeat and surrender. 'After four years of arduous service marked by unsurpassed courage and fortitude,'" Slocum quoted from brokenhearted memory, "'the Army of Northern Virginia has been compelled to yield to overwhelming numbers and resources. I need not tell the survivors of so many hard-fought battles, who have remained steadfast to the last, that I have consented to this result from no distrust of them; but, feeling that valor and devotion could accomplish nothing that would compensate for the loss that would have attended the continuation of the contest, I have determined to avoid the useless sacrifice of those whose past services have endeared them to their countrymen. By the terms of this agreement, officers and men can return to their homes and remain there until exchanged. You will take with you the satisfaction that proceeds from the consciousness of duty faithfully performed, and a grateful remembrance of your kind and generous consideration of myself. I bid you an affectionate farewell.' Those are the words of Robert E. Lee. There is more sensitivity, honor, and gentility in those words, Dobbins, than in all the pettifogging hyperbole of all the scheming hypocrites in Yankee land."

Stunned, Dobbins worked his mouth, jowls jiggling, for some moments before he could produce any coherent words. "I—I never . . . understood."

Slocum felt purged. He drew a deep breath and spoke in a light, almost cheerful manner. "Good. Then be good enough to remount. And you should be grateful you'll not be left behind to walk to McPherson."

Grumbling, though thoroughly shaken and cowed, the pig-eyed second-rate garment salesman remounted. That, Slocum thought gratefully, should put a muzzle on Dobbins. So emptied of rancor as to be oblivious of his surroundings, he nearly failed to hear the soft, throaty words spoken by Vivian Ballard.

"You were wonderful, Slocum. What next?"

What indeed? Slocum pondered it as he took the lead.

# 9

McPherson looked mightily attractive to the haggared passengers of the damaged stage. All expressed an intention of remaining awhile before hazarding the journey to Wichita. All except Vivian Ballard. She made her desires known immediately after a long, wearing session with the resident deputy U.S. marshal. It was vital, she declared, that she get to Emporia as soon as possible. She had already lost three days.

"So," Vivian went on to Slocum, "I want to leave at once for Wichita and my connecting coach to Emporia."

"The next stage isn't until tomorrow morning," Slocum reminded her.

"I know that. It isn't quite noon, and you're leaving today, aren't you?"

"Umm—ah, yes," Slocum said dubiously.

"Then it's simple. I'll go with you."

Surprised by this turn, Slocum let his jaw drop before answering. "It won't be easy. What about the roving Indians and rebel brigands?"

Vivian made a face. "You convinced me that real Southerners"—she used the Yankee term—"had nothing to do with all that. As to Indians, you haven't seen one and I haven't, so we don't need to worry until we do." With hands on hips, jaw jutted, she asked challengingly, "Well, what do you say?"

"Get together what you need. We'll probably need to hire

72

a packhorse, and we can leave by one o'clock," Slocum told her through a chuckle.

With the spontaneity of a young girl, Vivian rose on tiptoe and her arms encircled Slocum's neck. She gave him a warm, wet kiss, filled with thanks and relief. Passersby gaped. Vivian didn't care in the least. Neither did Slocum.

Two and a half hours later they rode out of McPherson, headed south, each leading a packhorse. One would carry Vivian's possessions when they reached the disabled stagecoach; the other bore supplies for a three-day trip.

Bursts of pale green brightened native oak, elm, black walnut and cottonwood. Through the once-naked limbs, now bursting with new life, Walter Black could see the palatial hunting lodge of Senator Victor Dahlgren. Constructed of large blocks of native limestone and rough-hewn timbers, it had more the appearance of a medieval castle than a cottage hideaway. It was located some twenty miles east of Topeka, in heavily wooded hills. Black's chest swelled in pride at being asked to a meeting in such a prestigious place. It had to be important, and Black had greater appreciation for the fancy invitation he had received the previous week. He slapped the loose reins on the rumps of a pair of matched bays and the surrey gained speed. What would come out of this gathering?

"Mr. Black, suh, you are expected," the costumed black porter announced when the newspaperman reined in under the white-pillared portico. "Step down and go right in."

*Class,* Black thought, fighting to keep a blank expression. State senators lived well, he reflected. Entirely too well, he considered, recalling how he frequently had to shift money from here to there and back in order to meet his publishing expenses. If this scheme of Cyril Anstruther's worked, his share would be more than enough to meet his needs. He alighted from the light carriage and affected a casual drawl.

"Thank you, my man."

Across the wide expanse of the access path the door opened before he could knock. Another black man, dressed as a butler, took his hat and cane. "Come right in, Mr. Black. The senator is expecting you. This way, please."

Walter Black followed the butler down a short span of hallway to a large, bright, airy rotunda, its rock walls interrupted by tall, wide windows that extended upward two and a half stories to where the dome began. The view, and the living plants sitting and hanging around the vast space, astonished him. This one chamber of the "hunting lodge" was larger than his entire house. A bar, he saw with relief, occupied one inner wall of slab mahogany panels.

"Ah, Walter, so glad you could make it," Senator Dahlgren greeted, playing the *grand monde* host.

"Thank you, Senator, it's a distinct pleasure to be here." He'd been thanking a lot of people in the last few minutes. He did not want to appear ingratiating, Walter reminded himself.

"Great events call for a suitable atmosphere," the senator burbled. "Come, get a drink. The servants will take care of your things and lay out your room. Dinner will be at nine tonight, and formal."

*Thank God he'd brought his cutaway, vest and white foulard.* Black acknowledged the information with a sparing smile and nod. At the bar he accepted a heavy tumbler, half filled with bourbon. At his request the bartender added a shot of seltzer from the syphon. The novel invention fascinated him and he availed himself of its use whenever one was present.

He sipped from his drink and noted that some thirty men were present, though they hardly filled the vast, circular room. He had received no indication of the purpose of the gathering, so had no preparation for what came after Cyril Anstruther called the group to quiet attentiveness.

"It's time, gentlemen, to get to business. The first pressing matter involves an uncooperative newspaper editor. I've become increasingly concerned over a dissenting voice in Emporia."

A sudden chill struck Walter Black's spine. His face paled slightly. Nonsense, reason chided him. He'd done his share, followed orders, written articles and editorials exact in every detail along the lines desired by these powerful men. It couldn't be he.

"With us today is Walter Black, editor of the *Light*. The opposition rag in Emporia, the *Telegraph-Intelligencer*, has not been giving people the 'right' slant on the troubles in the southeastern corner of our state. What can you tell us about the editor, Walter?"

Suddenly thrust into the center of affairs, Walter Black blinked owlishly and tried hastily to marshal his thoughts. He began brokenly, then improved as he went along.

"David Roberts . . . is a . . . serious journalist. He's . . . young, but that means . . . he's not become jaded by the pettiness and meanness of the world. He's idealistic . . . and the young women in Emporia at least think he's handsome."

"Uh—Walter, we didn't ask for a recommendation. What are his politics? Why has he taken a stand opposite of what we want everyone to believe?"

Black's brow furrowed. He'd not considered his competition in this light before. Words came hard. "The, ah, mere fact that his paper has a competitor means he has to take an opposed stand. It's traditional. In order to sell newspapers to people, often the same ones who read your competition, one has to present something fresh, different, in order to get them to part with their money. I'm not certain about his political stand. His editorials make him sound something like a Democrat from the South and a Kansas Republican combined. That is to say, he is a strong constitutionalist. He favors individual rights instead of the common good, and he writes in a manner that implies support for laissez-faire capitalism and strong local government instead of what we all know is a superior system: rule by an all-powerful, centralized federal authority, and all wealth in the hands of the ruling few."

"Hear! Hear!" Senator Dahlgren praised. "Man is incapable of self-government, with the exception of the elite, like ourselves. The masses need to be ruled, their lives and conduct planned and controlled for them by those who oversee their best interests."

Not taken in by the rhetoric of the collectivist, World Order and Obedience advocates, Cyril Anstruther chuckled and addressed Dahlgren sarcastically. "Everyone wearing the exact same clothes, eh? Everyone eating the exact same food at each meal, right? Everyone walking in lockstep to their exactly the same jobs in the jolly workers' paradise, hmm? Everyone married to the person chosen for them, having the exact proper number of children, making love only when the state says to?

"Oh, what a bleak, stale existence that would be. Don't be mistaken, I read your *Manifesto* by Marx. I found it dull, lacking in originality and spontaneity, plodding and unrealistic.

That's the trouble with all these utopian schemes." Anstruther paused to wipe his brow. "They never work. Under your 'ideal' system, Victor, I would probably be sweeping streets in New York City instead of hosting this gathering. Opportunity, combined with cleverness and the nerve to carry it off, should determine the elite, not some political formula." Then, to the editor, "Come up with something we can use, please, Walter."

"He is a bachelor. Lives alone in a housekeeping suite at the Tabor Hotel," Black began reeling off details, stung by Anstruther's sarcasm. "He often works late into the night on the day before the paper is set. So do I, for that matter. He takes his noon and evening meals at one or the other of two cafés and the hotel restaurant. He drinks only a little and that rarely. No, ah, involvements that could be used against him."

"One of those nights when he's working late, why not have some of Howard's men go in and simply shoot him?" Calvin Ruther asked.

"That, I think, would be a big mistake," Walter Black hastened to say. "One does not kill a member of the journalistic world and easily walk away from it. When one of us bleeds, we all bleed. Eventually, someone would find out the truth. Then every newspaper in the country would turn against you. They would dig and dig until your whole magnificent plan became exposed."

"Then what would you suggest, Walter?" Anstruther asked gently.

"Much as I regret the thought," Black said after a moment's contemplation, "I sadly fear my colleague in journalism will have to meet with an unfortunate, fatal accident."

"Well spoken!" Calvin Ruther praised.

Walter Black glowered at him. Cyril Anstruther waved over Captain Godfrey Howard and placed a fatherly arm on the younger man's shoulder. Quickly he related to him the consensus among those cabal members in the know.

"That, I think, can be easily arranged," Howard stated, eyes aglow and an odd, amused expression on his youthful face. "And by the way, I intended to bring it up at the formal part of the meeting. Might as well let you know now. We have successfully integrated the new men into the company and are ready to move against our scapegoat, Ewan McDade."

• • •

Sprawled at the fork of the Big and Little Arkansas rivers, Wichita showed little promise of developing into a metropolitan center. Under the goad of a dry Kansas the saloons had dried up, but the gamblers, whores, and specialty shops remained. They didn't lack for customers among the rowdier element that visited the plains community. Once the summer home of the Kansa Indians, the long triangle of land between the two rivers had been declared by its original occupants to be forever safe from the ravages of the "Twisting Winds." The powerful storms, spawned by the prairie, obligingly lifted their deadly black tails and skipped over the "land between two waters."

That suited Slocum quite well. Not until he came to Wichita had he heard of the Indian belief that tornadoes never struck within the fork of two streams. Then he must have had the phenomenon explained to him five times in the first half hour. If the future growth and prosperity of a community depended upon the enthusiastic promotion of its citizens, then Wichita would become Queen of the Plains, Slocum reckoned with amusement.

"I'd like to find several back issues of the larger newspapers," Slocum requested of the hotel clerk when he checked in.

"They got 'em over at City Hall," the earnest young man informed him. "A lot of books, an' volumes on law, too. Some of the ladies are talkin' of building an annex and havin' a library."

"My, civilization comes to the prairie," Slocum responded, amused again.

"It's mighty important, Mr. ah"—the youthful clerk checked the registry and continued hotly—"Mr. Slocum. Wichita started off as a wide spot on the trail, was a cattle town for a while. If the town's going to live, it's got to have, er-ah, refinements."

"Oh, I'm not making fun of it," Slocum assured him. "We had a fine library in Val—Ah, in my hometown," he ended cautiously, certain that Southern origins would not be well received. "I'll get settled in and go take a look."

Slocum found the city's accumulation of books, journals, and newspapers crowded into one high-ceilinged room off the lobby of the city building. He picked up several copies of the most recent papers, including the *Wichita Eagle,* and sat down to go through them.

"Damn!" It hadn't taken long for the short expletive to be forcefully drawn from him.

Accused, tried, convicted, and condemned in ink, he thought angrily. If anything, the story had acquired new life rather than fade away like most news items. It seemed to feed on itself, growing larger and more grotesque, instead of diminishing. He encountered several references to Ewan McDade, one that compared him to Quantrill. Slocum found he had a great urge to smash something.

"You seem to have found something of great interest," a matronly women with silver hair and the soft accent of Virginia spoke next to him.

"Yes. I find it hard to believe that anyone could be responsible for so many outrages and still be roaming around. That calls for considerable organization."

Her smile could be considered icy, and also condescending. "And how could those boys keep it together without someone being caught?" She warmed to him then. Few women, regardless of age, failed to do so. "I gather, from your manner of speech, that we have quite a lot in common. Have, ah, shared a common cause."

His surprise moderated somewhat by his recognition of her regional accent, Slocum brightened. "Then you don't believe these lurid accounts any more than I do?"

"Stuff and nonsense, I'd say. If it weren't so dangerous, and so terribly sad, that is. The war is over. At least for those of us who, ah, succumbed to overwhelming odds. I'll never say surrender," she added in a hissing whisper. "These are the acts of an organized military unit. Like Sherman's murderers who made war on women and children in Georgia."

"But Kansas has a reputation for violence related to the war and to the issues surrounding it," Slocum probed.

"True. And likewise true that seven of the twelve southeastern counties were settled by Southerns way back in the fifties. Many had slaves. But the organized violence in Kansas, the murders and night raids, were the doing of the Jayhawkers. The Redlegs." Thinly hidden anger seethed in her words.

Slocum nodded and produced a sympathetic smile. "I'm well aware of that. I served on Sterling Price's staff as liaison to

Mosby's irregulars and to Bill Anderson." The dowager raised one white eyebrow. "Perhaps I've said too much."

"Not at all, suh. We moved here after the war. I lost three sons to the cause of the Confederacy. I can never forgive the Yankees for that. Yet, I can assure you that none of the depredations you read of there have been done by Southerns. Not unless there are some, ah, white trash moved in with their firebrands and white robes. Did you know that one of the few survivors described the men responsible as having red legs? Do you find that significant?"

Slocum's bright, interrogatory expression changed to a black scowl. "Jayhawkers."

"My thoughts exactly, young man. Yet, our guardians of free speech and a free press have not seen fit to include that curious fact in any of their articles condemning us Southerns."

"Our former secretary of war, Judah Benjamin, said it best. 'The first refuge of scoundrels is a cry of freedom of the press,'" Slocum responded. "I think it would be wise to keep such conclusions to yourself, ma'am."

"And you, suh?" Her old eyes twinkled merrily.

"I think I'll follow it up and see where it might take me."

"God go with you, young man," the gentlewoman offered hopefully.

"Right now," Slocum offered through a spreading grin, "I'd rather have Jeb Stuart and about three hundred of his cavalry."

He found Vivian Ballard in the hotel lobby, her face alight with eagerness. "I have a seat on the early-morning stage for Emporia," she told him. "I can't wait to interview for this job."

"You haven't interviewed yet? You're not certain of the job?"

"I'll get it. I have confidence in my ability," Vivian assured him.

"Well, then, I suppose this is good-bye. I'll be leaving tomorrow for my friend's farm."

"It seems a shame. I wish you would come with me. We . . . ah, well. You'll remember me and write?" Slocum jingled the loose coins in his pocket. "And, of course, we have tonight," Vivian completed her thoughts.

Vivian rode him like a bucking bronco. Small white teeth biting at her lower lip, she drove her pelvic arch down against his rising body in such a manner that shivers of delight rippled through each of them. Slocum tightened the muscles of his lean, flat belly and slammed into her with the force of a pile driver. Vivian moaned and began to sway in a circular motion.

Alarms went off in Slocum's brain. This was—was too much. He was going to overload and evaporate in a cloud of pure sensation. Their rocking, pivoting motion made the bedsprings creak and snap. The people occupying rooms to either side in the Murdock Hotel would be getting quite an erotic entertainment this night. Ardor rose from Slocum's loins and he let out a soulful groan of sheer ecstasy.

"Now!" Vivian shouted. "Now—now—nownownow noooooooow!" A second mighty burst of completion washed over her and she slumped forward, her energies converted into tiny motions, while she mewed like a kitten. The rigid nipples of her firm, full breasts brushed tantalizingly against his heaving chest. Slocum increased his efforts and they rolled to one side, tumbled until he came up on top.

"Aaah, yessss," Vivian hissed. "Deeper, deeper, oh—God —ooooh—Gaaaawd."

She had never known she could be brought to three so magnificent climaxes, while her man maintained control well enough not to be caught up in the convulsions and frenzied action of her release. Slocum. He made it so good, so very good. Bright lights exploded in Vivian's head as she neared another fulfillment. She felt the pressure of Slocum's bony body against her sensitive breasts and squirmed to rub the tingling nipples on his skin.

His mouth found hers and his tongue probed her mouth as deeply as his stone-hard pestle ground into her quivering flesh. Nothing had ever been like this. She opened her eyes to see his face so close to hers, his own remarkable green orbs showing a lot of white as he rammed his way to the ultimate. Suddenly he gave a tiny cry and a hot pulse of life force jetted into her.

Slocum faltered for only a moment, shaken by the intensity of his orgasm. Then he continued as before, not the least diminished, it appeared, rather invigorated by his completion. Vivian shivered and raised her legs, allowing them to shake and oscillate, before clasping them tightly against his sides and locking heels at the small of his back.

"You're so fine, Vivian," Slocum whispered in gulps.

"You make me . . . feel like . . . a kid again," Vivian gusted.

"No kid could perform like you do."

"Don't stop. I want this to go on forever and forever," Vivian begged.

"We'll . . . see what we . . . can do."

An hour sped by before they reached the peak together and passed beyond into oblivion. Still rigid, Slocum withdrew and fell to one side. Like an eager pup, Vivian pounced on his reddened member and covered the sensitive tip with hungry lips. Slocum found energy to smile. What would the rest of the night provide? Wondering that, he entwined his fingers in her auburn locks and urged her to take more of him.

# 10

Outcrops of yellowed limestone and strata of bluish flint showed clearly above the tender green shoots. For as far as he could see, Slocum watched the rolling prairie ripple with windblown, hock-high sedan and buffalo grass. From the truncated bluff, he observed the McDade farm. There seemed to be little activity, limited to two women and a couple of hands. He saw no sign of Ewan or his children. After half an hour, satisfied that at least no Jayhawkers lay in wait for him, Slocum cantered down the slope and approached the house.

At a distance of two hundred yards, he halted and raised one hand. "Hello, the house. I'm alone and riding up."

"Come on in," came a firm, youthful woman's voice.

Slocum trotted Ol' Rip forward to a position in front of a tie-rail and reined in. Careful to keep both hands in clear sight, he studied the blank face of the white-painted clapboard building. A prosperous lawn of long-stem bluegrass thrived behind a low picket fence. Slocum raised one hand slowly and tipped back the brim of his Stetson Cattleman. Perspiration ran freely and he mopped at it with the back of his glove. The spring sun in Kansas turned on hot early, he noted.

"Who are you and state your business," came from an open window beside the front door.

"M'name's Slocum. I'm a friend of Ewan McDade. He served with me in the war."

"Captain Slocum? John Slocum?" the voice turned wondering.

"I used to be. Are you Aurora?"

"I be. Step down, Cap'n, and welcome to our place."

The door opened and the younger of two women, a Parker twelve-gauge cradled in one arm, stepped into the frame. She stood hipshot, bright blue eyes alight with welcome, while the older lady watched suspiciously from a window. The constant Kansas wind flirted with a strand of cornsilk hair that had strayed from the tight bun at the back of Aurora's head.

"Aurora McDade," Slocum said in a deep, warm rumble. "You're even more lovely than Ewan wrote to tell me."

A fleeting smile came and went. "And you're a flatterer, Cap'n Slocum, just like Ewan told me. Nine years and three children on this Kansas prairie leaves no woman looking young or pretty anymore."

"Then you're the exception that proves that rule," Slocum said with a sincerity that heightened her pleasure. "Now, where is that rascal and the children you mentioned?"

Aurora's expression changed from amused warmth to bleak resignation. "They're . . . not here. It's this—this terrible thing people are saying about . . . all of us." She sighed, decided to unburden her woes. "The children are with their maternal grandmother. Ewan—Ewan has been forced to go into hiding."

That possibility had not occurred to Slocum. "Won't that only make it appear that he . . . ? I mean," he tried to clarify his abruptly disordered thoughts.

"That 'only the guilty flee when none pursueth'?" Aurora quoted. "We had a long, difficult discussion of that before—before he left. He had to, Cap'n Slocum. We got word from a loyal . . . awh, hell, that makes it sound even worse. A friend. Harrison Monroe—he runs the big general store in Emporia—overheard some militiamen talking about orders to bring in Ewan and some of the other so-called leaders. He had to go, don't you see? They haven't come for him yet, but they're bound to."

"Which, as I said, only makes him look guilty," Slocum repeated with a frown. "Couldn't he have gone to the law?"

"The *law*? There is no law here now, except for the militia. 'All civil procedures are suspended, subject to review by military tribunal.' I think that's the way they say it. What it means is that we're living in a military tyranny not the least different from Reconstruction. And it's the same sort of damyankees runnin' it!" Aurora stamped her foot in frustrated anger.

Slocum quickly saw the spot he had been maneuvered into. Anything he did openly in defense of his friend would be interpreted as criminal activity. And, although he alone knew of his vow, if he failed to do anything, it would be seen as betrayal by Ewan and his ex-Confederate friends. The only neutrals in this sorry mess had to be the Indians who were dispossessed when the new state boundaries were defined in 1861, depriving them of most of the currently disputed land.

For a moment, a curious, vague idea struggled to be born of that. Then Aurora's voice distracted him. Slocum pushed the idea aside and summoned up his Southern manners.

"This is Ewan's mother, Eunice Glenndower McDade, Captain Slocum," Aurora made the introduction in the overfurnished parlor.

White haired and dignified, Eunice McDade rose from the piano stool and extended a hand, which Slocum clasped in both of his while he made a slight, stiff bow. He looked up with a smile and with warmth in his sea green eyes.

"It is my extreme pleasure to make your acquaintance, ma'am. You have a remarkable son who served bravely at my side."

"Thank you, Captain. Living here in this strange and troubled land I had forgotten such gallantry existed. You're here, of course, because of this unfortunate situation?"

"Uh—yes. More or less," Slocum stammered. "I couldn't believe that Ewan would be involved in anything illegal. I felt I must come and offer any help I could give."

"Your devotion to your men is in the finest tradition of our . . . ah, former country."

"Thank you. I would like to know more about what has really happened. The newspapers . . ." Slocum shrugged.

Eunice McDade sighed. "It's a familiar story, I would think. Greed over land and property has divided neighbor against neighbor, with the wealthy politicians of the northern part of the state seeking to dispossess those in the southern corner of what little we have left. Isn't that a familiar story? It's so much like the war . . . if only it would end."

Slocum noted the terrible sadness in her voice.

"There's more to Ewan's absence than avoiding arrest," Aurora injected, changing the subject a bit. "He and some of his friends are trying to gather evidence of who is really behind the raids and killing. I'll see that word is sent to him of your presence. You'll be staying the night, won't you?"

"Yes. Yes, of course. I want to talk with you more about conditions and, certainly, I want to see Ewan."

"Then that's all settled. I'm sure you could use some refreshment," Aurora stated briskly. "I'll arrange for that while Mother shows you to the guest room."

Once more the stray idea nagged at Slocum's consciousness. He caught at it, but it faded, mingled now with images of the rape of the South.

Halted in a swirl of black Kansas dust, the Corwin Brothers Express Line stagecoach ended its journey in Emporia. Amid the excited shouts of children and the homey camaraderie of the depot manager and the driver, a gangling teenager deposited a low step and opened the door facing the boardwalk. He handed out the lady passengers with a gallantry hardly expected by Vivian Ballard.

Product of a soddy on a '56 Boomer homestead claim, she had rarely seen good manners among her fellow Kansans. The majority led hard lives, trying to "prove up" their government land grant. They had little time for polished courtesies, and less for educating their children. What towns had grown up were peopled for the most part by failed homesteaders and by enterprising entrepreneurs who rarely shied from selling desperately needed supplies and equipment to the local farmers at five times the normal price. Given such a background, she found the youth's actions remarkable.

She repaid him with a beaming smile and a light touch to one cheek. Stricken with instant adoration, the lad brought one hand to the spot to touch it tenderly, while the late-afternoon sun made his skinny frame into an elongated, black exclamation mark on the thinly graveled dirt street. Vivian beamed at him again and looked around her at the enterprising business district.

Everyone seemed to dress far better than they did where she

came from, farther west. Tired and dirty from her trip, she decided that the next day would serve well enough for her interview with the school superintendent, Quade Purdy. When the last passenger had been disgorged from the coach, she spoke to the boy attendant.

"Could you recommend a decent hotel?"

"Wha—me? I, ah, oh, yes, of course. The Granger is right down the street, ma'am. Big place, built of fieldstone. Three floors and plenty of rooms. You can't miss it. There's big, round turretlike corners on the front. I—I'm through here until the westbound tomorrow morning," he blurted, taking a fearful chance. "I'd be pleasured to show you the way, ma'am."

Another of those radiating smiles. "Why, thank you. I'll have someone see to my luggage, then."

Brightening with his eagerness, the boy volunteered, "I can fetch it along, if you please, ma'am. Got a barrow right around the corner of the office."

Vivian clapped her hands in genuine pleasure. Such a show of consideration for a stranger, new-arrived in town, blinded her to his obvious infatuation. Here was that grand style she had heretofore only read about in books, or encountered back east. She accepted his offer on the instant.

On the walk to the Granger Hotel, Vivian asked casually, "What is your name?"

"Billy, ma'am. I—I'm pleased to give you assistance."

"My name is Vivian Ballard." She examined him. "Hadn't you ought to be in school?"

Billy glanced at the ground, then put his cobalt gaze on her lovely face. "Yes'm. Only there ain't any school. Hasn't been for a while. We're supposed to get a new teacher."

"That's what I'm here for," she informed him. "If we're fortunate I shall be the one."

Sobered by this, Billy gulped. "Y-you're the new schoolmarm? You sure don't look . . . ah, I mean, you look mighty fine and all, too nice to be a . . . that is, I expected some old battle-axe," he ended lamely.

"How do you know I'm not a battle-axe?" Vivian teased.

"You're too—too . . . aaaargh!" Billy ended in embarrassment.

Vivian checked in and ordered a tub and plenty of hot water sent to her room. Then she turned to her guide. "You can bring those up, if you will, please, Billy."

"Yes'm." The bellboy, a grizzled old-timer, gave Billy a thunderous glower.

Up in the circular third-floor room—Vivian had requested one of the turret accommodations—Billy put down her two large travel bags and unslung the overnight carpetbag from his shoulder. Vivian showed signs of sudden unease.

"I—ah—this is, ah, rather difficult. You were so courteous at the depot, I feel like we're more friends than that you were some sort of menial. But, here . . ." she blundered on, rummaging in her clutch purse for a two-and-a-half-dollar gold piece. She handed it to the astonished boy.

"I—uh—I . . . th-thank you, Miss Vivian." Dumbstruck, Billy could say no more.

Vivian correctly read his condition and acted sincerely, if impulsively. "You're right, you do deserve more." So saying, she reached out and enveloped Billy in a big hug. Then she kissed him on the forehead.

"Oooo-eeeee!" Billy squealed in embarrassed delight.

"Thank you for all you've done. Now, get along. I have my bath coming."

"Golly, Miss Vivian, I—I ain't never . . . oooo-eeee," he wailed again as she put a hand to his back, between the shoulder blades, and hustled him to the door.

Twenty minutes later, immersed in streaming water made the richer by a fragrant bath oil, Vivian relaxed and let the strain and stain of her rigorous journey dwindle away. Yes, tomorrow would be time enough for a visit to Mr. Purdy, she reasoned. Now, if only she had John Slocum here, life would be complete.

Oh, indeed, even the most ordinary of baths would become an electrifying experience if Slocum's lean, hard form occupied the copper tub with her. He had been such a magnificent lover. Thoughtful, gentle, and fiercely virile when called upon to be so. What a powerful, masterful lover he had been. Vivian noted the tingling in her loins and the swelling of her nipples. Oh, God, he doesn't even have to be present and he sets a person on fire.

At Aurora's insistence, Slocum stayed a second night, waiting for Ewan's return. On the morning of his second day at the McDades' Culloden Farms main house, he was "making himself useful" by mending some corral rails at the large stock barn. Aurora found him there.

"John! Er—Captain Slocum, I'm scandalized. You are our guest. You're not expected to labor in return for hospitality."

"A thing needs doin'," Slocum responded in calm philosophy, "it itches at me until it gets done. Your pardon, ma'am, but with Ewan away, the little chores are catchin' up to being big ones. I thought I'd lend a hand."

Although this was her first exposure to Slocum, Aurora was charmed, like most women. "You're too kind, Captain. I came to fetch you to break—" She broke off, listening.

"What is it?" Slocum asked, concerned.

"Nothing, I suppose," Aurora answered with a frown and shake of her head. "I thought I heard hoofbeats."

His hearing dulled by years of guns going off in close proximity, from light squirrel rifles to huge thirty-two pounder cannon, Slocum still possessed the gift of perception sharper than most. He had heard nothing. Turning, he set to twisting a wire that would hold two rails in place. Aurora made as if to touch his sleeve, then paused, hand to the bodice of her dress.

"There it is again. I . . . "

Slocum heard it now. A lot of horses, at a fast lope. He dropped his tools and retrieved his cartridge belt and holster from a nearby post. Aurora gaped at him while he strapped on the leather band. Then understanding dawned.

"You don't think it's . . . ?"

"We'll know in a minute. I'd suggest you hurry back to the house. Keep that shotgun handy if you can."

"They'll be after Ewan. Since he's not here, we shouldn't have to worry," Aurora offered in lame hopefulness.

Dark hats, along with the silhouettes of men's heads and shoulders, appeared above a dip in the prairie. They grew in size, a billow of dust behind them, horses showing at last, legs churning. Aurora had started for the house; now she fairly ran. Slocum recognized the blue uniforms of Union troops as the body of riders came close enough to pick out detail. Paying him little mind, the formation halted in front of the house. A man in an officer's hat, with flowing yellow locks and shining gold epaulets, called out.

"Inside the house! I have an order for you to produce one

Ewan McDade forthwith. Come out at once. And I warn you to make no show of resistance."

Nothing moved for a while. Half a dozen of the men, led by a sergeant, gave their full attention now to Slocum. From their lax attitudes, he had little expectation that they constituted any great threat. After three long minutes, Aurora appeared on the porch, the Parker shotgun at her side.

"Ewan McDade is not here. What do you want?" she stated cold and evenly.

"Ewan McDade is declared outlaw. It is your obligation as a 'reconstructed citizen' "—he made the term a sneer—"to surrender his person to us."

"I said he isn't here. Now go on, get off our land."

"It won't be yours for long," the officer snarled. Then he produced a scroll, which he unwound and read from in a loud, carrying voice.

" 'By order of the governor, made this twenty-seventh day of April, to all who see these presence: Greetings. Be it known that on this day and by my hand, the rebel insurrectionist Ewan McDade is hereby declared outlaw. All his lands, livestock, and possessions are forfeit to the State and his person is ordered surrendered dead or alive to the proper authority. Failure to comply with this Executive Order, and the rendering of aid or comfort to the outlaw, McDade, will result in such punishment as the Court shall decide, not to exclude the penalty of Death.' It is signed by the governor of Kansas. Now produce Ewan McDade or suffer the consequences."

Breaking one of his primary rules—never buck authority until the rules are known—Slocum spoke up. "The lady has already told you that he's not here. Why don't you do what she asks and get out of here?"

The round-headed, baby-faced officer turned his wrath toward Slocum. "Who are you?"

"Answering a question with a question? My, my, Captain, how rude. I might ask the same. Who the hell are you?"

"I am Captain Godfrey Howard, commanding Company Jay, Kansas State Militia, which fact should quell your insolence."

Slocum took in the troopers' uniforms, complete with red flannel leggings. "You're a mob of murdering Redleg scum, is what you are. I'll tell you for the last time. Ewan McDade is not here. Ride on out before some of you get badly hurt."

"You'll not threaten us," Howard snapped. He turned back to Aurora. "Inasmuch as this house and these outbuildings are known to have been used to harbor insurrectionist fugitives, I am hereby exercising my plenipotentiary powers to deal with them accordingly. Sergeant, take a detail of ten men and set these places afire."

"How dare you!" Aurora blurted, indignation changing to anger. "You can't do this." Howard gave her a lopsided, chilling smile.

"Yessir, with the greatest of pleasure, sir," Sergeant Banks responded. "Larson, Miles, Peterson . . . ," he named off ten men. "Light your torches and come with me."

The troopers produced prepared firebrands and ignited them with lucifer matches. When they burned with steady flames, the sergeant started out for the barn where Slocum stood. He watched them approach to within fifty feet. Two of them grinned the twisted rictus of a born vandal. All had eyes glazed by a lust for destruction. Slocum raised his left hand.

"You've come far enough. Your orders carry no authority here and are false at best. Stop before you commit an illegal act."

"Get out of our way, you grayback scum," Sergeant Banks snarled.

One of the troopers jumped his mount forward and hurled his burning brand. Slocum's right hand snapped across his belt line and came back with a .45 Colt Peacemaker. He swung it into line and cocked back the hammer in a smooth move, so that it fell free the moment his fingertip dropped inside the trigger guard. The big 250-grain slug struck the arsonist in the right side of his chest.

His horse reared and threw him. Slocum took a single back step and fired two quick rounds. One slug crippled the shoulder of another blue-clad trooper and the other clipped the lobe from a barn burner's left ear. Sergeant Banks howled in rage and fumbled at the flap of his black holster.

The instant his revolver came free, he screamed in terrible anguish as Slocum's bullet smashed into the cylinder and sent enormous energy up his arm, to flay nerves and torture muscles. Banks dropped the damaged weapon and wheeled about. Numbed to immobility, he could not even wave his right arm at the captain.

"He fired on us! Get him . . . get him," he shrieked in a hysterical tone.

As proof of his individual courage, Captain Godfrey Howard signaled for twenty men to follow him as he charged the short distance across the barnyard. Slocum triggered his last shot, which wounded another soldier and cleared him from the saddle. Loading gate open, Slocum made a hasty retreat toward the barn while he ejected spent cartridges. He slid two home and plucked a third from a belt loop. A quick glance over his shoulder told him he had run out of time.

Only the length of his horse's neck and head separated Captain Howard from Slocum when the officer raised his saber to deliver a decapitating stroke. From the porch, Aurora's shotgun boomed. Taken at that distance, the shot stung badly and deflected his blow but did not seriously injure Godfrey Howard. It gave Slocum a chance to blast a bullet into the forehead of the sorrel mare, unhorsing Howard.

Slocum jumped to the side and dodged another inexpert saber stroke from one trooper. Howard came up, dusty and enraged, to yank a soldier out of his saddle and take the horse. Slocum used his last two rounds to telling effect.

A pair of Redlegs fell from their mounts, one wounded in the thigh, the other with a grazed head. Then Howard came upon him and began to flay with the saber. Slocum parried blows with his six-gun barrel, ducked and dodged, yet he felt the burning sting of edged steel biting into his flesh. Howard tried to recover a missed stroke with a backhand swing, which slapped Slocum alongside the head with the flat of the blade. The ex-Confederate went down into enveloping darkness with an excruciating din of battle roaring in his brain.

Slocum's defeat, head and shoulders in a welter of blood, broke the battle craze that had engulfed Godfrey Howard. A swift check showed him far too many of his men disabled by the brief encounter with a single man. Shaken by the implications, he ordered them to regroup.

"Burn the barn and that grain elevator," he ordered when reason at last stilled his panting breath. "We'll not torch the house this time," he concluded. Then he addressed Aurora.

"You have acted in defiance of the laws of the land. Take warning. We will be back. When we come, we want Ewan McDade. I'll also finish the job of destroying this hotbed of sedition. And I'll haul off the corpse of this renegade criminal who attacked my men."

With a sweeping gesture, which under other, more dignified circumstances would have been dramatic, he pointed at Slocum's supine body. Then he raised his arm, saber and all, and gave the signal to form a column.

"Column of twos to the left, foor-waard hoooo!"

Behind him, Aurora sobbed in sudden relief and horror. Slocum dimly heard the thud of hooves and tried to rouse himself. He uttered a feeble groan and fell back into the blood-soaked dirt.

# 11

Purdy Feed & Seed occupied an unprepossessing position on a side street off Crawford Avenue, in Emporia, one block short of the west side of town. A spur of the AT&SF railroad extended to there and ran west toward Marion, sixty miles away, thence in a wide curve north to Herington, and finally to Topeka. There had been talk of running another spur line over to Wichita, but so far the Atchison, Topeka, and Santa Fe people had done nothing about it. Purdy obviously did a good business. A constant haze of grain dust, chaff, and fine powdered wood hung over the three tall elevator buildings.

Built entirely of wood with thick walls designed to contain dust explosions if any happened to occur, the elevators were the most stable structures in town. Each outer wall—six layers of edge-on two-by six-inch timbers, alternating in oak and pine—weighed a good fifteen ton. Inner walls were less thick, at twenty inches in depth. But for all the designer's caution, the buildings would no more contain a major explosion than would a balloon withstand a child's firecracker. That fact was entirely unknown to the men and youths who labored there. A separate structure, not nearly so imposing, held the office and scale dock. It was there that Vivian Ballard found Quade Purdy.

She introduced herself and, to his blank look, reminded him, "I've come regarding the teaching position."

"Oh! Oh, yes. Indeed. My . . ." He mopped ineffectually

at the thick layer of dust and chaff on his desk. "This place is simply impossible to conduct business in. I'll send for my surrey and we can go over to the school."

"I'd be delighted, Mr. Purdy. I'm anxious to see the facilities I would have to work with."

"Good, then. Hiram," he raised his voice to call.

A middle-aged, freed former slave appeared in the doorway. "Yassah, Mr. Purdy?"

"Go get my surrey, Hiram. Bring it around right smartly, mind. And don't be dawdling on the way."

"Oh, no sah, I mean, yessah, I'll fetch it right now."

Purdy caused one corner of his mouth to quirk in what might have been a smile. His eyes had not left their detailed inspection of the new candidate for teacher. She wore excellent clothes, revealing taste and reserve. Her good looks excited him, a condition he did not realize Vivian noticed at once. Most impressive, he found her refined speech and manners an excellent recommendation for hiring her on the spot. Caution, born of past failures to find the "right" woman for the position, decided him to delay until she had seen the school building and the available materials. He decided on small talk until the carriage arrived.

"Are you new to Kansas, Miss Ballard?"

"Oh, no. I was born here," she replied, genuinely surprised.

"Well now, that is a surprise. Your bearing, ah, manner of speech, suggest the fashionable East."

"After the normal school, I went back east to attend a woman's college, Vassar—have you heard of it?"

"Uh—uh, why, as a matter of fact, I have. Had you only completed secondary school, you would have qualified as a teacher, didn't you know?"

"Oh, yes, Mr. Purdy. Only I felt the normal school far better prepares a person. From there, the lure of college was entirely irresistible."

Despite his infatuation, Purdy's ingrained prejudices surfaced. "Highly educated women are often looked upon with suspicion in such backward communities as ours," he stated primly.

Taken aback, Vivian barely stifled a gasp. "Y-you don't approve?" she stammered, regretting the words as she said them.

"Oh, not I," Quade Purdy hastened to state. A new sensation

had washed over him, one that left his loins tingling. After all, everyone knew "freethinking" women all had loose morals. "I admire an intelligent woman who is willing to go against established custom. A college diploma would be quite an asset to our small school system."

*Don't patronize me, you old phony,* Vivian thought hotly. She forced a smile. "I find Emporia quite cosmopolitan, compared with Oakley. That's where I come from. Why, you even have an opera house. Are stage plays put on often?"

"Fairly so. We've even had Miss Lilly Langtree perform here."

"I'm liking Emporia more all the time, Mr. Purdy."

A small, light conveyance, more a trap than a surrey, jiggled up outside the door. Purdy looked up and brightened. He gestured to the doorway.

"Our transportation has arrived. Shall we go?"

Emporia's school board and its parents had lofty ambitions, Vivian discovered when they arrived at the school. Built of yellow brick, it rose two stories and blazed with reflected sunlight from dozens of windows. Someone familiar with the modern ideas of education must have designed it, she surmised. Bright and airy, it had an imposing flight of smooth, polished limestone steps that led to a set of four tall, glass-paneled doors. A proportionate fanlight of clear and stained glass above, faced in large blocks of glistening granite, completed the entrance. Purdy helped her from the surrey and oddly, it seemed to her, kept one hand as he led her up to the imposing gateway to knowledge.

"We know Emporia will grow," Purdy explained the daunting edifice. "While we were in a boom economy, people gladly voted for the necessary funds to construct this temple of wisdom."

"It's—awe inspiring," Vivian responded, genuinely taken aback.

"Here, I have the key," Purdy gushed on, producing the object in question and opening the left-hand center door.

Stepping through the portal introduced the front end of a short hall, widened into a sort of lobby, with offices to both sides. At the end of the hallway, another hall intersected at right angles, and another, smaller set of glass doors gave access to a large central courtyard, converted into a solarium by a four-sided glass dome that rose above the second-floor roof. It brought an involuntary murmur of delight from Vivian.

"I am even more impressed. How many teachers will operate this facility?"

"Fully staffed, sixteen, two for each grade, plus a music and voice instructor, an oratory and declamation professor, who will also teach Latin to the upper three grades, and a physical culturist. There will be three janitors—a fourth to operate the heating plant during winter. There's an office for the superintendent and a board room to this side, the principal's office, and accommodations for a full-time secretary."

"How marvelous. You've thought of everything."

Purdy produced an attempt at a modest smile. "We intend to become the Athens of the plains. The future lies in the minds of our youth."

Somehow Vivian got the impression Purdy was quoting someone else by rote, not entirely as dedicated to the advancement of knowledge as he pretended. It put an unpleasant edge on her tour of the facility. Purdy led her toward the long, intersecting hallway.

"The left wing is the performance hall, for music and forensics, the right is an indoor court for games. They both ascend two stories. The front and rear hallways in between are classrooms on both floors. There is a laboratory for teaching the sciences and a model kitchen for homemaking upstairs. The design is borrowed from the schools in the Kingdom of Bavaria, in Germany."

Such a vast educational program sparked a question from Vivian. "How many teachers have you presently?"

Purdy beamed. "Six, counting you, my dear. I'm sure the other five will return to their duties when they see your courageous example."

*I suppose that means I'm hired,* Vivian thought somewhat uncomfortably. "Are there not enough children to fill the classes?"

"Why, certainly," Purdy hastened to tell her. "Our shortage is in qualified teachers. Each teacher in the upper two forms must take two grades: five-six and seven-eight. It is the fifth and sixth grades where we have the vacancy."

"That calls for extra work," Vivian said through a frown. "But not so much as a one-room schoolhouse."

"Then you'll take it?" Purdy blurted with a note of eager relief.

"I—yes, I'll be quite pleased with this marvelous school. I am curious, though. When only one teacher quit, why did the others refuse to continue?"

Purdy sighed and rolled his eyes heavenward. "These are trying times in this part of the state. Surely you know of the depredations of the rebel outlaws? Well, there might be some behavioral problems in the district, ah, inherent in having some of that Southern trash enrolled here."

Through a frowning countenance, Vivian recalled Slocum's intense, yet moderate and reasonable, words about the South. On their journey to Wichita, she had urged him to quote more of his mentor and idol, Robert E. Lee.

"This is Lee on why the South chose to fight," he had told her. "'All that the South has ever desired was that the Union—as established by our forefathers—should be preserved, and that the government—as originally organized—should be administered in purity and truth.' And, of course, the heart of that was the rights of the states, about which he said, 'I consider it as the chief source of stability to our present system; whereas the consolidation of the states into one vast republic, sure to be aggressive abroad and despotic at home, will be the certain precursor of that ruin which has overwhelmed all those that have preceded it.'"

"But, John, none of that has . . ." His gentle, sad smile silenced her protests.

"Lee was a thinker, but also a visionary. Neither you nor I shall live to see it come to pass. But our children, or grandchildren, will witness the demise of this present, centralized federal tyranny just as surely as the Romans saw the disintegration of their republic into their period of civil war, and the birth of degeneracy and vileness of the empire."

At the time it had made Vivian want to cry for lost horizons. Now it wanted her to shout defiance at this smug Unionist. Purdy sensed her change of mood and took her by one elbow, directing her along the right-hand hallway.

"I'll show you the classroom where you'll teach," he stated, again alluding to a formal hiring.

Still off-balance, Vivian stammered, "Well, then, will I . . . am I . . . ?"

Quade Purdy produced a shark's smirk. "Hired? Why, certainly. I will so inform the school board. It's my feeling you will make a remarkable teacher, a real addition to our staff. Welcome to Emporia Central Grammar School."

"Th-thank you, Mr. Purdy."

"Please," Purdy cooed, patting her imprisoned hand. "Make it Quade. I like to be on a, ah, warm, personal basis with all my teachers."

In the room he exhibited the many marvels of a truly modern, progressive education system, one that in Bavaria produced after eight years students who could read, write, and speak fluently in two, often three languages. One from which mathematics produced no horrors for, nor held secrets from, the children. Vivian felt a remarkable delight. Then Quade Purdy got to a more unofficial aspect of accepting employment in the school district.

"Obviously there are a number of conditions we apply to teachers in our district," he began. "For my own part, there is one, ah, particular arrangement I like to have clearly understood from the beginning."

"If you are referring to men friends or overnight visitors, I have none and don't expect any in the future," Vivian offered, thinking Slocum gone from her life.

Purdy gave her a smile of praise. "In a way you have touched upon the subject quite accurately. It is not, however, regarding outside involvements to which I refer. Both the young women teaching here and I have found it most convenient to confine their intimacies exclusively to me."

"I beg your pardon!" Vivian Ballard protested angrily.

"Oh, I fear I have not made myself clear, my dear Vivian. What I meant was that the primary condition of your continued employment will be to make available to me your lovely body whenever I desire it."

"That is outrageous," Vivian protested. "It is demeaning, and debasing, and something entirely out of the realm of possibility."

Apparently untouched by her indignation, Purdy produced a winsome smile. "Ah, yes. Of course you have so many other employment opportunities. And certainly you have reserve funds enough to take you to those other places?"

Chillingly, the truth dawned on Vivian Ballard. She did not

have money to fall back upon. Hardly enough left, in fact, to provide for her first month teaching here, until she earned a paycheck.

"I—well, I can earn it," she stammered.

Purdy's voice turned ugly. "How? On your back? I can guarantee you that you'll not get any other job in this town."

Vivian recoiled as though slapped. She tried to form a sharp reply, only to have her shoulders slump in recognition of her dilemma. Purdy, for all his graciousness in the beginning, and no doubt the face he put forth to the community, was nothing but a lecher. A cold knot of defeat formed in her stomach.

"What I offer is simple," Quade Purdy continued in explanation. "You will have the opportunity to pursue your chosen profession, and be paid handsomely for it. You'll also have time to enjoy the refinement and comforts of community life, so important to the pedagogue. In return, all I ask is that you reward me from time to time for the advantages I've made available to you." Purdy produced a tight grin. "Only one man, once in a while, as opposed to scores of them."

With resignation came awareness of vulnerability beyond the norm. Quick thinking replaced outrage and defensiveness. "Mr. Purdy—Quade—I . . . well, I must say this has unsettled me. I've never had such an offer. It will take . . . er, I'll have to have time to consider my options."

Pushing on as though he hadn't heard her, Quade Purdy pressed his advantage. "There is no time like the present. I think that here would do fine. Right here, in front of the blackboard, will be a suitable first installment of your repayment for my patronage."

Words leaped to Vivian's defense. "I will not—I cannot. I mean, it's all so sudden. I am a woman of—"

"You are a woman of the world, who has traveled far from home and learned the libertine ways of the big city and high society," Purdy ground out. "Oh, I know full well the debased morality of the girls from Vassar. When I learned that you had attended that school for sirens, I knew fortune had blessed me."

"I won-wonder whether the other members of the school board would see your offer in the same light as you do?" Vivian challenged, gathering herself. "Please listen to me. I hardly know you. Nor you me. I meant what I tried to say earlier, when you interrupted me. I was raised, and still am, too much of a lady to go to bed with a man I've only just met . . ." *Forgive me Slocum,* she thought prayerfully. "I, ah, need time to adjust to this new world you present to me. I would like to make myself more . . . alluring. Wouldn't it be nicer in the proper setting? We can—we can investigate that avenue when I've had time . . ."

Purdy clearly didn't like it. His face became thunderous, a cloven-hoof gully pinched between beetle brows. The breath left him in a rush and he straightened his hunched shoulders.

"You're new to this, as you say," he remarked casually. "I'll accept you're having your way this time. I do advise you to make yourself ready for my first visit. After that, it is I who shall dictate the terms."

He turned sharply and stomped off with ill grace. Slowly Vivian followed and watched him mount to the surrey's single bench seat. He snapped the reins and rode away, which left her to walk back to her hotel. A fine beginning, she thought bitterly.

Pinpricks and tingles ranged inward from his extremities. Slowly weight returned, and a sense of warmth and pressure. Distant light played fitfully on closed eyelids. From far off, the bass rumble of troubled male voices set off echoes in his mind. Small, furtive movements established a firm support below his body. The clash and yell of battle faded away. In a burst of awareness, self returned.

Slocum felt about his body, identifying a mattress, bed sheets, and the heavy presence of a quilt. Gradually he became aware of lying on one side. Willing himself, he rolled over as a first step in sitting up. Agony exploded in his back and one leg. In spite of his innate caution, a loud groan escaped him. The murmur of voices ceased.

"Well, here's one rebel's proved too tough for Yankee steel," a familiar voice greeted him.

Forcing himself back on his side, Slocum opened his eyes to see Ewan McDade bending over the bed. With a scrape of boots five other men joined him. For a moment the vista swirled and darkened, then Slocum commanded his senses. He tried to smile. It made his head throb.

"Take it easy, Cap'n," Ewan urged, his sky blue eyes clouded with worry. "Someone did a fair amount of hacking on you. Musta been in a hurry, for he sure didn't make any of them count for much."

"You aren't the one it was done to," Slocum croaked.

Well-meaning chuckles filled the room. One man, heavier than the others, with large muttonchop sideburns and an officious manner, pushed through the throng.

"Come on now, make some room. I'm the doctor around here," he grumped. "The patient needs air."

"He could probably use some food to good advantage," Ewan McDade suggested. "Introductions are in order. Gentlemen, this is Captain John Slocum, late of Gen'ral Price's staff, under whom I had the honor and privilege of serving in the recent unpleasantness. Cap'n, this is your doctor, Judge Terrel. These other fellers are Jethro Pardee, Opie Tolliver, Nathan Fitzhue and Clay Armitage. They're neighbors and friends."

"Gentlemen," Slocum responded, a frown of confusion forming. "You said this was my doctor, yet you called him judge?"

"Weldon is a judge, right enough, not a doctor. That makes no nevermind, 'cause he's been thrown off his bench by the Jayhawkers and has doctored more horses and people of late than anyone else will do for the likes of us," Ewan concluded in his usual long-winded style.

Before any of the others could launch into well-wishes for the injured Slocum, or Ewan begin another oration, Aurora McDade entered the room with a tray of steaming stew and two slabs of fresh-baked bread. With Ewan's assistance, Slocum managed an upright position and began to spoon in the hot food.

"Eat up, and get a good night's rest," Ewan advised. "In the morning we're taking you to a safer place."

Startled by this, Slocum studied his friend of old. Ewan McDade had aged, certainly, but that had not affected his massive build, with the arms and shoulders of a blacksmith. Square and blocky, he stood six foot even, Slocum recalled. The bulk made him look much shorter. The expression of concern he wore emphasized his full lips, pursed now as usual when he contemplated an issue of importance. No, Slocum decided, time had not dealt harshly with his friend. But the idea of leaving didn't sit well with Slocum.

"Ewan, you're looking at the result of leaving your home places unguarded. Someone needs to stay here to protect the farm."

"The homes of Southerns in this part of Kansas have been burned before," Judge Terrel reminded Slocum. "Something you should well remember, judging by what Ewan's said."

"That's right," Ewan broke in. "And folks rebuilt after that and kept on going. That most of us are new here doesn't change that a bit. The enemy is the same."

"Meaning . . . ?" Slocum prompted, certain of the answer.

"Jayhawkers. Damned John Brown Redlegs. Best we can discover so far, they've been raidin' both sides with equal vigor. Kill our kind to show the Yankees that it's Southern rebels at fault; murder those on their side to have reason to go after us."

"They'd kill their own mothers, given a chance," Opie Tolliver opined.

"Who said they had *mothers?*" Jethro Pardee quipped. "I think they was littered by an abolitionist whore."

"Now, Jethro, you know better than that," Judge Terrel chided with a chuckle. "Abolitionists don't litter. They have few children, in fact, and never abide ladies of easy virtue. Because it's certain sure they don't know what to do with their dinguses, anyway."

Laughter filled the room. Slocum finished his stew and wished he had more. Someone lighted a pipe. The burning kerosene lamp, the rich tobacco smoke, and the presence of so many persons breathing in the room made the wounded ex-Confederate dizzy. He blinked owlishly and yawned. The walls seemed to ripple, then spin. Slowly the bowl and plate slipped from his hands. Ewan McDade caught them before they crashed to the floor.

"I think our patient could use some rest," Judge Terrel suggested.

"Right, boys," Ewan urged. "He's taken some bad cuts there; best we not overwhelm him with our blundering presence."

"Tomorrow," Slocum said drowsily. "Gotta . . . do som— someth—"

"Right. You'll be stronger tomorrow and we'll ride out of here for some place safe," Ewan assured him.

*No.* That wasn't it, Slocum's mind balked. Lacking strength to put words to his thoughts, Slocum let blackness slip over him and slept like the dead.

# 12

Intensely white shafts of carbide gaslight twinkled in the crystal fobs of ornate chandeliers in the dining room. A lavish meal had just been served in the palatial mansion of State Supreme Court Justice John Duffey. Topekans of power and influence gathered in small knots while servants cleared away the tables and a small ensemble tuned their instruments. There would be dancing later. Among those who sipped their brandy and puffed on fine Havana cigars, Cyril Anstruther held a rump court for his cronies.

"I hear that our enterprise is enjoying new success," Calvin Ruther prompted.

Anstruther nodded. "It has indeed. I can state with considerable assurance that it is only a matter of a few weeks now before we can expect a state sale of 'confiscated' land."

"And how soon after that will the militia rid the area of the last undesirables?" John Duffey asked, joining the group.

"They are well on their way right now," Anstruther answered. "The man to answer that is Captain Howard here."

Aglow with self-importance, Godfrey Howard filled his shallow chest like a pouter pigeon to make reply. "I think that I can say without fear of contradiction that by the time the state offers that rebel land for sale to, ah, 'loyal Kansans' my company will have rid the southern corner of the state of all elements in rebellion against authority and confiscated the land of those who aided and comforted them. You gentlemen can take possession of that property entirely unopposed within, ah, two weeks at most."

"I'd like to see it sooner," Ruther complained.

"Come now, Cal," Anstruther intercepted. "Every successful plan involves a lot of preparation and even more waiting. Rome wasn't—"

"Yes, I know, Cyril," Calvin Ruther bit off with his small, parsimonious mouth. "All the same, the longer we wait, the greater chance someone will discover what is behind all this."

Anstruther put a friendly arm on the banker's shoulder. "Cal, I would be the first to agree with you, if our goal were in the short term only. Look at what we intend to accomplish. Nine men, with lesser investors participating through us, will own ten thousand square miles of the southeastern corner of Kansas. Everything there will be ours. We'll put it to the plow, raise thousands of tons of wheat, all the labor done by tenant farmers in a series of interconnected cooperatives. And we, gentlemen, will reap the profit. Supply will never outstrip demand. Every day people stream into this country from Europe, from—from everywhere. They all have to be fed."

"What about cattle?" Justice Duffey asked. "That's excellent graze down there."

"Not enough profit," Anstruther snapped. "It takes three to four years to feed up a beef to slaughter size. With this new winter wheat, the farms can produce two crops each year, the other being late corn. The masses don't deserve meat. Let them be content with a bowl of porridge. It's more than they got where they came from."

"Perhaps, through the press, we can spread a rumor that meat is diseased? Or perhaps in some way harmful to their health?" Walter Black suggested. "It wouldn't take much to get everyone in the East afraid to eat beef or pork. Then they would have to feed themselves on our—er, ah—your cereal grains."

Anstruther shot from Godfrey Howard's side to the Emporia editor's. "That's inspired, Walter. An excellent idea. Do you think they could actually be sold on that idea?"

Black preened himself. "Of course. After all, everyone knows that if it's in print, it has to be the truth. 'America's newspapers,'" he qouted. "'Defenders of truth and freedom.'"

Let one editor with a large following pick up the story and before long there will be riots in front of every meat market in New York City."

"I like it better all the time," Anstruther beamed. "Look into it for us, Walter?"

Looking uncomfortable, Captain Godfrey Howard spoke what he had hesitated to reveal earlier. "I hate to inject a dark cloud on this otherwise sunny prospect," he began quietly. Reports of personal failure did not sit well with this worshiper of John Brown.

"What is this, Godfrey?" Anstruther turned to ask. "I thought you said your end would be cleaned up within two weeks."

"Yes, sir, and it should. I regret to say that our first expedition to capture Ewan McDade failed. We went to the farm— McDade was not there. I ordered the buildings fired, to deprive the renegades a refuge. Although, as I say Ewan McDade was not there, someone else was. After posting the notice of condemnation, I sent my men to torch off the barn. They were fired upon by a man that the McDade woman called to in warning. A brief fight followed. I lost one killed and seven wounded, myself included." Howard touched one of the sticking plasters on the right side of his neck and fought back the discomforting twinges in his arm and shoulder.

"Why didn't you make an end of it right then?" Anstruther demanded.

"I told you, sir, Ewan McDade was not there. In attempting to destroy outbuildings, we underwent some unexpected resistance from this fellow Slocum."

"Wha—?" Anstruther croaked from a face suddenly flushed and puffed with sign of his inner turmoil. "Who did you say?"

"Slocum, Mr. Anstruther. At least that's what it sounded like Missus McDade yelled when I sent Sergeant Banks and some men to burn the barn. He proved terribly mean and incredibly fast. Accurate, too, in that he obviously shot to wound, not kill. Private Keller would not have died had he not acted in a foolhardy manner. In the conclusion of the brief skirmish, I managed to briskly saber this Slocum about the head and back. I doubt that he could have lived through it."

Eyes glazed with a mad stare, Cyril Anstruther questioned Godfrey Howard further about Slocum. After a detailed rendition of every aspect of the armed encounter, Howard again

assured his superior that the sabering he had administered
should insure death.

"For all our sakes," Anstruther responded, visibly shaken,
"you had better hope so. In fact, you should return and make
certain. Slocum is tough and resourceful. He lived through a
hailstorm of Yankee lead with hardly a scratch. And he's not
a forgiving man." He paused a moment, considering. "In the
event Slocum survived your carving enterprise, I am hereby
offering a bonus of five thousand dollars to the man who finds
and kills John Slocum."

Out in the middle of the tallgrass prairie a quirk of nature, aided
by the literalness of the human eye, conspired to conceal from
ground-level view a huge, deep gorge. The native Osage and
Kiowa knew of it, as did the Delaware and Cherokee who had
been transplanted there by the white man. Also, Slocum discovered, the wide-ranging young men of former Confederate
families knew it well.

It was there that a stronghold of sorts had been established by those threatened by Captain Godfrey Howard and his
Jayhawk Militia. There, also, that Ewan McDade brought Captain John Slocum to recuperate. One man, Steven Varney, eyed
Slocum with suspicion until Ewan McDade made the introductions. Then he stiffened to a reasonable position of attention
and saluted smartly.

"Sergeant Steven Varney, late of Hull's Brigade, at your
service, suh."

Despite his fevered, painful wounds, Slocum returned the
gesture. "At ease, Sergeant. What brings you to this stalwart
band?" The moment he asked, Slocum regretted it.

Varney's face clouded and darkened with anger. Hot eyes
bore into the wounded ex-Confederate and a slight tremor affected Varney's voice. "M-my sons. Nathan and Davey. They was
hung by the goddamned Redlegs. Th-that's Davey over there."
He pointed to a skinny, undersized twelve-year-old. "He was
too light to be hung proper. Survived, witnessing his brother's
death and that of two cousins."

"What had they done?" Slocum asked, new to tales of ran-
dom violence.

"Rustlin' cattle, according to the murdering blue-belly bastard who hung them. Tell me, Cap'n, how can four tadpoles,

twelve, thirteen, fifteen, and sixteen, rustle their own cattle? I vowed over Nathan's grave that I would have justice. Davey, well, I had to bring him along. He was marked by the Redlegs for death."

"I . . . see," Slocum said quietly.

After an ample meal and an hour's rest, Slocum inquired further into the conditions of the supposed rebellion. What he heard left him with more questions than answers. Rather hesitantly, his powerful constitution still flagged by the recent attack on his body, he posed those queries.

"Don't misunderstand me. I'm not doubting any of you. All I want is to get this in the proper perspective. First, are you certain, those of you here, absolutely certain that none of the Southerns round about have had anything to do with the attacks on your Unionist neighbors?"

A chorus of denials answered him. Several men moved restlessly and fingered their weapons. Slocum asked several more questions about who might be to blame. Again the flat denials that any Southern had been engaged in even a limited, personal feud with a neighbor. Then, Steve Varney came forth with a suggestion.

"Those filthy Jayhawkers proved themselves ready enough to murder children. Who's to say they didn't set it all up themselves? If they would kill our women and children, hell, it'd probably be nothin' for them to do in their own kind."

Before Slocum could find some objection, Ewan offered further enlightenment. "Steve has a point there, Cap'n. We've got proof enough that all the atrocities committed against our neighbors and friends have been done by a militia company commanded by Captain Godfrey Howard. There's stories about that Howard is batty as a pet coon. He is supposed to actually believe that he has been possessed by the spirit of John Brown. Sho'nuff, Cap'n, that puts him in there with the all-time lunatics. But it don't interfere with his barn burning and murdering women and children. What's to say—and I believe every man and woman we've talked to over the past three weeks—that they didn't lay a little groundwork in advance of coming after us?"

"That sounds a little preposterous," Slocum began, to quickly quiet further protest by the men who ringed him and Ewan.

"We've been looking around," Ewan explained. "And listening. A lot of listening, and reading the big-city news-papers. Although Reconstruction has officially ended, and never applied to Kansas anyway, there are certain radical elements in the Kansas legislature, and among wealthy land-owners, who maintain that Reconstruction's provisions, or something exactly like them, should be enforced in Kansas. Within the ranks of these politicians and financiers, an organized force appears to have been formed.

"Behind their bluster, we've come to suspect, is a desire to obtain, by any means, the land of all former Southern sympathizers in the state. In the process, they seek to disenfranchise us in such a manner that we can't even make appeal through the courts. If that were to happen, you can be sure we would resort to violence. And something a lot worse than they ever imagined."

"Yes, suh, and that's why we're glad to have an officer of your impeccable reputation to join us," Varney injected, with a nod to Slocum.

"There has to be some other way to address the problem," Slocum suggested, ignoring the compliment.

"There might be," Ewan acknowledged. "Lincoln and his horde of lawyers and opportunists may have murdered states' rights, but we, as individual citizens, still have the right to petition for a redress of grievances. Sergeant Varney is under-standably vehement about this, but what we've discussed so far is seizing the ringleaders and taking them before a United States court. There they would have little chance of influence getting them off."

Slocum brightened. For the first time he could see Ewan McDade's keen intelligence guiding these desperate men in a reasonable direction. "Why not try the state courts first?"

"The cabal formed out of those with special interest in our land was large enough to get the present governor elected. Before last year's election it seemed no one wanted him. Yet, when the votes were counted, he's the one who won. So, to the point of your question, with that sort of power, they had no difficulty in acquiring the militia to enforce their will in this part of the state. That the troops sent by the adjutant general are former Kansas irregulars—Redleg Jayhawkers—is no coincidence."

"To what purpose? Regular troops would do, following orders, right?"

"Our point exactly, Cap'n," Ewan responded. "Regular troops could be depended upon to bring a swift end to insurrection. *Provided there was any.* Men lacking in conscience and morality, like the Jayhawkers, could be depended upon to *create the appearance* of an insurrection."

"Killing their own people is a little extreme, isn't it Ewan?" Slocum tried one final time to shake his friend's determination.

"Oh, c'mon, Cap'n. You were there, in Missouri and Arkansas," Ewan countered with a groan that could have signaled extreme suffering. "You saw the toothless old men, grannies, little children, all gunned down by the Jayhawkers. A-and the infants, mere babes, with their brains dashed out against fence posts by that Redleg scum. We fought them together, remember? And I'm here to tell you, *they haven't changed one bit.*"

Convinced in his own right, Slocum asked several more questions, more to have an understanding of the scope of what Ewan had discovered than in any attempt to dissuade these dedicated men from their search for justice. What developed, he considered to be most formidable.

"Jimmy, wait for me!" the class troublemaker bellowed in nerve-slashing soprano. Hard leather soles drummed on the oak floor as he bolted from the room into a glorious spring afternoon in Emporia.

"Thank goodness," Vivian Ballard sighed in relief. She patted a stray whisp of hair back into her auburn bun and started for the blackboard at the front of the room.

School had ended for the day. The large brass bell in the cupola over the front door had pealed the dismissal half an hour earlier. Her troublesome ten-year-old had been detained for that period and given five solid swats with the ever-present hickory switch for inking the braids of two girls. Since the teacher's rod of authority was thicker than Slocum's thumb and as rigid as his—ah-ah, don't get off on that, she chided herself—Vivian considered the punishment harsh. Unfortunately it seemed to be the only way to get his attention. Vivian smiled at her own thoughts.

It would be one more day before the first week of resumed school ended. Already she had formed opinions of the personality and aptitudes of nearly every child in her class. Odd that it should be so, Vivian reflected. Yet, every one of the fifth-and sixth-grade students had responded to her with such openness that she felt she had watched them grow from infancy. Take Jimmy Vale, the ever-suffering friend of her class clown, Bobby Latham. Jimmy was the "natural" target of less sensitive children, having to suffer a pair of overlarge gold-rim spectacles that caused him to stare owlishly at all he encountered. Perhaps, if he did not put up with the frequent cruelties of Bobby Latham, he would have a worse way in life. For all his hurtful pranks—tacks in the seat of Jimmy's desk, spitballs hurled from across the room by an improvised sling—Bobby had a genuine fondness for the frail, white-haired lad.

Which Jimmy reciprocated in what could best be described as hero worship, Vivian ruefully admitted. Jimmy was remarkably brilliant; Bobby could be, but didn't care. Who, she wondered, would wind up leading? And where? An unconsciously perceived flicker of movement passed across Vivian's range of vision. It arrested her hand as she reached for a long white stick of chalk.

A quick look around revealed no one else present. Funny. She completed the reach and raised the chalk to the board. In flowing script she began to write the questions for the next day's classes in history and geography. The children had been given the text pages, along with their reading assignment, and she expected fully half of them to make no effort to complete their outside study before classtime. Vivian's hand twitched involuntarily, which sent an irregular scrawl across the board.

Had she actually seen the shadow of a person's head and shoulders fall on the blackboard? Gradually a chill spread across her shoulders and down graceful arms. Could someone be watching her? Nonsense. She energetically erased the jagged line and continued writing.

*"Leea-niinggg, leea-niing on the crossss."*

Vivian dropped the chalk, which shattered noisily into three pieces, and whirled around. "Who is it? Is someone in the cloakroom?"

Ponderous silence answered her. Her chill grew to a creepy sensation, around which black-clad witches and red-eyed ebon cats capered and jibbered. Vivian shivered with self-induced dread. Telling herself she had a foolish case of the "vapors," she turned back to complete her work.

Vivian completed two more words. Behind her a board creaked. She started physically and a little yelp escaped her lips. Facing the cloakroom again, she reached for her hickory rod. A soft, breathy snicker sounded as though it came from behind the blackboard, in her teacher's supply area.

*"Leeeeaaaa-ningggggg."* The voice could have come from outside.

Mounting alarm put a brittle edge to her voice. "Stop it this instant! Do you hear?"

She slammed the hickory rod on her desk for emphasis. Instantly a bud vase gave a startled leap and fell over. A wide meander of water spread on her desk; the rosebud lay limp and broken over her copy of the fifth-grade reading text. The mocking laughter could have come from above.

"Oh, shit. Shit! Shit! Shit!" Vivian, on the verge of tears, exclaimed to no one. Imagination threatened to conquer her.

Quite carefully she walked to the cloakroom door. Hickory staff in the lead, she entered in a rush. Empty. Only a child's neglected jacket, left behind in the warmth of the afternoon. Vivian's shoulders sank in sudden relief. What had she been expecting anyway? She bit her lower lip in an effort to reject the answer.

*"Leeaa-ninggg on the crosssss."*

"Who are you? Where are you?" Vivian demanded shrieking now.

*"I'll beeee back, Viviannnnnnn!"*

The punishment switch clattered to the floor and Vivian raised both hands to her face. She wanted to weep, to rail and scream and howl her mounting fear. How could she? Fear of . . . what? A voice? One without shape or form? A little of that and she would be on her way to an asylum. A soft, sinister scrape sounded outside the cloakroom and terror iced her.

"Why, afternoon, Miss Ballard." Casper, the gray-haired, kindly senior janitor.

"Oh!" Vivian squeaked. "I was—I was getting ready to leave," she responded lamely.

"Ummm, my. Dedication. That's what kids need to get a good education, dedicated teachers. Have a nice evenin', Miss Ballard."

"Uh—thank you. The same for you, I hope. Oh, uh, Casper, were you working in the hall outside here a little while ago?"

"Down by Miss Appleby's room, yep."

"Were you, ah, singing something?"

"Me? Oh, no. I can't even carry a tune in a bucket."

"I—uh—oh, never mind." Vivian strode rapidly to her storage area and retrieved her light wrap.

With a casual toss she draped it over her shoulders and started from the room. "See you tomorrow, Casper."

"Sure enough, ma'am."

Vivian quickly put distance between her and the school building. While she stalked along the unpaved residential street toward the center of town, she tried mentally to rearrange the events that had startled her. It helped some, yet the strange feeling remained quite strong. And one nagging question kept gnawing at her. Would it happen again?

# 13

Slocum lay in the shade of a lean-to, face pallid, great beads of oily sweat on his gray-white brow. Infection had set in to the two larger saber cuts. Angry red welts ran across his right shoulder blade and the outer side of his right thigh. Judge Terrel had exhausted his knowledge of his healing arts and consigned the feverish man to the mercy of his Maker. Dimly heard, voices came and went in Slocum's consciousness, which knew neither day or night.

On the third day of his ordeal, an unfamiliar rumble overrode the protests of those who kept watch. "I don't give a damn, I know it works."

"What is that evil-smelling mess?" Ewan McDade asked.

"Oh, this?" the newcomer asked with disarming ease. "That rusty-looking liquid is made from scrapings from the inside of willow bark. It'll help him sleep and lower the fever. The other is a poultice of sulphur buds, buffalo-hump fat, and sphigmus moss. It's for drawing the puss."

"How's that going to do any good?" Opie Tolliver asked.

"I'll have to reopen the wounds, first, then smear it all around and cover the poultice with a strip of bandage."

"You sure you know what you're doing, Ross?"

A pink flush tinted Ross Six's coppery features. "I should. Before my family left the Nation, I was also known as Uowane Nuwote. It means Medicine Hand."

114

Ewan clapped his hands together. "Hell, I'm ready to try anything. Give it a go, Ross."

Someone lifted Slocum's head. A tin cup put pressure on his lower lip. Liquid spilled into his mouth, forcing Slocum to swallow. Bitter, the warm potion slid down his throat, bringing with it a soothing sensation. Then new pain exploded in his wounds. Slocum sucked in air through clenched teeth and his reason spun off into echoed darkness.

He awakened to sip again of the acrid brew. Time became a whirlpool. Gentle hands touched him and he awakened. More of the willow bark decoction and the musty-sour odor of the poultice. Slocum shivered and sweat and groaned. Three days had passed without his knowledge when he forced gummy eyes open and looked on three concerned faces with a steady gaze of lucidity.

"How long?" he croaked first.

"Five days altogether," Ewan McDade told him. "Looks like you could use a cleaning up."

"Uh—yeah. Wha-what happened?" Slocum mumbled as he ground knuckles into the gritty accumulations on his eyelashes.

"Your wounds festered. Judge Tolliver did all he could and gave up on it. You have Ross Six to thank for still being here."

Slocum rolled his eyes toward the bronze face hovering closest to his supine form. *"Osio,"* he spoke with rising inflection.

Ross Six beamed. He nodded curtly. "I thought that might be the case. Our family used to be called Sixkiller. As a *Tsalaghee* you surely know the name?"

Slocum inclined his head slightly to the barrel-chested, hawk-nosed man. "My mother was a Monroe. Of course they all 'went white' before the American Revolution."

"And later provided the country a president," Ross added. "You were a real test of my abilities, brother. Now you must eat, build strength. I have some stew ready."

"With more of that stinking stuff in it?" Slocum asked, lips twisting in distaste.

Ross chuckled. "No. That is behind you now."

"Then I'll eat it," Slocum offered.

With a heavy sigh, he relaxed onto the pallet of rough saddle blankets. Weakness hovered about, probing his defenses. How easy it would be, Slocum thought swimmingly, to ease back into that soft, yielding oblivion.

A pot of potatoes bubbled fiercely on the wood-burning cookstove. Savory aromas came from the oven compartment where a beef roast slowly browned. Vivian Ballard fought a losing battle against stray strands of her auburn hair that floated cloudlike around her head. She had located a small, one-bedroom house in Emporia and settled in two days before. This would be her first full meal cooked in her own kitchen.

She had invited two fellow teachers, elder spinsters, Maude Cross and Charity Welsh. They would be there any moment and she had yet to get the flour off her face and change to more festive clothing. For a while, at least, everything could take care of itself, she reckoned. A knock at the front door added to her anxiety. Wiping her hands on a gingham kitchen towel, she started through the house.

"I've come to discuss your, ah, additional services," Quade Purdy informed her when she opened the door.

"Not tonight," Vivian said sternly, and not for the first time. "I have guests coming for supper."

Purdy looked hurt and confused for a while. "Tonight will be a perfect time. There'll be a full moon."

"Which I'll not be watching, with you or anyone else. Now, please go away," Vivian demanded as she shut the door in his face.

Once more the tingling sensation of an alien presence oozed along her spine as she made for the kitchen. Set the potatoes on an asbestos pad, the peas, too, she planned in her head. That would allow her time to dress. She completed her task and had turned away from the stove when the kitchen door emitted a loud bang and slammed backward against the wall. The glass partition shattered and rang musically as it fell to the floor.

Quade Purdy stood in the doorway, the front of his trousers distended by the pressure of his erection. He breathed roughly and eyed her with malignant lust. Instinctively, Vivian backed away. Purdy parted parched lips and his tongue came out to wipe them.

"I'm gonna have my way with you, woman. Best you fix your mind on that."

"Like hell you will," Vivian challenged.

He lunged for her and she struck him in the face with a half-closed hand. Startled, yet not checked, he thrust his powerful legs against the linoleum flooring. Springing forward, Purdy's one hand grabbed her wrist. Fingers used to gripping heavy grain sacks closed with crushing power. Vivian cursed him in a low voice.

"There's not a woman with a pretty turn of ankle that wouldn't be glad to lay with me," Purdy snarled. "Not a one who worked at the school who didn't."

"Damn you, let me go!" Why didn't she scream? The thought sped away the moment Vivian had it. Her free hand reached out desperately for some object to turn into a weapon.

Purdy yanked her to him and ground his rigid phallus against her pelvic mound. It made her want to vomit. Desperately she slapped him and gouged at one eye. Purdy yanked his head out of her way. His grip tightened and he used his other hand to claw at the bodice of her dress. With a powerful jerk he ripped her clothing to the waist. Eagerly he began to paw her exposed breasts. Shaking with rage and humiliation, Vivian took a quick backward step.

Overbalanced, Purdy stumbled forward. Vivian made quick use of her knee in a sharp upward thrust. The swiftly rising limb made jarring contact with his crotch, mashing his testicles, which brought a satisfying bellow of agony. Purdy bent double, both hands clutching his savaged scrotum. Vivian sprang to the counter, where she snatched up a cast-iron skillet.

With a full-arm swing, she smashed the heavy metal utensil against the back of Quade Purdy's head. Rocked by the numbing blow, Purdy grunted and turned partway toward her. Vivian hit him again, this time above his left ear. She felt something give and dropped the skillet in revulsion. Quade Purdy, blood running from one ear, slumped to the floor. For several long minutes, panic took over.

Vivian ran to the sink. Several rapid strokes on the hand pump brought a dipper of water. She splashed it on the bleeding, unconscious form. Quade Purdy didn't move or respond in any fashion. Uttering a little cry of desperation, Vivian ran from the kitchen. Her eyes darted from one object to another without seeing any of them. In the small living room she stood at the center of a Persian rug and turned this way and that, knuckles crammed into her mouth to keep from screaming. A cicada started up on the trunk of a tree outside the window. Startled, Vivian dashed into her bedroom.

She came to her senses there as she fumbled with a change of clothing. She must have killed him, she reasoned. She had to get away. Her word would mean nothing against the death of a pillar of the community like Quade Purdy. Without conscious direction, Vivian clothed herself in her riding habit. The last button fastened, she hastened to assemble a few supplies. Her most trying moment came when she had to return to the kitchen for food.

A flour sack accommodated her provisions and she rushed away from the house to the livery stable. By the time she had rented a horse and it had been saddled, she had calmed enough to try to formulate a plan. Where could she go? Perplexed, she accepted the hostler's assistance to mount and headed her mount toward the outskirts of Emporia. Which way?

South, she decided on impulse. She would go south to find John Slocum.

Still unable to move without discomfort because of his wounds, and chafing at it, Slocum set about doing what he could to aid his friend, Ewan McDade. His first job, he decided, would be to establish some sort of organization and designate leaders. To that end he asked Ewan to assemble those men considered most likely to be followed by the rest. They met in late afternoon, on the day Ross Six had given Slocum a long session in an improvised sweat lodge.

"The way I see it, you have three things to accomplish at the same time. The first is to protect your families and your property. Second is to investigate these men responsible for the land-grab attempt. Lastly, you have to get somebody in government to listen to your side of things. I think the easiest approach is to solve the last problem first. A delegation has to be organized to present your situation to a court."

"What good will that do, even if we go to Topeka?" one Southern asked accusingly.

"That's right," another added. "I'm willin' to bet they're all in on it."

"I've said it before. No one listened then, maybe you will now. If you can't get satisfaction from the state, go to the federals."

"Damyankees don't listen to Southern complaints," Steve Varney objected.

"Not here in Kansas, perhaps," Slocum pressed. "So you go to Washington City. Among you it should be possible to gather enough money to send, say, three men to Washington to talk to the United States attorney general. Kansas was a free state, so you won't have any trouble getting in to see someone in a position to help. After that, it's up to those who go to sell your story to that person."

"Who should go?" another exile asked.

"That's up to you. Pick them and get them started," Slocum stated.

In half an hour, three men had been selected, among them Judge Terrel. Arrangements were made for them to get money, cross over into Missouri, and take the train back east. They departed, with the best wishes of everyone, at five in the afternoon. Then Slocum turned to the next priority.

"It might be possible to put a stop to all this faster if we had some law on our side. I want two men to head west, to Dodge City, by train. There's a deputy U.S. marshal there who is far enough removed from the politicians in Topeka to be trusted to listen before he acts. If we can get him here, we stand a better chance. Whoever goes should also head out tonight."

His idea met immediate approval and two men set off. Slocum touched on his next point.

"Are there any of you who are not known by sight to those you suspect of being involved with the Redlegs?" Slocum inquired.

"Well, ah, there are a few," Ewan allowed. "Thing is they're fairly straightforward fellers, might not be too good at snoopin' around legislators, senators, and the like."

"They'll have to learn," Slocum dictated. "Pick the ones you consider most reliable and qualified and send them off to Emporia and Topeka."

With that accomplished, the meeting broke up for the evening. Slocum ate his supper heartily. He noticed only a few twinges of pain whenever he raised himself from the ground or twisted his body suddenly. He spent a restful night and once more submitted to two hours in the sweat lodge before breakfast. Immediately after, the general meeting of exiles reconvened.

"This part can get mighty sticky," Slocum warned them. "So far any unbiased observer would have to admit you have no structure as a unit of irregulars, no organization whatsoever. The minute you agree to this step, that's all blown out the window like smoke."

"Meaning what?" a narrow-faced, nervous ex-Confederate inquired.

"There are roughly enough men here to form a company. We'll need to do that, with a captain to lead, officers to command the platoons. It'll be just like the army. Three platoons of four squads each. Everyone mounted. Preferably, those troops should be men without families, young, well armed. One platoon will guard the farms and families, on a rotating basis. Another will patrol for sign of the Jayhawkers. The third will form a quick-response mobile strike force to go wherever needed."

"It 'pears you've given this a lot of thought," Opie Tolliver opined. "Would you be willing to command this company of, ah, rangers?"

Slocum's mouth pursed and his cheeks went hollow as he gnawed on the inner linings. "I can't move around, keep in touch with the troops," he protested.

"Seems like, for a while at least, you might do better stayin' around here, runnin' things. Comes the time we need someone used to runnin' a company-sized lash-up, you'll be feeling up to it," Quinten Andrews advised.

A chorus of voices joined in agreement. Strongly disinclined to accept such a responsibility, Slocum raised his hands in protest. He shook his head and tried to wave the enthused Southern men to silence. Gradually they complied.

"Let's hear it for our new captain, boys!" a lean, far-eyed Tennessean roared in the eventual silence. "Hip-hip . . ."

"Hooray!" Three times the ancient cheer rang through the gulley.

"If that's what you all want, then I can only say that I insist on Ewan McDade as my executive officer. He's every bit as good at field craft as I am. Besides, he's one of you. He should be leading," Slocum told them.

"No offense to Ewan, but you're a real captain, led a real company. Ewan'll do just fine doin' what he did before. There's some of us officered in the war, can organize the platoons easy enough. Lord knows there's plenty sergeants among us. We'll handle the details, Cap'n," Opie urged. "You take care of the big plans."

"All right—all right," Slocum responded, with what he considered dangerously close to a note of pride. "Then the first thing we need to start is recruiting more men. And I mean *men*. No boys under sixteen. Those of you who are sure you can bring back three or more new recruits, ride out tonight and get started." Another cheer answered his first order. "Now, tomorrow, we have to set up a staff. That Frenchman, Napoleon, said an army travels on its stomach. So we'll need a supply and commissary section. There are special ways of easily getting information about your enemies. Those who served with scouts or irregular units know how. You can teach others. That needs to be started at once.

"Another thing," Slocum went on. "In the event of attacks by the Jayhawkers, we need a means of rapidly sending messages. Flat as this country is, heliograph sounds good to me. Does anyone know how to build one and operate it?"

That brought scant response. "I used to be a telegrapher," one Southern boy announced. He had a long, gawky neck and the slender frame of a stripling. "I know the dots and dashes. Shouldn't be too hard to make 'em with a mirror instead of a sending key."

"That's the idea," Slocum encouraged. "Everyone pool your knowledge and resources and we'll get this going."

By morning the first volunteers began to arrive. Men streamed into the gulley all through the day and for two following. Slocum took time to interview everyone with a special talent. Three in particular, who had experience with explosives, he conversed with for a long time. From them he took ideas that would, he hoped, come to their aid in the future. By afternoon of the third day a patrol schedule had been established that enabled the men banished from their homes to rest easier. The far-flung members of the patrolling platoon would see each threatened place twice a day.

Still Slocum would not be content. He organized drills for the men, set some to digging caves in the walls of the wash to cache food and other supplies. With each following day he worked miracles of creative staff function. On a crude map of the area, the location and movement of the militia took on a definite pattern. Slowly, it became obvious, the McDade farm was being cut off from any support, isolated like a lamb cut out by wolves.

"We can't let this keep on," Opie Tolliver complained when the last red *X* appeared on the map. "That's five farms burned out, the folks run off. Why haven't our boys been able to prevent it?"

"Spread too thin," Slocum explained. "We have to put more men in the field."

"When?" Opie snapped.

Ambulatory now, Slocum stood and strapped his gunleather around his waist. "Now," he answered with soft menace. "Let's go find some bluebirds with red legs."

# 14

He'd been pushing cows around since he turned eight. That made five years. Clell Tyree couldn't think of anything more boring than spending all day sitting on a horse, walking slowly around a lot of stupid, four-legged critters with big, fat middles. How he wished that sometime something exciting might happen. Experience taught him not to expect that wish to come true. On that particular sunny, blue-sky afternoon, filled with meadowlark song, fate dealt him a different hand.

He saw the dust first. A rising brown smudge against the horizon. Then the mounted figures came into sight topping a swell in the prairie. A lot of them. They would cross his present eastward route about a mile ahead. The spirit of adventure goaded Clell out of his doldrums. Drubbing blunt spurs into his pony's ribs, he worked up a fair canter, which would put him much closer to the large body of men.

They weren't looking his way, Clell decided after a hard fifteen-minute run toward the soldiers. He could see that now. They wore blue uniforms, like the Yankees who had invaded their home in Georgia that Momma talked about. Clell hugged his pony's neck and urged more speed. He had to see where these blue-bellies were going.

To the south, he knew, lay Mr. Crawford's Triangle C Cattle Company spread. Paw and Mr. Crawford always held roundup together to exchange any strays that had crossed over the unfenced boundary between their ranches. Mr. Crawford was from South Carolina. His son, Timmy, was the same age and Clell's best friend. Clell knew the danger the Jayhawkers represented. He had gotten close enough now to see the red leggings they wore, and identified them. Best he find his brother, Clell decided, swinging away and forcing his gentle mount into an unaccustomed gallop.

His back to the column of Jayhawkers, Clell didn't see the puff of white smoke that came when Sergeant Banks spotted the little lad. He did feel the sharp, burning pain along the outside of his right arm and hear the crack of the rifle. He also, much to his horror and embarrassment, wet himself. Then Clell devoted all his energies to getting out of range and locating his brother, who rode with the Southern scouting patrol.

"They'reheadedfortheTriangleC!" he blurted out in a spill of words when he came upon Wayne Tyree's squad.

"What? Say that again, li'l brother," Wayne responded as he rose up from pouring a cup of noon coffee.

"Jayhawkers. A whole lot of 'em," Clell panted. "They're ridin' for Mr. Crawford's place."

"How long ago?" Wayne's sergeant asked.

Clell studied the sun. "Half an hour, maybe."

The sergeant ruffled Clell's snowy mop of hair. "You done good, boy. We got time to get the word to the cap'n."

Nightfall of Clell Tyree's fateful day found Captain Godfrey Howard and his company in position to attack the large headquarters of the Triangle C. He sat his Morgan mare in contentment, looking down at the three large barns, extensive corrals, four implement sheds, a long, low bunkhouse, three wells with covered copings, two smaller houses for Crawford's grown sons, and the rambling, two-story main dwelling. Fast-growing elms and cottonwood trees had been planted to provide future shade. A woman's touch could be seen in the flowering window boxes and knee-high privet hedge around the inside of a white picket fence.

Prosperous. Of that, Godfrey Howard had no doubt. He roused himself from his reflections and turned to Sergeant Banks.

"We'll not burn the buildings. Fire those haystacks, run off any cattle and the horses, and kill everyone."

"You—ah—sort of like this place, eh?" Banks asked in a familiar tone.

"I do, Ike. I'm sparing it, in hopes I can convince Mr. Anstruther to let me have it as my bonus for a job well done. Of course, you'll have a share in it, too."

"I'll accept gladly," Banks said through a chuckle. "But before we divide up all the chickens, we'd better see to gettin' them hatched."

"Right you are. Form the company in two lines of skirmishers. And pass the word on sparing the buildings."

"Yes, sir."

In two minutes the troops stood ready to move out. Full darkness lay over the shallow bowl that housed the headquarters of Crawford's ranch. The moon had yet to rise. Captain Howard checked the alignment of his men and gave the signal to advance.

"At the walk, forward . . . hoooo!"

Briskly the troops started out. As they descended the long, rolling swale toward the main house and hay barns, pairs of soldiers dropped off to ignite torches and set fire to the haystacks that stood drying on the plain. Faintly at first, the sound of hoofbeats impinged on Captain Godfrey Howard's consciousness. A sudden swell in volume sent his gaze to his right.

Riding in military formation, a large body of men seemed to rise out of the ground as they topped a ridge and broke into a gallop toward the militia's flank. A muffled curse from Sergeant Banks brought his attention forward again in time to see another contingent charging toward them. A moment of confusion followed for the militia officer.

Who could they be? They rode like regular troops. None of the Southern rabble had organization. Unable to satisfy his curiosity, Captain Howard was about to call out when a terrible, keening cry split the night air.

*"WOH—WHO—EY! WHO—EY! WHO-EY!"*

Shrill and eerie, the rebel yell came out of the past in all its horrifying splendor.

They arrived at the Crawford ranch with no time to spare. Young Clell Tyree had begged to come along, and had been refused. He went off into the camp in the wash to sulk and pout. His message, delivered in the same excited rush, electrified the hundred and twenty-eight men in camp. By then, Clell had ordered his thoughts enough to report an estimated force of over a hundred and seventy. Slocum quickly organized the strike force into two wings. Although outnumbered by two to one, he had confidence in their fighting ability. Surprise would be on their side, also. They would ride together and deploy in an L-shaped formation to carry the attack to the enemy.

Now, toward them raced that enemy. Faint starlight glinted off the edge of an officer's saber at the center of the front rank. Despite the slight, nagging tenderness of his larger wounds, Slocum insisted on leading this first major skirmish in the field. He swung his headquarters escort toward the dim light of that blade. If it proved to be the man who had hacked him, Slocum wanted to settle with Howard in a decidedly unpleasant manner.

"Volley fire, First Sergeant," Slocum bellowed. "And fast, too, before we close our own lines."

"Sir! By the volley . . . FIRE!"

Seven saddles emptied in the wake of the wall of yellow-orange flame from the muzzles of sixty rifles. Slocum found the result satisfying, considering the range and the irregular motion of their horses. Off to his left, from the militia's right flank, came an answering volley.

Nine of the fourteen men detailed to fire the haycocks lay on the ground, pools of their blood spreading. Two more screamed in agony, limbs shattered by bullets. Slocum nodded in appraisal.

"Once more, if you please." The old, familiar commands and calm remarks returned so easily. Slocum felt warmed by them. Another sheet of fire erupted from his right and left.

A great curtain of burning powder momentarily lighted the heads of the militia horses. The militiamen had overcome their initial shock and returned fire with vigor, if not accuracy. Slocum noted two men down, both wounded but able to recover their mounts.

"They're closing up," First Sergeant Varney shouted. "There, at the middle."

Those would be the most dedicated, Slocum considered from experience. The others would be simply looking for a way to get out of the line of fire. His flankers hit the concentrated knot of militiamen and swarmed around them. In less than a minute, the main force would hit them as well.

"My God, they've got an army," Captain Godfrey Howard blurted.

His plans in disarray, the militia commander could hardly still his panic to formulate any countermeasure. At last he hit upon the best defensive—if not tactically wise—decision. Yanking at his reins, he called out to those around him.

"Halt! Rein up and form a dismounted perimeter." Fitting his actions to orders, Howard swung from his saddle. "Scoop out firing pits so you'll be below ground level. Pile up the dirt for breastworks. Hurry, men! They're about on us again!" Howard's usually soft, effeminate voice rose in volume to a shrill timbre.

"Kneel . . . take aim . . . fire!" Sergeant Banks commanded of the defenders.

With the speed and power of a whirlwind, the ex-Confederates washed over the thirty or so men around Captain Howard. Three militiamen died screaming. Two horses went stiff-legged and dropped to the ground. One former reb jumped his horse over the still-upright Howard. Guided by instinct, the young captain plunged his saber into the straining animal's belly.

In the next instant Howard let out a howl of pain when the horse's momentum ripped the sword grip from his hand. Seemingly from everywhere the frightening, unearthly rebel yell wrapped around the disorganized soldiers.

*"WHO—WHO—EY! WHO—EY! WHO-EY!"*

"Oh, God, make them quit that," a youthful reinforcement wailed near to his commander.

"Shut your mouth, you yellow bastard," Captain Howard snarled.

*"WHO—EY WHO-EY!"*

"Oh, Lord, please, *please!*" the frightened young trooper moaned.

Rifle fire crashed from all around them. Again the ghostly taunt of the rebel yell worked its sinister magic on the bewildered and frightened militia. Those old enough to have served in the Union army had generally avoided contact with the disconcerting battle cry by the expedient of making war on helpless civilians. Those too young to have ever faced a rebel charge knew a terror like none before. It turned the bowels to water and freed the bladder to gush like a Niagara.

*"WHO—EEEEEY!"*

"I can't take it anymore, *I can't!"* another green trooper shrieked.

Before Sergeant Banks could reach to restrain him, he jumped up out of his half-completed hole. The other frightened reb hater bounded upward, mouth working unheard in the thunder of galloping hoofs as the ex-Confederates charged again. Muzzle flashes illuminated the bedeviled youths.

A bullet crashed through one side of the prayerful militiaman's head and out the other. Bits of bone, brain, and blood splashed in Godfrey Howard's face. Howard wanted to scream in terror and revulsion and to run and keep on running until he could never see a rebel on horseback again.

"Shit!"

Slocum had taken careful aim, intent on blasting the life out of Captain Godfrey Howard. The precipitous action of the frightened trooper had put a different target in his sights. When the hammer fell, a 250-grain slug splashed the young soldier's brain into pudding, which saved the life of the malevolent Jayhawk leader. Slocum sought to sight in again, only to flash past the shallow defenses and into the dark.

"Turn back and do it again," he commanded in disregard of the correct orders.

"We broke 'em, Cap'n!" First Sergeant Steve Varney roared. "They're runnin' like scared rabbits. Look at 'em go!"

"Have the trumpeter sound Recall and Advance as Skirmishers. We're going after them, First Sergeant," Slocum shouted back, caught up in the fever of battle.

*"WOH—WHO—EY! WHO-EY! WHO-EY!"* The yell came from behind.

*"WHO—EY! WHO-EY!"* To be answered from in front of the fleeing column of militia.

"Won't they ever give up?" a harried militia corporal plaintively asked of no one.

"They won't follow us over that ridge," his lieutenant assured him.

"You said that about the last ridge . . . sir."

Mounted men suddenly appeared on their right. The tardily rising moon paled to dimness in a sheet of muzzle bloom. Three men, including the frightened corporal, fell from their saddles. Instantly the rebels whirled and rode off in the darkness. A wild glaze fixed in the lieutenant's eyes.

"They're behind us, in front of us, on the sides. What the hell is going on?"

"Steady there," Captain Howard advised from the officer's front. He had only a moment before he silently asked himself the same question. "Another mile and they won't dare pursue us. We'll be too close to Chanute."

"The way they fight, that town ain't big enough to scare 'em off," an anonymous voice opined.

Disgusted with the defeatist sentiment, Howard spurred his mount forward to the head of the column. Sergeant Banks heard him coming and turned in the saddle.

"Face it, Cap'n, we've been whupped good and proper."

Anger stung the last vestige of fear from Godfrey Howard's consciousness. "Then we pull ourselves together and go after them again. And we keep on hunting them down until the last rebel scum is dead."

## SEDITIONIST MASSACRE!
### PEACEFUL MILITIA TROOPS MURDERED IN SLEEP!

Below those somber black headlines, editor Walter Black wove a tale of marvelous fiction, blended of fabrication, falsification, and misinformation. A dedicated practitioner of the scrivener's art, he spared nothing to see that truth didn't get in the way of bombastic yellow journalism.

"Two nights ago, twelve miles south of Chanute, the peaceful night camp of a company of our valiant Kansas Militia was treacherously and viciously attacked by a band of villainous rebel insurrectionists. Outnumbered by three to one, our brave militia acquitted itself with valor, claiming the lives of nine scurrilous villains. Twenty-three brave boys fell dead and nearly fifty were wounded by these misbegotten followers of the Starry Cross. The cloak of civilization must be put aside when dealing with such vermin. A pestilence on the land, these slavers showed no mercy to those helpless men, still asleep in their blankets when Bloody Insurrection descended upon their bivouac."

He had a good deal more to say, all in like purple prose. Slocum set aside the copy of the *Emporia Light* from which he read the first few paragraphs and sighed in disgust. They had struck the marauding militia on his orders, in expectation of bringing about an end, or at least a stalemate, in the Jayhawker-manufactured conflict. It appeared now that all he had succeeded in doing was turn the entire state against these vulnerable and desperate men who fought for their homes. It would have been better, Slocum thought, if he had never come.

"How many children is that?" Cyril Anstruther's male secretary asked, pen poised over the sheet of foolscap on his knee desk.

"Four. Ages fourteen, thirteen, eleven, and eight," Anstruther answered, adding their names.

"And the wife?" the secretary prompted.

"Aurora," Anstruther breathed softly, eyes fixed on a prismatic rainbow caught in an imperfection of the leaded glass in the bay window of his tastefully appointed study. "Add Eunice, his mother, and might as well include his mother-in-law, an old battle-axe who lives in Fredonia."

"My, you've gathered quite a lot of information on Ewan McDade," the secretary commented. "Your usual thorough undertaking, of course."

Rankled by this condescending familiarity, yet unable to reprimand for it because of years of like lapses, Cyril Anstruther responded with a snort. "I want twenty copies made and circulated in the right places. You know how to take care of that. Then we shall see how these rebel scum like death sentences on every member of the McDade family and a reward of ten thousand dollars for accomplishing it."

"Sort of two birds with a single stone, what?" the dandified secretary quipped.

"Exactly," Anstruther allowed, his hands clasped in a choking gesture. "We're rid of the McDades and that should smoke Slocum out where I can get a shot at him."

# 15

Too many men, Slocum thought as he studied the deep, wide gorge in the tallgrass prairie. This place could not be kept secret much longer. Supplies, particularly ammunition, had dwindled. The addition of some thirty more volunteers didn't help that situation. Still concerned with the logistics of handling a force of nearly a hundred and fifty, Slocum descended from his vantage point and went to the brush hut he used for a headquarters.

"The hunting's gone to hell around here," he told his staff officers and troop leaders. "Never was that good, not enough to feed this many men. We need fresh goods. We're low on food, ammunition, medical supplies, and we could use a farrier. There must be two dozen horses need shoeing."

"Where do you figure on getting all this?"

"At Emporia, Opie," Slocum answered. "What's the name of the general store owner who is sympathetic?"

"Harrison Monroe," Ewan McDade supplied. "He was with General Stand Wattie. They didn't surrender until six months after Appomattox."

Slocum produced a slim smile. "Another Cherokee in the woodpile, and maybe a relative at that. Good enough. We'll take four wagons, big ones. And an escort of twenty men. They can hole up outside town."

"You said 'we.' You shouldn't go, Cap'n," Ewan protested.

131

"Why not? Too many of your faces are known. I'll ask for volunteers from the younger boys—er—troops."

"When do you plan to go?" Opie Tolliver asked.

"Within an hour," Slocum told him. "We'll need one wagon to haul grain for the horses. Get the volunteers and wagons ready. Now, for the next item. We did well at Crawford's. We lost only nine men killed. Eleven with wounds of varying seriousness. Considering the size of the battle, that was remarkable. But we have to do better."

For half an hour Slocum outlined his observations from the fight and made suggestions for cutting their losses. The wagons and young drivers appeared on time, along with two squads from Ewan's headquarters platoon. With a creaking of wooden wagon boxes, they started up out of the gorge. Once clear of the cleft in the ground, Slocum sent out scouts to both flanks and in front. He felt terribly vulnerable and trusted his far-reaching eyes more than their combined firepower.

"We're going to avoid the enemy, not fight him," Slocum advised Wayne Tyree, who drove the first wagon.

Ten miles north of the gorge, one of the advance scouts appeared suddenly and galloped toward the caravan. Still a quarter mile off, he began to wave his hat wildly. Slocum trotted forward to meet him.

"Militia," the excited young man yelled. "About fifteen of 'em, six miles ahead and ridin' this way."

"Ride ahead and tell the others to pull back. We'll be heading . . ." Slocum studied the terrain. "West. Want to get that ridgeline between us and the militia."

"Yes, sir," the youthful scout panted.

At once he set off at a hard run. Slocum returned to the wagons. He directed them toward a low ridge some two miles away. He wore a rueful grin when he observed the disappointed faces.

"I know we outnumber them. But they're a lot more mobile than we are. We'll have to run the teams a bit to cover ground. Make sure you've got a good seat and stretch 'em out."

Slocum's cavalcade made it with time to spare. Belly down on the reverse slope of the ridge, Slocum watched the searchers ride past. They had to be blind, he reckoned, not to see where four sets of wheels turned off the established road. Some effort had been made to obliterate the tracks, yet a man with the height advantage of a saddle should be able to note the bent grass and broken turf. Must be that these troops hadn't any scouting experience, Slocum allowed. Cautiously he worked his way backward until he could stand up. Time to get rolling.

"Sergeant," Slocum called to the NCO. "Send three men down the trail to watch our rear. The rest of you get 'em rolling."

"Yessir," the volunteers chorused.

For the next five miles, the wagons continued northward beyond the ridge. The flank scouts had not reported in and Slocum considered it a good sign. They had less than fifteen miles to go to Emporia when one of the three men rode in from the west.

"Blue-belly patrol t'other side of the Arkansas. Don't reckon they'll cross the river."

"Keep an eye on them," Slocum advised.

To add distance between them and the patrol, Slocum returned to the road. The pace increased. Ahead the road dipped into a long downhill stretch bordered by tall outcroppings of limestone. Beyond that the road ground slowly upward to the nominal elevation of the prairie. A bend masked the continuation of the ruts they followed. The wagons hit the bottom of the declivity at a fair clip and the teams leaned into the strain of uphill progress.

Suddenly five figures appeared around the bend above. The lead man reined abruptly and stared downward. He turned and spoke to his companions and they broke into a brisk trot.

"I think we have trouble," Wayne Tyree observed as the men advanced.

"They're Redlegs, right enough," Slocum murmured. "If we can bluff them we're home free."

Hard-faced and suspicious, the Jayhawkers proved not to be in a bluffing mood. At a distance of fifty feet the leader called out for the wagons to halt. Slocum signaled for the drivers to rein up. A twisted smile splitting his face, the leader started forward.

"Where you bound?" he called.

"Emporia. A little shopping," Slocum answered.

"Mighty lot of you for such a simple chore," the Jayhawker remarked.

"Surely you've heard there are dangerous rebels around these parts," Slocum quipped.

Counting the number of guns against him, the Jayhawker suppressed his flash of anger. "What's to say you're not some of them?"

Slocum shrugged. With a sweeping arm gesture, he included the wagons and remaining escort. "Would we be riding into town open as can be if we were?"

That brought a frown and a moment's contemplation. "Did you meet any of our company further down the road?"

"We did. They let us go about our business. I don't see why you're giving us a hard time."

Sharp anger flared. "You'll think hard time," the leader snarled. His hand dropped toward his holster.

Slocum's short move across half his waist produced the big Colt .45 before the hapless Redleg could open the flap covering his weapon. Hollow clicks came from the hammers of .45-70 Springfields, in the hands of the escort. Slack-jawed, the five Jayhawkers stared at a ring of deadly muzzles. Slocum took note of the chevrons on the man's uniform tunic.

"Sergeant, it would be nice to spend the day chatting but we do have important business to take care of. If you'll sort of easy-like take out your weapons and hand them over, we'll arrange for a nice place for you to relax until we return."

"Goddamn rebel—," the Jayhawk sergeant began, then broke off as a Springfield muzzle menaced him between his shoulder blades.

"The guns, then dismount. You won't be harmed, only tied up and left until we get back here. If we have trouble and don't manage . . ." Slocum let hang with a shrug and a crooked smile.

Under Slocum's direction, three of the large wagons parked behind Monroe's general mercantile, at the loading dock usually used to take in merchandise. The other used the alley to approach the feed and grain store of Quade Purdy. This back-way approach would increase their chance of not being recognized by any casual passssersby. Slocum rode around and tied up Ol' Rip in front of the store. Harrison Monroe greeted them warmly and passed on the best wishes of several people in the community who secretly harbored a partisanship for the beleaguered Southerns. Immediately the drivers, helped by Monroe and his stock clerk, began to load sacks of flour, rice, sugar, and beans. To that they would add slabs of bacon, hams, and a plentiful supply of dried, jerked beef. As an afterthought, Slocum suggested a barrel of pickles and another of apples. Harry Monroe donated two five-pound tins of coffee to the purchase of five more, and kicked in for a flat wooden case of .45-70 cartridges. From the storeroom, cases of rifle, shotgun, and revolver ammunition would nearly fill one wagon. Slocum mentioned something about looking for a case of dynamite and left the younger men to their labors.

Out on bustling Commerce Street, Slocum located a farm and builders' supply. A bell sounded cheerily above the door when he entered. Peering from behind gold-rimmed half-spectacles, a clerk with black sleeve protectors and a green eyeshade glanced up.

"What can I do for you?"

"Do you carry dynamite?" Slocum asked.

The clerk frowned his obvious disapproval of such a request. "Yes, we do. How much will you need?"

"Would five cases be more than you can deliver?" Slocum totaled up and asked.

Eyebrows racing for his receding hairline, the clerk swallowed. "You must have a lot of stumps," he offered haltingly.

"Rocks. I've got a whole field that grows nothing but rocks. Big ones, the size of my horse. So I'm going to make little ones out of them and build a house."

"You'll want the fast type, then," the fussy little man blurted.

"No. Sixty percent will be good enough. I don't want to send those rocks to the next county, just crack 'em a little," Slocum allowed, his mood relaxed for the first time since the expedition to Emporia began.

He arranged for the proprietor to load from his rear dock and returned to the street. He sought the best source for information in any town, a center of community news and personal gossip. Slocum wanted to find a saloon. It took him twenty minutes to locate the last public barroom in Emporia. With Kansas going dry, city by city, the liquor emporium had an aura of tragedy and despair about it.

Slocum's approach, he felt certain, would guarantee a free

and easy exchange of the latest idle banter. "I'd like to purchase a small keg of whiskey and a barrel of beer," he announced upon reaching the glowing expanse of mahogany.

"That's a mighty ambitious order, mister," the bartender opined.

"Gonna be a wedding," Slocum lied smoothly.

"Father of the bride?" the apron asked. To Slocum's curt nod, he added, "Congratulations." Then he flashed a grin. "I reckon I can handle it, though. What'er you drinkin' now?"

"Give me a beer," Slocum requested.

"Comin' right up," the genial barkeep acknowledged.

Slocum stood at the center of the bar. From the end on his right hand came the whiny voice of a barfly. "I still think she done all right. That randy goat needed takin' down a notch."

"Wilber, you've got whiskey on the brain. Ain't no way for a schoolmarm to act, whanging the school superintendent with a skillet," his boozy companion argued.

"She was right purty, with them long limbs and coppery hair," Wilber remarked. "Still it weren't no reason she had to put up with a lecher like Purdy."

"Where'd you get the idea that's what caused her to brain him?"

Wilber sniggered and rapped his empty schooner on the bar top. "What else? Wouldn't be the first one ol' Quade tried to put the pork to. I hear tell he's a regular rue-*aay*."

"And I hear, Wilber, that he ain't got enough pecker to trouble a prairie chicken. Reg'lar pencil prick."

With lovely and willing Vivian Ballard in mind, Slocum signaled his interest by ordering a round and producing a grin. "What's this about old Quade Purdy getting his comeuppance?" he initiated his inquiry.

In short order he got a great deal more information than he had expected. Wilber proved a literal fount of knowledge on the subject. He concluded his highly colorful account with remarks on the outcome.

"That new teacher, the one with the dark red hair, whomped him sure enough, then hightailed it out of town."

"Anyone know where she went?" Slocum probed.

"Naw. Not that anyone's saying anything. Headed west for a while, then turned south. I got that from Hiram down the livery."

"Is she wanted for murder?" Slocum prompted.

Wilber wrinkled his brow. "Nope. Not even for battery. Ol' Quade survived an' ain't makin' too much noise about it. He causes a lot of fuss and his wife will figger he's been foolin' around, which he has for years. Quade got him a cracked skull and a whale of a headache. His story is that he don't have an idea why she just up and attacked him. He'd gone over to that Miz Ballard's place to discuss a matter about the school. At least that's the story he told the police. All of a sudden, he claims, she ups and grabs an iron skillet and whaps him a good one."

"It coulda happened that way," Wilber's companion suggested. "You know wimmin do funny things. Why, I recall my Sophie. Ev'ry month, when she got her curse, she'd sort of like go off her nut over the simplest things. Like clockwork, ev'ry blessed month. One of the reasons I left her and moved west."

"But nothin's known about where she went?"

Both drunks shook their heads solemnly. "She musta left right away she done it," Wilber offered. "With him layin' on her kitchen floor, cold as a stone crock in a springhouse."

"Gentlemen, gentlemen," a braying voice addressed the occupants of the saloon from the doorway. "The difficulty in finding this wondrous establishment has left me utterly parched. I must imbibe in spiritous waters this very minute or perish."

Slocum recognized that voice and tensed himself. In the tail of his vision he caught the familiar, corpulent figure of Harvey Dobbins and grimaced. Dobbins advanced to the bar and loudly smacked down a silver dollar. Slocum studied him in the mirror behind the bar.

If anything, Dobbins had put on more weight. He fairly waddled when he walked and his fat jiggled with each breath. He, too, stared into the mirror and his face underwent a drastic change from forced joviality to bleak terror. Unwillingly he turned toward Slocum.

"Why, as I live and breathe, if it isn't that knight errant of the high road, Slocum. What brings Southern trash like you to Emporia, Slocum?"

Two men at a side table started at this pronouncement and held a brief, whispered conversation. One of them departed hastily. Slocum noted it and began to frame a comment that would allow him to depart with equal alacrity.

"Still traveling around in ladies' undergarments, Harvey?" Slocum asked with heavy sarcasm.

It brought sniggers from Wilber and his fellow barfly. It also turned Harvey Dobbins's face bright crimson. A nervous impulse sloshed beer from the schooner the barkeep had set before him.

"I see you remain a coarse, vulgar bastard, Slocum," Dobbins said with asperity.

"I'd call you out for insulting my mother . . . if you were a man," Slocum growled.

Slocum's hand hovered dangerously close to his six-gun and Dobbins noted it. He paled and the trembling of his jowls increased. "N-now see here—"

"To hell with it," Slocum snapped. He slapped a pair of double eagles on the bar. "That's for the order I made," he informed the barman, then turned away and started for the door.

"Not so fast, reb," the man who remained at the table barked as he stood.

Slocum saw the red leggings he wore. He also saw the Red-leg's hand on his revolver butt. Two quick steps and the next thing he saw was his own cocked fist fly forward and connect with the Jayhawker's jaw.

Driven backward into his chair, the Redleg sent it crashing on its side. Completing his follow-through brought Slocum up close before the man had a chance to fall. Two short, fast blows under the ribs and another right cross to the jaw dumped the Kansan in a heap on the sawdust. Slocum stepped over him and started for the door.

"A wagon will pick up the barrels and the driver will pay any balance due for them," he stated far more calmly than he felt.

" . . . inside right now. One of those rebel marauders." The voice caught up to Slocum as he stepped onto the brick side-walk. The other man from the table turned at the slam of the door. "There he is. That's the one."

An instant, angry mob formed. Led by three Redlegs, the howling crowd surged toward Slocum. Slocum spun on one heel and ran along the walk toward the entrance to an alley. Fifteen men streamed behind him.

With thirty feet to spare, Slocum swung into the dirt alley and sprinted toward the rear of the buildings that presented blank walls to the narrow passage. Five of the mob tumbled into the space behind him.

"Keep going," one advised the others. "Cut him off at the next street."

Slocum put on speed. He reached the rear of the buildings, fronting another alley, and turned left when an old-timer in shirtsleeves opened the back door. In two long bounds, Slocum reached the entrance and bolted inside behind the oldster, who vigorously shook a small rug.

Slocum worked his way down a dim corridor that smelled of boiled cabbage and stale tobacco smoke. He reached a sort of lobby when the mob swarmed in behind him. Slocum jinked to the right, toward a staircase, then bent low and hurried on tiptoe to the registration desk and crouched behind it. Reacting to his disappearance, the vengeful men thundered up the stairs. Slocum gave them two long, tense minutes, then came from behind the desk.

With an affected casual air, Slocum strolled out of the front door. Down at the corner, one of the Jayhawkers turned to look back and saw Slocum.

"There he is!"

# 16

Slocum did the only thing he could do. He fled without thought or plan. Several more citizens of Emporia had joined the mob. One waved a rope, knotted into a hangman's knot. Ahead, Slocum saw a man step out of a shoemaker's shop. He duplicated his first escape by entering the store in a rush. He vaulted the counter and ran for the back.

No door. *Think fast*, Slocum told himself. "Sorry," he yelled over one shoulder to the cobbler as he hefted a chair and threw it through the window.

He dived out a minute later, to find himself in a dead-end alley. A quick look around showed him three Jayhawkers menacing him from the mouth of the cul-de-sac. Three to one. He'd faced worse odds. So far no real harm had been done. The six-guns in the hands of the hard-faced Redlegs convinced Slocum that such a luxury had come to an end. The one in the middle started to raise the muzzle of his converted Remington .44.

"Don't!" Slocum shouted, raising his left hand up and away from his body. "Can't we talk this over?" He delivered the last word as his right hand closed over the butt grips of the .45 Colt.

It came free and across his body in a smooth movement. Slocum's thumb had already eared back the hammer. A slight pressure of his finger on the trigger and the big revolver bucked in his hand. Greasy white powder smoke rose to obscure the trio of Jayhawkers.

Slocum fired through it and heard a man grunt and the sound of a fallen body. He sidestepped and loosed a third round. A jink the other direction brought him clear of the smoke and he saw one man on his knees, hands clasped across his gut, with blood trickling between his fingers. Another lay dead two feet away. The third discharged a wild shot that cracked over Slocum's head. He answered with a bullet to the Redleg's right shoulder.

His man went down as though it had been a fatal shot. A long, pitiful groan came from the fellow with the belly wound and he slumped to the earth, dead from internal bleeding. Slocum ejected his spent rounds and reloaded, then holstered his Colt. Hurrying past the defeated trio, he kicked the weapon away from the man with the shoulder wound, then stepped onto the street. Cross over and around the next corner he would find Monroe's general mercantile. He would be safe then.

Unfortunately the mob had other ideas for Slocum. They had divided into three groups and set up the hue and cry in earnest. While two segments of the aroused citizenry chased off in wrong directions, a calmer, quieter group, made up of Jayhawkers, began a sweep back through the streets Slocum had fled along. They came upon their three comrades and the death of two fueled their fury. Still they hunted like well-trained pointers. Their slow, methodical pace allowed Slocum to retrieve Ol' Rip from in front of the general store, mount, and sedately walk the animal over three blocks before increasing to a fast trot.

Slocum rode west. He had discussed the eventuality of trouble and the wagon drivers knew that if he did not return within two hours, or if his horse came up missing, they were to take a northerly direction out of town. They were not to swing south until well beyond the settled area. While the angry Jayhawkers and their local sympathizers fruitlessly searched the town, Wayne Tyree and the other drivers proceeded out of the city unmolested.

"They've even identified you by name," Ewan McDade said angrily as he slapped down a copy of the *Emporia Light*. "This Captain Howard has taken the killings quite personally. I agree that we should disband, spread out, but where are you going?"

"Where they least expect me," Slocum told his friend.

Four days later, Slocum appeared in the state capital, Topeka. Judicious investigating by friends of the beleaguered Southerns had developed the locations frequented by the powerful cabal. They had not come up with Cyril Anstruther's name, though Senator Dahlgren and Justice Duffey frequently appeared in reports. Armed with those two names, and dressed in the finery of a prosperous businessman, Slocum presented himself to the second-floor headwaiter at the Fontainbleu Restaurant shortly before noon.

"Yes, sir?" Icy tones greeted Slocum.

"I am expected in the private dining room," the ex-Confederate responded, trying to put a note of condescension in his voice.

"Your name, sir?" A blue norther would have been warmer.

Slocum gave an offended sniff, and felt foolish doing it. "Dieffenbeck."

In the restaurant staff's absence earlier that morning, Slocum had checked the reservations list and selected a name, beside which had been written the notation "new guest." Then he had sent Mr. Dieffenbeck of Dodge City a note saying the luncheon meeting had been delayed a day. The maître d' ran a long, bony finger along the sheet in his book.

"Aa-a-a-ah, yes. Senator Dahlgren has left word that he was called away on short notice and will not be here. Since this is your first visit, he has asked that I introduce you in his stead."

Gratified that his reconnaissance had proven fruitful, and been graced by fortunate circumstances, Slocum nodded curtly. "Thank you. That will be quite satisfactory."

"This way, please." A check mark was made beside the name, and the maître d' walked along the hall in a mincing manner. Slocum followed.

The stuffy, self-important headwaiter might have been the chamberlain at Buckingham Palace when he swung wide the tall oak doors and announced Slocum as Augustus Dieffenbeck of Dodge City. He went on to provide the imposter with valuable information by advising the gathered conspirators that Mr. Dieffenbeck was a land promoter.

Justice John Duffey rushed forward to take Slocum by the hand. He wrung it with all the energy of a campaigning politician and steered the bogus Mr. Dieffenbeck through the room, making informative comments about individual participants. At the far end of the room, Slocum was given a diminutive glass of sherry and was invited to sample the caviar.

Slocum had never had a fondness for fish roe. Curing them in salt in wooden casks had done nothing to improve his appreciation. He found that the tiny toast point triangles, chopped onion, and egg yolk went down all right and he concentrated on taking more of them with each helping of what he considered little more than fishy-tasting black tapioca. Beluga sturgeon or not, the gelatinous mass smelled like a bullhead left too long in the sun.

"So, you're thinking of consolidating your interests?" Duffey asked him.

"More or less," Slocum responded noncommittally. "Land speculation is risky out Dodge way. Too much like a desert. I need something solid, with fast turnover."

Several years ago, a long, boring train ride with a land speculator had provided Slocum with an ample lexicon of the trade. At the time he had barely avoided yawning in the man's face. Now he took time to offer thoughts of gratitude. A man who had introduced himself as Calvin Ruther nodded sagely.

"There'll be plenty of that in this operation," Ruther offered.

"What, exactly, is going to happen? Victor Dahlgren never did tell me everything," Slocum invented.

Justice Duffey gave him a quick overview. At the conclusion of it, Slocum forced a frown and spoke hesitantly.

"What I don't see is how we make more than a single profit on the initial sale of land we have to purchase in the first place."

"Oh, that's the beauty of Cyril's scheme, ah, Gus," Wendel Jorden inserted. "We'll sell these Dutchies land, all right, but not adjoining parcels. Sooner or later they'll want to move on to where they have their own communities. We buy back and sell to the next crop of immigrants, always keeping some for ourselves. That is, what land we don't have under tenant farm cultivation. There'll always be an ample flow of money."

By the time a uniformed waiter rang a small bell and announced that the buffet line was open, Slocum had learned a good deal about the cabal's intentions. One small thought nagged at him.

"I know Victor Dahlgren, and I'm sure this isn't his grand

design. Someone mentioned a man named Cyril. Who is he?"

"He's the real brains behind this, Gus," John Duffey informed Slocum. "Cyril Anstruther."

For a moment, Slocum thought he might expose his unauthorized presence, but years of masking his expression prevented him from revealing his shock and anger. *Cyril Anstruther.*

In the annals of the Confederacy, the name Anstruther ranked with that of Benedict Arnold in Yankee history. Cyril Anstruther had been a major in the Army of the Trans-Mississippi. He had been in charge of a large shipment of bullion to Richmond, the treasury of the state of Arkansas. Anstruther stole it and left behind twenty soldiers, some mere boys, bleeding and dying. Worse, he ran to the North.

Once behind Yankee lines, Anstruther provided all the information he possessed on Confederate positions and strengths. He was said to have later ridden with Sherman's bummers on the march through Georgia. He had known and hated John Slocum from the first day the young officer arrived at General Price's headquarters. The enmity was equally returned.

When Anstruther committed his treachery and defected to the Union cause, Slocum had not been surprised. He considered it typical of Cyril Anstruther and that made him damned angry. Anstruther's personal hatred of young Captain Slocum flourished in the light of Union popularity. It took no goading or promise of reward for him to accuse Slocum of personally committing all sorts of atrocities, none of which happened, all of which he swore to be true. The traitor's lies could have gotten Slocum hanged if he had remained in Georgia during Reconstruction.

Slocum had left his home and wandered in the West, ignorant of Anstruther's perfidy, until some years later when he spent a winter jawing with a former army scout who had served with Sherman. From that time on, Slocum vowed to right the wrongs done to him. Now chance conversation connected Anstruther to the callous conspiracy that threatened to rob the decent people of Southern lineage of all they had salvaged from the war. If anything, that knowledge inspired Slocum to outdo his earlier performance.

"Then it's agreed?" Justice John Duffey asked of the men seated around the table, amid the remains of their gastronomic orgy. He rose and extended a hand diagonally to Slocum. "Congratulations, Gus. You're now one of us."

Slocum left the cabal's meeting with a big grin of triumph. Not only had he penetrated the core of the vicious plot, he had also put himself much closer to settling accounts with Cyril Anstruther.

*"Goddamn that man!"* Cyril Anstruther produced a startled look and visibly fought to regain his usual icy self-control. "I'm doubling the bounty on Slocum," he went on in a tone closer to normal.

"You have to admit, Cy, that he's slicker than a fresh oyster," Senator Dahlgren said somewhat admiringly.

"He used your name to get right into the heart of our operation, don't forget that," Anstruther entered censoriously.

"Ummm. And if John Duffey hadn't bumped into the real Dieffenbeck the next morning at the railroad depot, down here in Emporia we'd never have been the wiser. Oh, he *is* slick."

"It's time to give these rebel scum an object lesson," Anstruther decided, then called loudly, "Howard. Come in here."

Godfrey Howard entered the room from the hallway where he had been straining his patience cooling his heels while the big shots ate breakfast. "Yes, Mr. Anstruther?"

"Alert your company, Captain Howard. We move out today for the McDade farm. We're going to raze it to the ground."

"We, sir?" Howard repetitiously asked, not certain he had heard correctly.

"Yes. I'm going along. Slocum has to be with the rebels. We're going to show him what his impertinence has earned. And, Howard, we will leave no witnesses."

Smiling wolfishly, Godfrey Howard saluted and departed at once. Over thick fingers laced atop his swelling belly, Victor Dahlgren studied this unexpected aspect of his associate's personality. He had never suspected Cyril Anstruther of recklessness. Although good enough in itself, this campaign against McDade in order to spite Slocum could backlash on them. One thing was obvious. Cyril wasn't thinking clearly, or coolly.

She had been wandering for days across an undulating sameness of tall spring grass that came close to rubbing her horse's belly. She had no idea where she was going. The unsettling memory of slamming a skillet into Quade Purdy's head kept her overly cautious. As a result, she hid, or fled, each time she spotted riders anywhere near her. To Vivian Ballard they represented a posse, charged with apprehending her and bringing her back to a gallows for murder.

Nearly as nagging, another problem troubled her. Vivian had exhausted her meager supplies the previous day and had no hopes of replenishing them. All her caution came to nothing when she reached a wide wash and dismounted to lead her horse down the near bank.

Vivian looked up from the swirl of dust at the bottom, when she reached it, to find five men quietly sitting their horses and watching her. She gulped back a cry of desperation and tried to throw herself into the saddle.

"Afternoon, ma'am. We've been watchin' you fer a spell an' if you don't mind, you seem to be lost."

At least he hadn't started with that ritual about being under arrest, Vivian thought fleetingly. "I—I am . . . sort of," she stammered out.

"Mayhap we can be of some service to you, then? I'm Corporal Granger, Woodson County Volunteers."

Vivian noted then that one of the men had unfurled a small banner attached to a stout wooden pole. The breeze caught it and exposed the stars and bars of the Confederacy. Sighing in relief and apprehension, she spoke with mounting hope.

"C-Can you take me to a man named McDade? Or to J-John Slocum?"

A smile bloomed on Corporal Granger's rugged face. "That we can, ma'am. You acquainted with Ewan or the cap'n, ma'am?"

"I, ah, don't know Mr. McDade, but I do know Slocum and he's spoken highly of his friend," Vivian answered honestly, if not completely.

"Well then, best you climb on that critter of yours and we'll lead you to camp."

"That's—that's wonderful of you, Corporal. I—uh, I beg your pardon for imposing, but do you have anything to eat?"

"Our patrol's ended for the day," Granger told her kindly. "There'll be a good, hot supper waitin' back at the gorge."

"And John Slocum, too," Vivian appended.

"Yep. He oughta be back by now."

• • •

That's odd, Aurora McDade thought at the sound of pounding hooves. The patrol had been through only three hours before. They wouldn't be back until shortly after dark. Who, then, could this be? She remained several seconds longer at the clothesline, two pins clenched in her teeth, a sheet flapping to her left where she had secured it moments before. Then, miragelike, the heads of men appeared over the sea of tall, waving grass. Their blue uniform coats came next.

Aurora dropped her bag of clothespins and ran for the back door of the farmhouse. Right inside, propped against the wall, was her shotgun. She took it up before she rummaged in a drawer for additional cartridges. Aurora didn't think through why she might need them. It proved to be a grim premonition.

This time the Redleg troops made no pretense of serving "lawful" papers. They spread out in the farmyard and began to set fire to torches they would use to destroy the remaining buildings. Aurora shot one from his saddle when he raised his arm to throw the flaming brand. Severely wounded, he began to howl and thrash on the ground. Quickly she loosed the other round and dodged back further into the kitchen to reload.

"Get her," Cyril Anstruther demanded.

"Corporal, take three men," Captain Godfrey Howard ordered.

Four Jayhawkers dismounted and started for the house. Aurora appeared in the doorway and blasted two of them into eternity with a load of 00 buckshot. The corporal and remaining trooper leaped apart as though on springs. The Redleg NCO returned fire, somewhat wildly, a moment before his face disappeared in a spray of blood. Aurora McDade darted out of sight again.

"Goddamnit, are you going to let one woman hold you up," Anstruther railed at the befuddled troops. "Get in there after her. Go in the front way."

One Redleg ran to the front door and kicked it open. The flat report of a rifle came from inside and he staggered backward, clutching his belly.

"Damn Yankees, get off our place," Eunice Glenndower McDade shouted from the hallway. With delicate attention to detail, she reloaded the Heys rifle.

Flames gouted from the outbuildings. Two barn burners

started for the house. A double load of shot from Aurora's Parker twelve-gauge turned them back. Captain Howard called for more men to approach the house from another angle. Three of them got in close and hurled their torches through windows. Flames began to crackle inside.

"They've got to come out," Howard informed Anstruther.

"Good. I want them to be easily found."

Unworried by the cryptic remark, Howard directed other of his men to their work of destructiveness. One trooper sat at the officer's side, a board attached to a pointed stake in his left hand. Long minutes passed while the fire in the house increased in intensity. Still no one came out. When yellow tongues broke through the roof and a dense column of smoke formed, Anstruther rose in his stirrups and called out in his most persuasive voice.

"Come on out, you'll not be harmed. No reason to throw your lives away."

Another minute, by the big Ingersol watch in his hand, went past. Anstruther drew a deep breath, preparatory to calling again. Then, through the gray smoke that billowed from the front door, a woman stumbled into the open, her face darkened with soot, hand to her mouth while she coughed. Behind her came a gray-haired figure. Captain Howard raised a hand, checking his men until the ladies cleared the conflagration.

Undaunted in defeat, Aurora McDade stopped near Cyril Anstruther's horse and glowered up at him. Knowing what the result would be, Anstruther smiled in amusement. Then he nodded to Howard.

"All right, Captain Howard. Kill them both."

# 17

It would add a day and a half to his return. Slocum decided on spending the time. For all that the patrols kept constant watch, he felt certain his consideration would be appreciated by Ewan McDade. So he headed Ol' Rip south and west after skirting Emporia.

This precaution allowed him to approach the farm from the same direction as on his first visit. His earliest indication of something wrong came from the sight of large, black carrion birds circling high in the sky, beyond the sandstone ridge he climbed. Before topping the rise, he halted and dismounted. Belly down, Slocum wormed up to the crest and looked beyond. What he saw brought immediate alarm and a twisting sickness to his gut.

Only blackened, charred studs and heaps of brick, cracked sandstone, and burned wood remained of the buildings. A few thin wisps of smoke still rose from the piles of ashes and charcoal. At that range, he could not identify the huddled lumps in the yard. Other, larger mounds in the corral area had to be dead livestock. Bile burning in his stomach, Slocum remained motionless, eyes shifting to examine the entire area in detail. Satisfied at last that no one lay in wait, he edged backward, stood, and mounted.

Slocum brought Ol' Rip in at a fast canter. Each yard closer brought him more information. It had to have been the

Jayhawkers, he decided. They had been considerably more thorough than on the previous visit. Outside of a few buzzards, gorging themselves on the carrion, he could see no living thing. At his approach, the ungainly birds squawked offendedly and wobbled into their awkward takeoff runs. The odor of blood and death mingled with the acrid stench of burned wood. Recognition came a good while before Slocum reined in near the huddled forms on the ground.

"Awh, damn," the ex-Confederate breathed out softly. "Damn them all."

Gently he straightened both dead women. Then he knelt, Aurora McDade's head cradled in his hands. He winced and fought with rising furor brought on by the grotesque, lopsided expression her morbid features held, caused by a bullet fired into the back of her head. A short way off a paper fluttered in the steady fifteen-mile-per-hour wind. Slocum rose and walked to it.

It turned out to be a notice posting the property against any and all trespass. It also identified the property as contraband, confiscated by the state of Kansas. Slocum uprooted the sign and ripped the single sheet from its backboard. That he tore into small bits and let the wind carry away. Then he went around to locate and destroy the others. After that he found another note, pinned in a fold of Aurora's dress.

*"You can thank John Slocum for this,"* it read.

Slocum looked at the sky, his grim expression turning to one of shame and guilt. "You bastard!" he shouted uselessly.

Anstruther. Somehow he had found out about the impersonation and ordered this in retaliation. For a long minute Slocum considered what he would do if he caught Anstruther alone. Then he dredged out a partially damaged shovel in the toolshed and began to dig graves for Ewan's wife and mother. Saddened and guilt-ridden by the unnecessary murders, Slocum knew he had to carry the terrible news to his friend.

In the deep, wide wash where the self-styled Volunteers had their headquarters, Slocum found Ewan sitting alone, staring blankly at a glowing bed of embers left from the noon meal. *He knows*, Slocum thought. McDade might have read his friend's mind by his answer.

"Patrol came in early this morning. Told me about it. They had been on the long leg of their search area, didn't get back by the place until after dark. By then it was all over. Th-they didn't do anything for them, had to search for those who did it, send word in here. Happened yes—two days ago, now."

"I—I gave them decent burial, Ewan. I'm truly sorry—"

"I know all the words," Ewan cut him short. "God knows I've heard them enough lately. I'm sorry," he went on, his mood altering slightly. "I'm grateful for what you did. I'll arrange a p-proper funeral when this is over."

"That might be sooner than you think. I managed to penetrate the cabal and learned their next big meeting will be in Emporia." Slocum went on to describe the luncheon buffet and the topics discussed. Then he added, "There was a note, pinned to your wife's dress." He told Ewan the contents.

"Bullshit," Ewan snapped. "They're only using you to make it hurt more. Howard was behind it. That son of a bitch did it because he likes doing things like that. So they'll be in Emporia a week from Friday. That's where we'll wipe out every last mother's son of them. We've got a lot of planning to do."

Slocum lay naked in Vivian Ballard's arms atop a blanket. Despite his lingering feelings of guilt and grief, he had agreed to spend some time alone with her. After the camp had settled down for the night they had slipped away upstream to a spot where a rock outcropping had formed an eddy, creating a large, deep pool. Their earlier words of warm welcome and mutual desire quickly turned to deeds. Slocum spread the blanket and they embraced. When the kiss ended they swiftly removed their clothing. Moonlight turned their skin alabaster as they made flat, shallow dives into the water.

Still endowed with a bit of winter chill, the liquid stung and tingled. Passion soon overcame nature and Slocum's phallus rose in spite of the cold. Vivian hugged him again and her hardened nipples pressed against his chest. She thrust her pelvis against his erection and moaned softly. Their lips joined, played lightly together, and parted.

"Oh, God, Slocum, I was afraid I'd never see you again."

"You almost didn't. When I saw what had been done to Ewan's wife and mother I wanted to head right back to Topeka and personally kill Anstruther with my bare hands."

"And why didn't you?" It wasn't a taunt; Vivian had a genuine interest.

"It would have achieved nothing."

Sensing the ranks of goose bumps on her breasts and the urgency of the pressure from Slocum's member, Vivian pushed back slightly. "Let's get out. Any more of this and I'll loose the urge."

"I don't think I can," Slocum advised her.

They climbed from the water and lowered themselves to the blanket. A light touch here and there and ardor warmed them like a friendly fire. In moments, Slocum had insinuated a hand between her long, lovely legs. He flirted with the firm mound of her cleft, which parted in eager acceptance. Slowly he pressed his advantage while Vivian held his manhood in a tight grip and slid it against her silken belly. They both knew when the moment arrived.

Slocum entered her with a rush. Their bodies became singing instruments in an erotic orchestra. Point and counterpoint pulsed as Slocum strove to bury himself. Impaled on his wondrous lance, Vivian cooed in delight and bent every effort to bring rapture to the man she adored. Their long absence from each other made the lovemaking even more delightful.

Each long, powerful stroke worked them toward frenzy. Far too soon for both of them, their bodies surrendered to the primal siren song and exploded them into head-swimming oblivion.

Now they lay quietly, enjoying the warm night air and heady scent of blooming sage and wildflowers. Slocum ran a finger down Vivian's spine. She stiffened reflexively as it made progress.

He reached the rounded hillocks of her posterior and cupped one firm, dimpled cheek. Vivian leaned over him and closed lips around the bronze medallion of his right nipple. Slocum started to chuckle.

"Don't leave a suck-mark there. I'll never be able to explain it."

"You're distracting me, you terrible man. I'm trying to let you know how much I care about you."

"Might try that a little lower. I'm sure I'd get the idea."

Obligingly, Vivian began to work her way down the midline

of Slocum's body. She encountered the puckered cicatrix of an old gunshot wound and stopped.

"You never told me how this happened."

"I didn't duck in time," Slocum said lightly.

"There . . . has to be more to it than that," Vivian prompted.

"There is," Slocum agreed. "But this is a night for happiness, not frightening stories. I wound up in bed for three weeks."

"Alone?"

"What kind of question is that?"

"A serious one. Didn't you know I can be a terribly jealous woman?"

"For your information then, I was alone. But you have ample evidence that I didn't come to your bed a callow youth."

"I do. I just want to make sure this"—she tapped the scar with a finger—"wasn't done by an outraged husband."

They laughed together and Vivian continued her downward journey. Slocum sucked in a long draft of air when she reached the base of his fully risen organ. Her lips toyed with it, worked around to the firm sack beneath, then started up the sensitive underside. Slocum quivered with wild sensation when she closed over the exposed tip.

With the studious attention of a great scholar, Vivian worked diligently to take in all of his generous endowment. So powerful was her combination of lips, tongue, and suction that he went rigid and arched up off the blanket. Slowly, over an uncountable aeon of time, Vivian pleasured him and herself with this thrilling intimacy. Slocum had never encountered anyone quite so skilled in this fine art, and his jangled nerve paths threatened to reject any more intense discharges of sheer ecstasy.

When at last the dam broke and his reservoir of life force surged outward, they found an overwhelming communion of souls that slid them away into a far, starry universe. Panting and gasping, Vivian finally retreated from her prodigious efforts and stretched out beside a drained and bemused Slocum.

"There'll be more?" she asked hopefully.

Slocum languidly raised a hand to trail it across her bosom. "There'll be lots, lots more before morning," he promised.

Captain Godfrey Howard sat at breakfast in the Leighton Hotel dining room when a shifty-eyed, ferret-faced individual crossed

Emporia's Crawford Street and entered the street-side door. He
came to Howard's table, hat in hand. A narrow, pink length of
tongue flicked in and out in a reptilian manner, wetting thin,
too-widespread lips.

"Are—are you Cap'n Howard?" he began without greeting.

"I am, and I'm eating my breakfast, as you can see. I do
not appreciate being disturbed at this time. Whatever you have,
fellow, save it for later," Howard answered him haughtily.

"Ain't likely. I got something you'll want to hear. Pay well
for it, too."

"I'll be the judge of that," came Howard's snotty, trite reply.
"And I'll judge it later, as I told you."

"Wanna know where the McDade kids are?" the rodent-
visaged caller slurred out.

Howard's expression underwent an abrupt change. Eagerness that could almost be called lust burned in his eyes. "Spit
it out," he hissed in a low tone. "What is it you know?"

Surprisingly, the nervous individual stood his ground. "It's
worth a good bit, I'd say. You come up with the money, I'll
give up the kids to you."

"Talk to me, goddamnit!" Howard's face had suffused darkly with ill-concealed rage. "All I have to do is call some of my
men over and I'll have it out of you before they finish breaking
all your bones."

"Uh-uh, from what I hear, this is prime information. You
part with, say . . . a hunnard dollars cash money and I'll consider tellin' all."

Howard came partway out of his chair. "You wretched animal . . . ," he blurted.

Flinching back, the informer made to dart for the door.
Howard's arm moved with superior speed. Hard fingers closed
around the betrayer's scrawny wrist. He winced and a look of
genuine fear entered his eyes.

"No!" he gulped. "Wait. I heard you would pay for information on the rebs. Ain't nobody else around gonna tell you
what I know. Bein' a gen'leman an' all, Cap'n, you'll for sure
pay me?"

"If it's worth it, yes."

"Well, then, they're at their grandmomma's."

"She's dead," Howard said coldly.

"That was Miz McDade. I'm talkin' about old lady Stillwell.

She's got a place on the edge of Fredonia. Kids've been there since the troubles began."

"You're . . . sure of this?"

"Swear my life on it, Cap'n."

*Gotcha!* A thin smile cracked the ice of Howard's face. "That's exactly what you're doing. If I, say, happened to send some troops over there, what would they find? There an ambush waiting?"

"Oh, no. No, sir. No one knows I've come to you and no one's guardin' the place. Swear it on my . . . ah, I swear."

"If my men do go by there and you're telling the truth, you'll receive double that hundred dollars you asked for. Until then, we'll keep you right close. Sergeant," he called out in a raised voice.

Sergeant Banks entered from the hotel lobby. "Yes, sir."

"Form a detail, one large enough to overcome any minor opposition. You're going after the McDade children."

"Right away, sir."

Nothing stirred on the sloping lawn between the Stillwell house in Fredonia and the small stable at the back of the lot. A line of Osage orange trees masked the country lane that led past the west side of the property. Removed from the town by three blocks, the old family place had an air of permanence and exclusivity. Tall cottonwoods and a trio of medium-sized junipers graced the front of the building. From the branches, mourning doves kept up a doleful chorus. Beyond the line of hedge trees, invisible in the glory of a setting sun, sat Sergeant Banks and a dozen men.

Banks had been studying the house for some while. Two small children had played with a hoop and sticks until summoned inside to wash for the evening meal. A velocipede, one of those newfangled, chain-driven devices, leaned against the front porch railing. So far they had seen nothing more of those they had come to take captive. Banks gave another gnaw to the Osage orange twig in his mouth and threw it away.

"Time to be movin', boys. With them set to table, shouldn't be any problem at all. Jacobs, take half the men and hit the front door. Rest come with me."

On foot, Sergeant Isaac Banks led the rush across the lawn to the kitchen door. A burly, barrel-chested Jayhawker threw his shoulder into the panel above the latch and it flew open; the glass pane shattered from the impact and rained down on the floor inside. Hattie Stillwell looked up in shock and surprise, then made a fast grab for a large butcher knife.

"Get out of my house," she demanded.

One of the McDade girls screamed in fright from the dining room. Five men had crowded into the kitchen. They looked with amusement at the little, bright-eyed lady with the knife. Savory odors of a rich stew rose from the stove. At a signal from Sergeant Banks, one of the Redlegs barged into the dining room and grabbed up the youngest McDade child.

"My man can snap her neck like a matchstick," Banks delighted in telling Hattie.

"Wha-what do you want?"

"First for you to put down that knife. Then you can look into feeding us. We're going to be guests for a while."

"You'll do nothing of the sort," Hattie rejected.

"All secure in front, Sergeant. Caught a skinny kid about twelve or so trying to sneak down a rose trellis."

"Well then, everyone is rounded up. Mrs. Stillwell, put down the knife or we start killing grandchildren."

Hattie Stillwell's defiance slumped with her shoulders. "What is this all about?"

"War, Mrs. Stillwell. And like last time," Banks went on, amused by his cleverness, "it's between the North and the South. We're here to clean up some of the trash."

"I thought I'd find you here," Captain Godfrey Howard informed the traitor.

Avarice lighted the too-close-set eyes of the informer. "They was where I said?"

"Exactly."

"What about my reward?"

"Oh, that," Howard said casually. "There's one other small service you must perform to earn it."

Color washed from the ferret-faced man along with his expression. "N-now that wasn't part of the agreement."

"Oh? I pay the money, so I make the rules."

"Wh-what is it?"

"That's better. I have a message here I want you to deliver to Ewan McDade. No, don't open it. You're not to know its contents. I'm positive you'll have no difficulty finding him," he added through a thin, wintry smile.

Billy-Bob Sawyer thought he would piss in his pants. He'd never been so scared in his life. The two-day ride from Emporia to the big wash had gone without difficulty. He had made sure he was not followed. No way Billy-Bob Sawyer would lead the enemy to his friends. Now, those brats were something else.

Wouldn't anybody do harm to kids. Particularly an officer of the state militia. He'd make his money and the fighting would be stopped and no one would be the wiser. Billy-Bob had it all figured out. Until he ran into the security patrol.

"What the hell you doin' here, Billy-Bob?" his friend Aaron Grayson asked.

At least he and Aaron *had* been friends. That had been before the drinking and Aaron being promoted. Billy-Bob began to sweat.

"I—I've got something for Ewan McDade. Some sort of message. I don't know what it says. I cain't read, you know that."

"Who sent it?" Aaron asked, suspicious.

"I cain't say. Got told to talk only to Ewan."

"He's not going to be happy to see you, Billy-Bob. Not after you bein' throwed out for gettin' drunk on watch duty."

"B-but I got this message," Billy-Bob protested.

"I'll take charge of that." Aaron extended a hand, his expression demanding.

*Oh, Lord, they suspect me already,* Billy-Bob wailed silently in his mind.

# 18

Ewan McDade read the note from Captain Godfrey Howard, then read it aloud, his voice rising toward hysteria with each word. "A detachment of my troops have your children and Hattie Stillwell in custody. You have forty-eight hours after receipt of this demand to come to Emporia and turn yourself in or your children will be killed one per day until you do, or we run out of brats."

Stunned silence filled the wash. Ewan's expression clearly revealed how this terrible news affected him, after the murder of his wife and mother. He stood now, face livid, hands trembling. His deep blue eyes seemed bottomless. A tremendous effort of will kept the tears he needed from flowing. Shaking a fist, he raised it and his face to an unresponsive heaven.

"How could a just and loving God allow such vileness?" he shouted from the depths of his despair.

Broken by circumstance, Ewan could no longer think rationally. For several seconds he mumbled to himself, then raised his voice in a cry for vengeance.

"Godfrey Howard wants me to come to Emporia. I'll go to Emporia, by God. I'll go and take with me the awful wrath that Quantrill visited on Lawrence. Every Redleg and Yankee sympathizer will die. The town will burn for days."

"No, Ewan. That's not the way," Slocum urged his friend.

"What else can I do?" Ewan asked rhetorically. "Should

I turn myself in like he wants? He'd only kill me and the children. You know that."

"Yes, Howard's that kind of sick bastard," Slocum agreed. "We have to stop him and we have to free your youngsters, too. Doing that takes time. We have two days' grace. It would take that long to get to Emporia anyway. Before we do anything, it has to be carefully planned. Ewan, we were going to hit them in Emporia when the cabal met there. At the same time we can take care of Howard. Plan it, work it out, make sure everyone is ready and get them in position. That's what you can do. I'll leave at once for Fredonia. I'll take along enough men to effect a rescue if they're still there, or to hunt them down if not. Keep active, man, fill your mind with every detail of how we'll get revenge on Godfrey Howard."

Slocum had used all his argumentative skill in his attempt to sell Ewan on a reasonable course of action. He waited with deep concern while emotions played across Ewan's face. He recalled that McDade had not been entirely in control from the moment he saw Billy-Bob Sawyer. That set off another jarring chain of images in Slocum's mind. He started to say something when Ewan spoke in a calmer, quieter voice.

"You're right, of course, Slocum. I—I've let my feelings push out reason. We can't move until we're ready. We have to know where everyone is. Maybe—maybe Billy-Bob can tell us the layout in Emporia."

"There's something I wanted to ask you about Billy-Bob," Slocum began, then whispered the rest to his friend.

Dark red suffused Ewan McDade's face before Slocum concluded. His eyes took on a wild, glazed appearance and he began to shake again. Slocum patted one broad shoulder and spoke quietly.

"Let me handle it."

"I . . ." Ewan shook his head, fighting for calm. "I'd probably make a mess out of it anyway. Go ahead."

Slocum walked over to Billy-Bob and asked him a couple of questions. The fear in the man was so obvious Slocum wondered how it had been missed before. He asked another question, deliberately harshening his voice. Billy-Bob tried a clumsy evasion. Rattlesnake quick, Slocum backhanded him.

"Tell me that again, Sawyer. You just happened upon the note? There's no address on it. You say you can't read, so you didn't know what it said. How'd you know who should get it?"

"I—I—I, ah, well, it came from that Jayhawker. That Captain Howard." His shifty eyes danced from side to side. "He, ah, dropped it on the ground and I knew whatever it was might be important."

"Sure, and pigs fly, Sawyer. I want all of it," Slocum growled. "Every detail."

"I—I—I can't say anythin'," Billy-Bob bleated.

Slocum reached across his midsection and slowly drew his .45 Colt. "Yes, you can. And you will, or I'll blow off your kneecaps one at a time, then shatter your elbows. You don't talk then and I'll shoot away your balls."

Billy-Bob had no way of knowing Slocum would never make good on those threats. He knew the man only by his reputation as a tough, relentless leader of irregular troops during the war. Yet, there had been some stories going around about bloody doings out on the frontier that had Slocum's name in them. His bowels turned to water and his bladder let go. He soiled himself and stood with his urine running into his boots. Terror, as much as shame, blocked his throat. Slocum unstoppered his vocal cords by ramming the muzzle of his six-gun into the traitor's stomach.

Grimacing with pain, Billy-Bob spoke. He sang, wailed, pleaded, babbled out all his guilt. Slocum looked on in growing disgust. When Sawyer ran down, Slocum turned to Ewan.

"There'll have to be a trial."

McDade raised a quizzical eyebrow. "Oh? For what?"

"Treason. It's your duty. I'll get ready to ride out. Opie," Slocum turned his remarks to the young rebel officer. "Pick a detail, say fifteen men. We'll ride by one-thirty this afternoon."

"Right away, Cap'n."

Slocum turned back to a quietly sobbing Billy-Bob Sawyer. "Wha-wha's gonna happen to me?" the wretched traitor blubbered.

"If I'm right, they're going to try you, convict you of treason, and give you a proper traitor's end."

Half an hour after Slocum and his detail rode out of camp, the jury found Billy-Bob Sawyer guilty of treason. Hands tied behind his back, head covered by an old shirt fitted under the noose, Billy-Bob Sawyer was hanged by the neck until dead.

• • •

Fortunately, Fredonia was considerably closer to the encampment than Emporia. Slocum's detachment reached the area in early morning of the next day. Roosters still advised everyone that the time had come to open their eyes, and the setter hens hadn't taken inventory of the eggs under their feathers. An all-night ride had left them tired, though not too spent for the job at hand, Slocum reasoned. He sent Opie and another man forward to scout the area around the Stillwell home and waited with the others. Right then he would have killed a pride of lions with bare hands for a cup of coffee. He could swear time ran backward while they kept busy staying out of sight.

"Someone comin', Cap'n," Sergeant Buhler advised.

Slocum had heard the horse. He nodded and eased himself up from his place against a cottonwood. Opie Tolliver came around the bend. His face wore an expression of good news. A lot would depend on what Opie considered good, Slocum admitted.

"Unless Miz Stillwell's taken to boarding horses, the Redlegs are right there in the house," Opie announced when he dismounted.

Slocum listened to the details and made a hasty basic plan, then set out. The short ride to the Stillwell homestead took more time than it seemed to him it should have. Slocum recognized the symptoms. He was getting geared for battle. They dismounted a safe distance away and approached the blind side of the house on foot. Slocum studied the two-story dwelling from hiding in the line of Osage orange along the property line where a creek ran.

What he observed necessitated a change in his plan. It appeared that one man alone would have a better chance of success in freeing the children. All he needed to do, Slocum told the others, was get inside. To do that he would need a sharpshooter to cover him in the event something went wrong at the front door. Opie was the best they had. Slocum selected three more men to cover the front and positioned the others to provide good fields of fire on all likely escape routes. Then he told everyone to get some rest. They would have to wait, perhaps until dark, for the right opportunity.

Changeable as always, the Kansas weather came to their aid earlier than that. Clouds built in the west and southwest, piling

high, with huge, black bellies. Lightning flashed between the
behemoths as they approached. The low, gentle breeze whipped
into a gale. Before the rain actually reached them, Slocum told
the men to stand by and led Ol' Rip away toward town. The
sky turned black and the deluge hit ten minutes later.

In twilight gloom, Slocum rode at a gallop to the front of
the Stillwell house. Rain and pea-sized hail lashed at his face.
He threw himself from the saddle, his slicker and so'wester
flapping in the maelstrom. At the door he pounded with a fist,
a hollow boom audible to the waiting rebels.

"I've come with a message from Howard," he shouted over
the tumult.

A moment later the door opened. The hand inside Slocum's
slicker flashed outward with his .45 Colt held ready. He jam-
med the muzzle in the Jayhawker's gut and disarmed him.
Using the man as a shield, Slocum entered, leaving the door
standing wide. Three men sat in the parlor, their movements
interrupted by his abrupt appearance.

"None of you move and no one will be hurt. Where's the
children and Mrs. Stillwell?"

Howard's men proved more fanatical than Slocum expected.
Two of the three went for their guns. One shot Slocum's captive in an attempt to get him. With the corpse to absorb bullets,
Slocum took time to precisely shoot the two armed men, then
threw the dead one into the arms of the third. Taking the risers
three at a time, he headed upstairs. Shouts of alarm came from
behind him and he heard a scream when one of the Redlegs
precipitously ran into the exposed area of the hall. Opie was
doing quite well.

On the second floor, the shrill screams of a woman and two
girls added to the confusion. Slocum stopped short at the first
door he came to and kicked it solidly under the knob. It flew
open and Slocum fired instinctively at the sight of a Jayhawker
who tried to swing his revolver in line with a small boy.

Slocum's bullet punched through the militiaman's right shoulder and deflected downward into his chest. The Colt dropped
from his uncontrolled fingers and he made a strangled, gargling
caw before he dropped to his knees. Slocum picked up the fallen
six-gun and turned to the boy.

"How old are you?"

"Fourteen. I'm Corey. Did Paw send you?"

"Something like that. You look three years younger."

"I'm the runt of the litter," the lad said easily, not sensitive about his slight build.

"Can you use this?" Slocum asked, extending the revolver toward the boy.

A big grin answered. "You bet."

"Good, get his spare ammunition. I'll need you to help protect your grandmother and the other kids."

"Right with you," Ewan McDade's eldest child chirped.

Already Slocum had returned to the hallway. Two hardcases had managed to reach the top flight of stairs. A pair of hot rounds blasted down the well discouraged them. One man sprawled with a painful flesh wound. The other ran all the way to the landing, which put him in Opie Tolliver's view. Opie's big rifle boomed and the man slammed back against the wainscoting.

He convulsed and slid to a sitting position, leaving a wide, wet smear of crimson on the wall. Slocum hit the next door with his shoulder and followed it into the room in a roll. He came up squeezing the trigger. It tripped and the hammer fell on an expended cartridge.

Damn. He knew better than that. He should have counted. Before the stunned Jayhawker could fire, Slocum dived under the bed and made a grab for the top of his right boot. From it he took his old favorite, a nicely balanced .36 Colt Navy caplock. The flat, notched hammer came back and he poked the muzzle forward, almost into the face of the Jayhawker who stooped to find his supposedly helpless attacker.

The .36 ball took him between his upside-down eyes. At once the little black hole spouted blood and fluid under pressure and Slocum rolled out of line with it. He popped another cap and the .36 made a flat, smoky report. The other man in the room howled in pain and released a girl of nine or ten.

She added insult to his injury by kicking him in the same leg Slocum had shot. By then the ex-Confederate had come from under the bed and scooped up his empty Colt. He opened the loading gate and quickly ejected the spent cartridge cases. He had two rounds in the cylinders when a sharp report banged outside the room.

Young Corey McDade stuck his head in the room. "One of them tried to make a run with Emilie."

"And?" Slocum asked as he worked. Two more rounds in place.

"He died before he hit the bottom of the back stairs."

"Don't get too cocky, boy. What happened to your sister?"

"She ran back in the room."

"Damn. Now we've got to get her out of there," Slocum swore, adding a few more colorful words.

Slocum found the door locked. Corey called to his sister and was answered by a frightened squeak and a bass snarl. He exchanged glances with Slocum and the big man nodded. Bracing himself, Slocum kicked in the door. He and Corey fired at the same time.

Slammed by two slugs, the Jayhawker holding Emilie lost control of his reflexes and threw his revolver toward the ceiling while his thigh muscles flexed and sent him backward to sprawl on the bed. His legs twitched while his heart pumped out the last of his blood. Shrieking, Emilie ran to her brother with tears streaming down her face.

"It's awful. Those terrible guns. They scare me, they scare me," she wailed.

"If we din' have 'em, Sis, you'd be dead," Corey told her in simple practicality. "Still . . . I think . . . a-after seein' th-that one . . . I'm gonna be sick."

"Do it in the corner and hurry," Slocum snapped, forcing himself to be hard, show no sympathy. "We've got work to finish."

Sounds of a fierce firefight came from outside the house. Slocum found a window at the back of the house that over-looked the stable. Two men lay dead at the wide-open door to the small barn. Five more streamed out on the lawn, firing as they ran for the back door. Caught in a Confederate cross fire, they fell one by one. The sky turned white with a close-by lightning strike and thunder more fierce than cannon shook the building. A new, streaming, gray deluge washed out the scene below. Slocum turned back to the unopened doors.

"You men in the rooms, listen to me. Your friends are all dead or wounded. You have no way out. Killing your hostages will only get you slow, terrible deaths by torture. They are only children and one old woman. Where's the glory in that? Give up now, let them go unharmed, and save a lot of grief."

"Fuck you!" a defiant voice responded, muffled by a closed door.

By something else, too, Slocum speculated. Probably a mattress. Let him find out about that, he decided as he pumped two rounds through the polished wood at belt level. A groan followed and a soft thud. Then came the excited voice of a younger boy.

"You got him! You got him!"

Before Slocum could smash in the door a gun fired inside and the child screamed. "Jimmy!" Corey shouted, and added his weight to the door.

It barely opened and Corey squeezed in. He heaved the wounded man aside and followed him with the mattress. Then he looked for his little brother.

Jimmy McDade stood by the stripped bedframe, left hand to a freely bleeding scrape along his right arm at the shoulder. "Will I have a scar, Corey?" the little lad asked hopefully.

Corey said a word his father would have razor-strapped him for. "You little rat. I oughta wring your neck," he chided gently, unable to stop the flood of relief that ran wetly from his eyes.

Slocum herded them into the hall. "Keep your brother and Emilie back. There's two more to go."

A doorknob rattled and a Jayhawker came out, hands up. A small girl, only a toddler, came behind him. "You're right, mister. I can't do in a little girl. Don't shoot me."

Slocum settled for Emilie tying the captive with strips of bed sheet while Corey held a gun on him. He reached the final door. A shot came from inside and a big slug showered splinters from the outside of the wooden portal. Crouched low, Slocum tried the knob, found it turned easily. The unlocked door flew open and Slocum dived through, searching for the desperate Redleg. He saw him from the corner of his eye. Far off to one side, his six-gun already lined up on Slocum, there would not be time to avoid the bullet.

Not ready to die, Slocum roared his defiance and made what effort he could. The tailing edge of his vision caught a flash of something white, then came a crash and musical tinkling. The militiaman's revolver discharged in the midst of that.

The bullet struck high in the wall, beyond Slocum's head. He rolled and came up with the hammer falling on his Colt

Peacemaker. Stunned by the pitcher that had struck his head, the Jayhawker reacted too slowly. Slocum's bullet caught him in the chest a full second before he finished cocking his revolver.

"I knew Ewan would not let us down," Hattie Stillwell said in a voice steady if burred by age. "He sent the very best. Thank you, young man."

"And thank you for that quick work with the pitcher," Slocum responded, warming to her aristocratic charm.

Coming from someone younger it might be called a giggle; Hattie Stillwell gave it dignity. "I've always wanted to hurl one of those across a room and see how it would break."

Eyes avoiding the dead man beside her bed, she hurried to the hallway. "Come, children, you shouldn't be exposed to such terrible sights."

Slocum went to the window and threw back heavy drapes. He made a signal seen in the hedge trees. Swiftly the rebel forces rushed to the house with mounts for the freed hostages. A few weapons popped from time to time, while Slocum led the grandmother and her brood to the ground floor. On the screened back porch they sloshed through rainwater and out onto the steps. Only a light mist remained, the storm now expending its fury off to the northeast.

Making a self-conscious gesture toward the horses, Slocum spoke into the silence. "We've a long ride ahead, ma'am. Sorry we couldn't find a sidesaddle."

"Lands, I'll make do. This is war, isn't it?"

He looked around at the sprawled bodies and back at the house. "Yes, I suppose it is," Slocum sighed sadly.

"Then let's get on with it," Hattie Stillwell declared stoutly. "There's bigger enemies than these brigands."

*She's right about that, too,* Slocum silently acknowledged as he dragged himself to his horse. Smelling blood, Ol' Rip snorted and edged away. Bone weary and starting down from his adrenaline rush, Slocum barely managed to control the skittery horse long enough to mount.

"Back to the wash," he commanded. "We've got a pleasant surprise for Ewan."

# 19

Ewan McDade wept with relief for the safe delivery of his children, mixed with an echo of grief for their mother's untimely death. He welcomed them and the returning ex-Confederates—two had been killed in the brief skirmish at the Stillwell house—with unbounded joy. Then he undertook the painful task of informing the youngsters of the deaths of their mother and other grandmother. To Slocum he poured out his gratitude.

"Anything you want . . . hell, everything I have, is yours, old friend. You've saved my family. It's all—all I have left of Aurora and so precious to me. Your name and glory will never die, so long as there is a McDade on this earth."

"I, ah, don't need your generosity, Ewan," Slocum stated quietly, consumed with his own grief and borrowed guilt. "I only wish I could go back, do it all over, maybe save them from what happened. Aurora and your mother, as well as the children. I should have killed Howard when I had the chance."

"And wound up dead yourself. You didn't know the extent of the man's depravity then. None of us did. Now, come, listen to this." He led Slocum away to talk strategy.

"We're over two hundred strong," Harrison Monroe informed Slocum. "Yes, I got tired of fence sittin'. I pulled a dozen men out of Emporia and came to join up while you were gone."

"We outnumber the Jayhawkers now, Slocum," Ewan emphasized. "Here's what we came up with. It's pretty much how you outlined it. You and a picked force of ten men will infiltrate town shortly after sunrise on Friday. You'll direct them in locating Anstruther and his corrupt friends. At eight o'clock that morning, we will attack from three directions, splitting up the Jayhawkers. Once they're isolated, we'll exterminate them. Under cover of our engagement, you'll move in on the cabal.

"Remember, we need to keep some of them alive to prove our accusations," he added. "Once that riffraff in uniform see the heads of the money men falling, they'll play Billy-be-damned getting out of there. If all goes well, peace will return. Then we can let the law take over."

"What about Anstruther and Howard?" Slocum asked coldly.

Ewan looked at the ground, studied his boot toes. "I'd like to see them hang. The bastards deserve to swing for what they've done. But, chances are, with all their money and influence, they can wangle their way out of it. If killing them quick and clean helps bring an end to all this, I'm for it. Oh, we're going to send a scout unit out tomorrow to get final details of the layout in Emporia."

"Good. I want to go with them," Slocum said tightly.

McDade eyed him askance. "Isn't that taking a big chance?"

"Maybe, maybe not. But I need a close-hand, personal feel of the layout. We can get a look, then meet you on the way and give a final briefing." Slocum reached for a pot of coffee with one hand and patted Ewan on the shoulder with the other. "And don't worry so. I'll stay on the edge of town if necessary and let the boys go in and peek around."

## RENEGADE MILITIAMEN
### HOLD CHILDREN HOSTAGE

Dave Roberts looked up from the first copy off the press of the single-page extra his *Telegraph-Intelligencer* would run. He was taking a chance. He knew that. Sentiment ran high against the Southerners in Emporia. Yet, he had been so outraged upon learning that at least some of the militia had resorted to using children in an attempt to get at the supposed Southern insurrectionists. Captain Howard had denied any involvement, at least of his troops. That didn't matter. The telegraph message from the *Intelligencer* stringer in Fredonia had stated positively that the bodies at the Stillwell house had been in uniform. They had worn red leggings, too. Rescue of the hostages had happened five days earlier. Dave's stringer put in the telegram that he had been prevented by the militia from sending word until then.

Although a staunch Unionist, Roberts neither wrung his hands nor lost any love over the Jayhawkers. He considered them cut of the same cloth, if a bit more shabbily, as Quantrill. Two wrongs did not make a right, cliché or not, Roberts told himself.

He had sided with the Union because he felt its cause to be just. That did not make him a fanatic. The war was long over, still Howard and his entire company flaunted their red leggings. Howard claimed to have been at Harper's Ferry with John Brown, but that would have made him around eleven years old at the time. Howard had also been quoted as being possessed by the "spirit of John Brown."

He claimed to have felt the presence of the bloody-handed old abolitionist in the moment after the executioner sprung the trap and hanged Brown. If he had in fact authorized the taking of a woman and children as hostages, Roberts thought, it certainly indicated Howard walked in Brown's footsteps. Well, the paper would be out in a short while and people could make up their own minds. Dave looked up and saw a young lad on the brick sidewalk. He hurried to the door.

"Tommy, go round up the other boys. We have an extra to put out."

"Yessir, Mr. Roberts," the freckle-faced youngster chirped.

Dave Roberts returned to his desk and the effort of trying to make something interesting out of the article Maude Young had written on the local society doings. Maude tended to ramble, he acknowledged with a sigh, and to get sidetracked, into homey little anecdotes about the subjects of her column. Gossip, in other words. Stripped of all excess, her latest would hardly fill two inches of an inside-page column. He became so absorbed in his efforts that he took no notice of the growing crowd outside the newspaper office.

Angry voices cut through his concentration only an instant before the door slammed open and the irate mob, led by a large number of red-legged militiamen, burst into the office.

Three Jayhawkers headed his direction, while the rest of the mob spilled out into the composing area.

"Smash everything!" shouted a beefy, barrel-chested Jayhawker with sergeant's chevrons on his blue tunic. "Wreck the presses."

"You men get out of here!" Dave roared. "You're breaking the law and you'll be punished for it."

Then the irate citizens swarmed over him. Fists pounded his face and ribs. Two burly Redlegs bore him to the floor and another began to kick him. Unable to fight back, Dave battled a wave of dizziness that swept through his jumbled mind.

"Get a rope!" someone shouted.

"That's right," Sergeant Banks bellowed. "We'll fix this rebel-lovin' traitor."


"Somebody's sure raisin' hell over there on Crawford," Nathan Fitzhue observed as he and Clay Armitage accompanied Slocum down the next street over in Emporia's business district.

"You know Yankees," Armitage remarked casually. "They likely to get upset over anything. Could be an election, or a bare-knuckle contest, maybe a dogfight."

"Or a lynching," Slocum added as he pointed ahead.

Part of a mob had spilled into the next intersection. Yelling and capering, one of them waving a rope, they made progress toward the large native oak that stood in the center of the main intersection, a block from the courthouse. After a gap of about ten paces, the rest of the shouting throng came along, dragging a man in white shirt and dark trousers. The sleeve protectors and short apron marked him as possibly a clerk.

"Who is that?" Slocum asked.

"Looks like that newspaper man, Davey Roberts. He's at least been fair about the troubles," Fitzhue informed Slocum. "Even did a piece sayin' how the accusations against us got to be proved before anyone can legally do anything."

"Seems to me not everyone likes his position," Slocum remarked.

A carrot-haired boy with a face made brown with freckles rushed up to them, a single-sheet newspaper in his hand. "Somebody help," he appealed in a frightened voice. "They're tryin' to string up Mr. Roberts. I sell papers for him." He showed them the extra.

Slocum read the headline. "That must be what set them off. We'll help, boy. You run for the town law." To Fitzhue and Armitage he issued swift orders. "Round up the rest. Get your horses and be ready."

"Someone get a horse," Sergeant Banks commanded.

Quickly two men stripped the saddle from a roan gelding and led it into place under the spreading boughs of the oak. Led by the Jayhawkers, the mob cheered. Rough hands yanked Dave Roberts upright. One of the Redlegs stood in front of him, swiftly winding a hangman's knot. Blood trickled from one corner of the newspaper editor's mouth. His left eye had swollen and showed a purplish smear of bruise.

His savage beating made it necessary for the two Jayhawkers to keep him upright. The knot finished, its maker slung the coil over a thick lower branch and another willing Redleg made it secure to the post of a tie-rail. Again the crowd cheered. On the fringe of the mob, his back against a redbrick building, Walter Black stood smirking.

Now they would be rid of the meddling do-gooder and no one to carry tales of a murder to curious ears in other places. Sergeant Banks secured Dave's hands behind his back with a leather thong. The pair who held the editor hoisted him onto the bare back of the nervous, snorting roan.

"Hold that animal down," Banks demanded. "Be a shame if we didn't get him hung all right and proper."

Shouts and jeers drowned out the sound of drumming hooves. Banks checked the tautness of the rope and stepped back a pace. He removed his blue kepi and gripped the brim tightly. Poised to swing it down and slap the roan's rump, he produced a wicked grin.

Opie Tolliver, who had been with another group scouting Emporia, took careful aim with his big Sharps. Mighty thin target, he reminded himself. Gradually he took up slack. When he saw the Redleg sergeant raise his arm to spook the horse, he squeezed through. The big hammer dropped.

Bright yellow-orange flame spat from the muzzle and the Sharps bellowed. Three blocks away, the rope around Dave Roberts's neck parted with a loud, flat pop and bark sprayed when the big .54-caliber slug buried itself in the oak limb. Opie moved at once. A quick glance beyond the cloud of powder smoke showed him the rope falling slack in the same moment people scattered at the back of the crowd as Slocum smashed through them at a full gallop. They flew to both sides with cries of alarm while Ol' Rip churned out two more long strides.

That brought Slocum up beside the stunned editor. He grabbed the reins of the horse Roberts sat upon and thundered away down the street. Slow to come out of shock and react, the Jayhawkers grabbed at their six-guns. Opie put another powerfully destructive round downrange, to knock a kepi flying when the heavy bullet shattered a Redleg's head. Confusion and panic prevented more than two shots being fired toward the fleeing riders. At once the ex-Confederates mounted up and fired a wild volley in the direction of the suddenly disorganized lynch mob.

No longer intent on seeing an innocent man hanged, the good people of Emporia scurried in all directions. Laughing and hooting the rebel yell, the scouting party rode out of town.

"I can't say it often enough, how grateful I am for your rescue," Dave Roberts spoke softly to the ring of men around the low campfire.

Safe in the big encampment at the wash, he had eaten a hearty meal and drank his fill, constantly thanking the men who had saved him. Now he took a long pull on a tin cup of beer, somewhat flat but tasting like ambrosia to the fugitive editor. He wiped his lips with the back of his hand.

"I've been suspicious of this entire affair for some time. Learning that some troops, who had to be from Godfrey Howard's command, had taken children and a woman hostage, I became almost convinced that the events that have happened the past month didn't occur as we had been told."

"You're damn right about that," Steve Varney told him.

Quickly Varney told his story. Following that, Dave Roberts listened for two hours to tales of the depredations committed under a pretense of law by the Redleg militia. Each new revelation further saddened the editor. When he heard of the murder of Aurora and Eunice McDade, Dave wept openly.

"What has our state come to?" he lamented.

"What has the country come to?" Ewan McDade countered. "Kansas isn't the only place this centralism, this ownership of everything by the powerful few, is being put forward. Marse Robert had it right. The war was fought to impose an all-powerful federal tyranny upon the people of this nation."

"Lee?" Dave queried. "Lee said that?"

"From the start. And after, too," Slocum added. "He said Lincoln was inclined to be too lenient. He wasn't assassinated by a conspiracy of bitter Southerns. He was murdered when he wouldn't carry out the programs demanded by the money men in the North."

"I—I don't know if I can believe that."

"You're seeing it on a smaller scale right here," Ewan informed him. "Many of us lived through it during Reconstruction."

"Tell me—tell me more . . . about Howard's men and what they've done," Dave invited.

For another hour they did. Then the atmosphere changed drastically. It had a feeling of danger and pending explosion. The air seemed to crackle when anyone moved. Huge clouds that had been gathering all evening erupted into eye-searing networks of crazy-quilt lightning. It flashed horizontally from one black mass to another, rebounded off the earth, turned the darkness into day. Peal after peal of ground-shaking thunder ripped at their ears. Each flash revealed a weird, sickly green tinge to the sky. Everyone ran for shelter.

Wind whipped the flames of the hastily abandoned fire, while the band of Southerns peeked from their rude dwellings. Someone coughed, cleared his throat. The tense, unnatural quality of the air set nerves on edge. Someone decided a song would ease the growing malease.

*"We are a band of brothers, and native to the soil, fighting for our heritage we won by honest toil. And when our rights are threatened, to fight we do prefer. Hurrah for the Bonny Blue Flag that wears that single star."*

Half a hundred voices joined in the chorus. *"Hurrah—hurrah! For Southern rights hurrah! Hurrah for the Bonnie Blue Flag that bears that single star."*

An enormous blast of thunder drove the words from their throats. In the silence that followed it began like the low, distant murmur of a freight train. It grew in volume, the railroad analogy becoming more distinct. A swift hiss of rain and a drumming scythe of hail proclaimed the cataclysmic approach of the most monstrous of nature's aberrations. The temperature dropped twenty degrees in thirty seconds.

With a bull roar, a thousand locomotives hurtling overhead at once, the heart of the storm raced down upon them. A long, jagged spear of lightning illuminated the hideous, black, snake-like tail of the funnel cloud undulating sinuously through the air. Seen from the front, a thin nimbus of blue white delineated either side. Black thunderheads tinged green formed a perfect backdrop. Objects in camp began to whirl away.

Shrieking, a man flew off with his brush lean-to. Still the deadly tip of the horrifying twister had not yet reached them. Ominously the finger of death sped toward the lip of the wash. Nothing could be heard save the outrageous wind. On the tornado came. Then, with the speed of its inexorable rush, the murderous maelstrom picked up its whirling tube and skipped over the wide gulley.

Howling ferociously, it dwindled and the tumult diminished as it hurtled off to the northeast. In the slowly returning quiet, Slocum found Vivian clutching tightly to his shoulders. Sopping wet, she ground against his chest.

"Oh, Slocum, Slocum," she murmured in shattered fright. "Make love to me, make me know I'm still alive."

In a rush, Slocum found that he too had an overpowering, raging need to excise the devil storm in the ritual of procreation. Lifting her, he carried Vivian off into the darkness. In the slippery mud at the creek bank, they made fast, powerful love.

Tumultuously he drove into her. They gasped and groaned and pounded their bodies together in a welter of completion. Then, lingeringly, they made love again, and again. The first gray hint of false dawn found them still entwined, Vivian deeply impaled on Slocum's rigid, well-used member.

# 20

Wearing a false beard and a long, black "preacher's" coat, Slocum and three men entered Emporia from the west, shortly after sunrise on Friday. The other seven in his special detachment would be doing the same from the north and east. They neared the center of town a bit early. Slocum reined in and they dismounted. He spent some time examining a new, fresh-smelling saddle in front of the shop where it had been made. The proprietor looked on, beaming with justifiable pride.

"It's a dandy, isn't it? You can have it for, aaaah, seventy dollars," he revised his asking price downward ten dollars for a "gentleman of the cloth."

"Nice workmanship. Wouldn't do for me, though. Too elaborate," Slocum invented. "Folks would get to thinking I didn't need the money in the collection plate."

That sally brought a chuckle from the saddlemaker. "I've got another, less fancy, inside. It's made on the same saddle tree as this, only not so much tooling and no silver."

Slocum gave him a polite smile. "Maybe next time, brother."

"Any time, Reverend."

"Another hour and we'll be able to walk in and take that saddle," Ross Six said softly as they walked away.

"This is not Lawrence and you're not Quantrill," Slocum chided the Big Cherokee.

175

Three minutes later, Slocum glanced casually around the four corners and the big oak, noted the bullet scar in a lower branch, and satisfied himself all of his men were in position. Nodding to Nathan Fitzhue, he started off toward the Leighton Hotel.

"Mr. Anstruther?" the clerk responded to Slocum's question. "Yes, he's staying here."

"What's his room number?"

"I'm sorry, but Mr. Anstruther and the other gentlemen have not come down from their rooms for breakfast. I imagine they are all asleep."

Slocum's eyes narrowed. "That still didn't give me his room number."

"Oh, it didn't, did it?" the clerk replied blank-faced.

Neatly shortstopped, Slocum gave a little nod and turned away. Outside, he and the other two headed for the livery stable where they would meet with the rest. So far Emporia showed no sign of an impending violent encounter.

Captain Godfrey Howard stood on the balcony of the Leighton Hotel and surveyed his men through field glasses. An uneasiness filled him. All of the important members of the conspiracy were inside, still sleeping off the previous night's lengthy indulgence in whiskey, poker, and willing, barely nubile female companionship. No, he amended. They might be shaving by this time. They were due downstairs for breakfast in thirty minutes. Still goaded by a vague restlessness, Howard left the hotel.

Unwittingly he provided valuable information to the silent watchers who gathered information for Ewan McDade's vengeance-hungry force waiting outside town. Preoccupied by the specter of yet another failure, and stung by a string of costly setbacks, Captain Howard walked the streets of Emporia oblivious to the careful interest paid him. At the intersection of Commerce and Crawford, he turned to his right, headed south. A block from the corner he stopped and signaled to men on the rooftop. Three troopers waved back in casual fashion. A former Confederate corporal made careful note of their number and location. Godfrey Howard walked on.

In the middle of the next block, he abruptly turned into an alley. Curious eyes noted this and a local youngster, whose family had Southern leanings, scampered in after the militia officer, rolling a hoop with a stick. He returned shortly and reported to the corporal.

"He went up the stairs to the doc's office. Must be three, four soldiers up there. I got close as I could. I heard him say something about covering the front windows. What're they gonna do? Use blankets?"

The corporal laughed. "It means they're to guard those windows and be ready to shoot from them."

Howard reappeared a moment later and started northward. New watchers kept track of his progress. For an hour the nervous, suspicious officer made his rounds of outposts. The importance of protecting Cyril Anstruther and his associates weighed heavily on him. At last he finished his inspection and started back to the hotel. Breakfast should be over now and he would make his report. While striding down Commerce Street, a block from the hotel, Howard automatically touched fingertips to his hat brim in a salute to a tall, thick-shouldered preacher.

Smiling, the man of the cloth returned the gesture. For a moment, Howard got the impression the preacher's three associates smirked rather than smiled. Still nagged by the security problems of the upcoming meeting, Howard dismissed his intuitive flash and proceeded toward the hotel. He'd nearly reached the front door when it struck him that the preacher bore a remarkable similarity to Anstruther's description of Slocum. Take away the beard and . . . Howard whirled around to find the party had disappeared. Uttering a muffled curse, he hurried off to the hotel to inform Anstruther of his preparations.

"We should have gunned him down right there," Nathan Fitzhue growled inside the livery barn.

"Oh? And alerted the whole militia force?" Slocum prodded. "The biggest problem with carefully laid plans is that they aren't carried out as designed. Someone acts too early, or doesn't act when he's supposed to. Keep a cool head, Nate, we'll have our chance."

Ewan McDade, his headquarters and first platoon rode through a cluster of cottonwoods on the west end of Emporia. They moved at a careful walk. Screened by the trees, none of

Howard's sentries positioned on that side of town noticed them. Behind the sixty-five determined Southerns lay the familiar limestone hills, shot through with blue veins of flint. Since the end of the last ice age, men had come here to obtain the easily workable stone, or to trade for the products of artisans who plied the trade of shaping spear points, knives, scrapers, and a plethora of other products. The grim-faced former Confederates either didn't know or ignored the heavy weight of human history their surroundings represented as they neared the edge of the grove.

Arm raised to signal the halt, Ewan McDade calmed his horse while others fidgeted around him. He probed in a small trouser pocket and produced his Elgin eight-day pocket watch. He watched it intently while the inset second hand made jerky movements. Twice it circled its little dial and McDade looked bemused as the minute hand slid to twelve, showing eight o'clock. Sighing to relieve tension, he drew his carbine and gave the signal for the advance.

Captain Godfrey Howard stood uncomfortably beside the head of a long table in the private dining room off the hotel restaurant. Just as in the army, he silently resented the presence of so many who considered themselves his superiors. For all that he clipped off his report in precise, militarily correct delivery. He completed his review of the security strategy and concluded with his momentary suspicion regarding the preacher.

"This may have nothing to do with ou— your meeting, sir," he informed Anstruther. "I encountered an unfamiliar minister on the street while I inspected the positions. He had three men with him. Although his face was unknown to me, his physique reminded me of my encounter with John Slocum. The preacher was bearded, but the planes of his face and his stature have kept me suspicious."

"You didn't stop him?" Anstruther demanded.

"I decided to, though when I turned he and his companions were no longer on the street."

"Send some men to find this preacher. You can question him at your leisure."

"Right away, sir. Thank you, s—"

The first shots of the opening battle interrupted Howard's response.

• • •

Sharpshooters placed in their own advantageous positions took out the sentinels on the west the moment Ewan McDade led his troops from the trees. Only the time it took for the sound of gunfire to reach the northern side of town elapsed before more marksmen eliminated the hidden militiamen. At fifty yards from the first houses, McDade and Tolliver set the men to a gallop.

A hundred and eighty heavily armed troops swarmed into Emporia. Carefully aimed shots now turned on ranking NCOs and young officers. Confusion spread through the defenders as their leaders fell. Despite the previous setbacks, they had not expected a disciplined, military assault. Panic struck home first among the overage and out-of-shape conspirators. In the two minutes it took Captain Godfrey Howard to rush to the lobby of the hotel, the reserved, blatantly superior men of means and power turned into a gaggle of badly frightened individuals.

When five horses clattered across the brick sidewalk and burst into the hotel lobby, the cabal fled upward. Like cats before a terrier, safety lay in getting higher. After shouting hurried, contradictory orders to Sergeant Banks, Godfrey Howard joined the stampede.

Slocum swung off Ol' Rip and went after him. His boots pounded on the stairs. From above, someone with enough presence of mind fired a shot that smacked into the plastered wall an inch from Slocum's nose. He ducked low and kept pumping up the carpeted risers. On the second floor, a movement and stentorian wheezing distracted his attention from Godfrey Howard.

One hand clutched over his heart, Senator Victor Dahlgren stared wild-eyed at the grim apparition of Slocum, who advanced on him, Colt .45 at the ready. Dahlgren raised his other hand in a pleading gesture.

"I can't . . . breathe. I . . . my heart," he gasped.

Slocum kept his eyes active, searching for any indication this might be a ruse, that Dahlgren wanted only time to produce a hideout gun. The corpulent state senator grew sickly pale, a tinge of green around his lips. Slocum took another step.

Dahlgren lost all control. He blundered through the nearest door. Slocum's swift gait brought him close before the portal closed all the way. He threw a shoulder into the effort and smashed his way in. Senator Dahlgren dropped to the floor beside the bed. His breath came in long, wet, sobbing gasps and tears ran down his face.

"I had nothing to do with it. Nothing. Cyril Anstruther gave the orders, Howard carried them out. You can't—can't kill an unarmed man," he begged.

Slocum produced a crooked, nasty smile. "I could make an exception for you. Where's Anstruther?"

"H-he went upstairs. His—room—third floor—rear."

"Put your hands behind your back," Slocum commanded.

Dahlgren began to whine for mercy. He blubbered and offered another feeble string of mitigations. Slocum's smile held more than a little sneer. He crossed to the kneeling man, never taking the muzzle of his .45 Peacemaker off the fat senator's head.

"I have money. Lots—of money. I can—can make it worth—your while."

"To do what?" Slocum snapped.

"To spare me. I-in my inside coat pocket. There is a billfold there, it contains two thousand dollars in currency. Take it. It's yours. Only, please, please let me go."

Slocum eased a hand around and delved beneath the expensive cloth of the senator's suit. He came out with the wallet. With a snap of his wrist he opened it. Sure enough, he found a thick sheaf of bills. He extracted them, counted and folded them double, then shoved them into a front trouser pocket.

"Th-then you'll let me go?" Dahlgren queried, the first faint glimmer of hope buoying him.

"No. I'll not do that."

"Why?" Dahlgren shouted the word. "You took the money."

"It will make a nice contribution to the Southern widows' and orphans' fund. Now, lay down on your face, hands behind your back."

Sniveling and moaning in terror, Senator Dahlgren complied. Slocum produced a length of rope coiled around his left shoulder and with spare efficiency trussed Dahlgren up like a pig. The corpulent senator squawked like a doomed rooster at the pressure of the rope around his neck.

"Wh-what are you going to do now?"

"I'll leave you to the tender mercies of Ewan McDade and his friends."

Senator Victor Dahlgren began to shriek like a terrified woman.

Out in the hall, Slocum heard the pandemonium that announced the arrival of the main force. Shots came from beyond the hotel, as well as inside. Men shouted and a few screamed in pain from wounds. Horses kept up a constant din. Slocum turned right and started for the stairs that would lead to the third floor. Only one more above it. Their earlier reconnaissance had revealed an iron ladder fire escape that led from the roof to the ground. Somehow, with all the vengeance-bound Southerns milling around down there, Slocum doubted that Anstruther and his lackeys would choose that means of fleeing. As Slocum climbed to the third floor, his head came level with the floorboards just as a heavy revolver roared close by.

Slocum felt the wind of the bullet's passage. A fraction closer and he would have lost his nose. Instead of ducking, he surged up the final three steps and dived into a roll along the carpeted runner strip.

The second bullet tore through the back of his vest and shirt. The skin over his shoulder blades stung and burned like hell. Slocum made a second roll and came up with his .45 Colt in the lead. He found his target and the hammer fell.

Justice John Duffey squealed like a pig when Slocum's bullet punched a hole two inches above his navel. Terrible things went on inside, the pain told Duffey, before the hot lead exited through his left kidney and he lost all interest in worldly things. Backed against the wall, he slid to a sitting position, his eyes already glazing. Slocum gave him a quick check, replaced spent cartridges, and started toward the back of the building.

*"You insufferable, puritanical bastard!"* Cyril Anstruther roared when he spied Slocum from the doorway to his suite at the far end of the hall.

He held a small-caliber revolver in his left hand. With the aplomb of a duelist, he raised it to shoulder level and fired at Slocum. The slug snapped past Slocum's left ear. It made Slocum's return round a fraction too late. Anstruther had leaped to the side and disappeared into the room.

"Damn." Biting off a curse, Slocum went after him.

"I might have known you'd be mixed up in this from the beginning," Anstruther accused from the marginal safety of his large suite. "Killing women and children was always your forte."

"Bullshit, Anstruther," Slocum answered him. "You seem to forget who it was did your dirty work. Captain Howard doesn't take orders from me."

"You were a dirty, sneaking guerrilla in the war and you still operate that way."

"Fine words from a traitor and a thief," Slocum snapped.

"I stole nothing," Anstruther denied, his voice rising. "The gold was given to me. It was rightfully mine."

"Now you're using it to buy misery for a lot of innocent people. You are a liar, a murderer, a traitor, and a thief, Anstruther. Give up now and I'll see they only send you to prison for life."

"Go fuck yourself, Slocum!"

Instead, Slocum dived into the parlor of the three-room suite. He fired two rounds on the way in. Neither struck anything of importance. Partly obscured by the powder smoke, Slocum scrambled behind a large upholstered chair and gazed over the room for a sign of his enemy. He saw nothing, but he could hear heavy breathing.

"You're out of shape, Anstruther. You wheeze like an old man. This is your last chance."

Anstruther put two bullets into the thick padding of the chair. Then, uttering a thin, wavering yell, he made a break for the doorway. Slocum rose up and brought his .45 Colt into line. Almost reluctantly his finger closed on the trigger.

Hot lead smashed into Cyril Anstruther's left armpit. Impact staggered him and he made an ungainly turn toward the source of his misery. Numbness spread from his left lung, punctured through by Slocum's bullet. A froth of blood oozed through his thin, soulless lips. Animal rage lighted his oddly colored, pale brown eyes when he focused on Slocum. His little revolver felt as if it weighed a ton when he forced his left arm upward, swinging it toward the ex-Confederate.

Beads of sweat formed on Anstruther's forehead, born of his terrible effort to squeeze the trigger. The .32 barked, then fired again. The first slug caught Slocum in his left shoulder. The second went into the ceiling as Cyril Anstruther reflexively bounded backward when a 250-grain .45 bullet drilled into his breastbone. Biting his lip against the onset of pain, Slocum watched Anstruther die. Then he set out after Godfrey Howard.

From the forth-floor hall, Captain Godfrey Howard listened to the sounds of defeat from below. With growing terror, he heard the progress of the angry men who spilled through the hotel. He also heard the pleas and death throes of the lesser conspirators as they were hunted down like rats. Cyril Anstruther's enraged shout brought home to him how implacable the Pale Rider had to be. If Anstruther didn't stop Slocum, Howard reasoned with a sick ache in his gut, he would be next.

He knew it when Anstruther died. Biting his lip, he fought to steady his hand. He drew himself up and leaned against the wainscoting on the wall. Braced, he extended his converted Remington model '60 and held on with both hands. Slocum appeared, framed by brightness that streamed up the stairwell.

With an evil grin, Godfrey Howard squeezed the trigger. The heavy Army model bucked in his hands. His bullet cleaned the hat from Slocum's head. Reflexively, Slocum returned the favor before he ducked, and shot Howard through the thigh. Screaming like a woman, Godfrey Howard collapsed to the floor. His six-gun abandoned, he began to claw and drag himself along the hall. Reverted to the cowardly wretch he had always been, Godfrey Howard began to sob and beg for his life.

"Please . . . please, don't—don't kill me. I didn't do anything wrong. I—I . . . I only—only followed orders."

Still aching from the wounds he had received from Anstruther and the mendacious Justice Duffey, Slocum slowly followed Howard down the hall. The debased officer's thigh wound pumped a steady flow of blood that stained the carpet runner and straggled over the floor to the mopboard. By then all anger had fled and Slocum looked on the pathetic craven with revulsion.

"Oh, no, I won't kill you," Slocum growled. "I wouldn't think of depriving those brave boys down there of the pleasure of hanging your sniveling, yellow-bellied ass." Howard moaned and closed his eyes to shut out the too-vivid images. "How did it feel to kill those women? Did you like it, Howard? What about the children? Especially the boys. I've seen your kind before. I'll bet you had a cock stiff as an iron rod while you killed the boys."

Shorn of all his secrets, Howard screamed his final defiance. "You bastard!"

With sudden ill timing, a door opened right beside the wounded militia officer. A woman stepped partway into the hall. In the wild desperation of the condemned, Godfrey Howard seized the woman and dragged her down in front of him. From his tunic pocket he snatched a tiny seven-shot .32 revolver. Rising on his good knee, he held the hideout gun to the woman's head.

"Let me go, Slocum. Let me get out of here or I'll kill her."

"I suppose I haven't any choice," Slocum said resignedly, while he lined up his Colt on the craven Howard's forehead.

"No you don't," Howard crowed.

But Slocum did. With cool precision, he drilled Godfrey Howard exactly between the eyes. So swiftly did Howard's savaged brain turn off that he flopped backward without ever firing the .32.

Victory brought the inevitable celebration. Apprised of the deceptions practiced by the cabal, the townsfolk of Emporia turned out a regular wingding for the terribly wronged Southern boys. At the height of the uproarious party, two events occurred that furthered the cause for joy. A United States marshal arrived from Dodge City, and with him Vivian Ballard and the McDade children. When the whooping and hollering subsided, the marshal cleared his throat and made an announcement.

"I have here a telegram sent all the way from Washington, in the District of Columbia. It says that a commission from the Department of the Interior, and a special prosecutor from the Justice Department, will be arriving within a week."

"We've won," Ewan McDade fairly shouted into Slocum's dour face. "We've really won now."

"Yes, you have," Slocum agreed, putting off his warm welcome of Vivian.

"You don't sound too happy about it, Slocum." McDade sounded disappointed.

"Oh, I am. Believe me."

"Then join the fandango," McDade invited.

"I will, in my own way."

"And what's that, John Slocum?" Vivian asked in a throaty contralto.

"I was thinking," he informed her in a whisper beside one ear, "of that huge canopy bed in Cyril Anstruther's suite. Instead of a wild hoorah, I'd sort of like to have a delightful romp with you right in the middle of it."

Vivian beamed. "That, my friend, can be arranged."

*A special offer for people who enjoy reading the best Westerns published today. If you enjoyed this book, subscribe now and get . . .*

# TWO FREE

## A $5.90 VALUE—NO OBLIGATION

If you enjoyed this book and would like to read more of the very best Westerns being published today, you'll want to subscribe to True Value's Western Home Subscription Service. If you enjoyed the book you just read and want more of the most exciting, adventurous, action packed Westerns, subscribe now.

Each month the editors of True Value will select the 6 very best Westerns from America's leading publishers for special readers like you. You'll be able to preview these new titles as soon as they are published, FREE for ten days with no obligation.

## TWO FREE BOOKS

When you subscribe, we'll send you your first month's shipment of the newest and best 6 Westerns for you to preview. With your first shipment, two of these books will be yours as our introductory gift to you absolutely FREE, regardless of what you decide to do. If you like them, as much as we think you will, keep all six books but pay for just 4 at the low subscriber rate of just $2.45 each. If you decide to return them, keep 2 of the titles as our gift. No obligation.

## Special Subscriber Savings

When you become a True Value subscriber you'll save money several ways. First, all regular monthly selections will be billed at the low subscriber price of just $2.45 each. That's

# WESTERNS!

at least a savings of $3.00 each month below the publishers price. Second, there is never any shipping, handling or other hidden charges—Free home delivery. What's more there is no minimum number of books you must buy, you may return any selection for full credit and you can cancel your subscription at any time. A TRUE VALUE!

## Mail the coupon below

To start your subscription and receive 2 FREE WESTERNS, fill out the coupon below and mail it today. We'll send your first shipment which includes 2 FREE BOOKS as soon as we receive it.

---

**Mail To:**                                                    12493
**True Value Home Subscription Services, Inc.**
**P.O. Box 5235**
**120 Brighton Road**
**Clifton, New Jersey 07015-5235**

YES! I want to start receiving the very best Westerns being published today. Send me my first shipment of 6 Westerns for me to preview FREE for 10 days. If I decide to keep them, I'll pay for just 4 of the books at the low subscriber price of $2.45 each; a total of $9.80 (a $17.70 value). Then each month I'll receive the 6 newest and best Westerns to preview Free for 10 days. If I'm not satisfied I may return them within 10 days and owe nothing. Otherwise I'll be billed at the special low subscriber rate of $2.45 each; a total of $14.70 (at least a $17.70 value) and save $3.00 off the publishers price. There are never any shipping, handling or other hidden charges. I understand I am under no obligation to purchase any number of books and I can cancel my subscription at any time, no questions asked. In any case the 2 FREE books are mine to keep.

Name _____

Address _____ Apt. # _____

City _____ State _____ Zip _____

Telephone # _____

Signature _____
(if under 18 parent or guardian must sign)
Terms and prices subject to change.
Orders subject to acceptance by True Value Home Subscription Services, Inc.

# JAKE LOGAN
## TODAY'S HOTTEST ACTION WESTERN!

| | |
|---|---|
| __SLOCUM AND THE PREACHER'S DAUGHTER #119 | 0-425-11194-6/$2.95 |
| __SLOCUM AND THE GUNFIGHTER'S RETURN #120 | 0-425-11265-9/$2.95 |
| __THE RAWHIDE BREED #121 | 0-425-11314-0/$2.95 |
| __GOLD FEVER #122 | 0-425-11398-1/$2.95 |
| __DEATH TRAP #123 | 0-425-11541-0/$2.95 |
| __SLOCUM AND THE OUTLAW'S TRAIL #126 | 0-425-11618-2/$2.95 |
| __MEXICAN SILVER #131 | 0-425-11838-X/$2.95 |
| __COLORADO KILLERS #134 | 0-425-11971-8/$2.95 |
| __RIDE TO VENGEANCE #135 | 0-425-12010-4/42.95 |
| __REVENGE OF THE GUNFIGHTER #136 | 0-425-12054-6/$2.95 |
| __SLOCUM AND THE TOWN TAMER #140 | 0-425-12221-2/$2.95 |
| __SLOCUM BUSTS OUT (Giant Novel) | 0-425-12270-0/$3.50 |
| __A NOOSE FOR SLOCUM #141 | 0-425-12307-3/$2.95 |
| __NEVADA GUNMEN #142 | 0-425-12354-5/$2.95 |
| __THE HORSE THIEF WAR #143 | 0-425-12445-2/$2.95 |
| __SLOCUM AND THE PLAINS RAMPAGE #144 | 0-425-12493-2/$2.95 |
| __SLOCUM AND THE DEATH DEALER #145 (Feb. '91) | 0-425-12558-0/$2.95 |
| __DESOLATION POINT #146 (March '91) | 0-425-12615-3/$2.95 |
| __SLOCUM AND THE APACHE RAIDERS #147 (April '91) | 0-425-12659-5/$2.95 |

| Check book(s). Fill out coupon. Send to: | POSTAGE AND HANDLING: $1.00 for one book, 25¢ for each additional. Do not exceed $3.50. |
|---|---|
| **BERKLEY PUBLISHING GROUP** 390 Murray Hill Pkwy., Dept. B East Rutherford, NJ 07073 | |
| | **BOOK TOTAL**      $ ____ |
| NAME_____ | **POSTAGE & HANDLING**   $ ____ |
| ADDRESS_____ | **APPLICABLE SALES TAX**   $ ____ (CA, NJ, NY, PA) |
| CITY_____ | **TOTAL AMOUNT DUE**   $ ____ |
| STATE_____ZIP_____ | **PAYABLE IN US FUNDS.** (No cash orders accepted.) |
| PLEASE ALLOW 6 WEEKS FOR DELIVERY. PRICES ARE SUBJECT TO CHANGE WITHOUT NOTICE. | 202d |